ZERO LIMIT

ALSO BY JEREMY K. BROWN

Ocean of Storms (with Christopher Mari)

Calling Off Christmas

ZERO LIMIT

JEREMY K. BROWN

47NORTH

This is a work of fiction. Names, characters, organizations, places, events, and incidents are either products of the author's imagination or are used fictitiously. Any resemblance to actual persons, living or dead, or actual events is purely coincidental.

Published by 47North, Seattle

www.apub.com

ISBN-13: 9781503946651
ISBN-10: 1503946657

Cover design by Damon Freeman

Printed in the United States of America

Dedicated with love, respect, and admiration to all the women in my life.
My wife, mothers, sisters, nieces, and goddaughters.
Keep on conquering.

Chapter One

There were times, usually in the morning, when Caitlin Taggart almost felt like she was still alive. Lying in bed, riding the line between sleep and waking, everything around her seemed sweet and warm and possible. Even her dreams felt almost tangible, as though she could reach out and dip her hand into them like a cool mountain stream. Then the alarm always shattered the stillness, jerking her fully awake. After a fruitless few seconds of lying still and trying to recapture the dream, Caitlin would give up and climb out of bed. She'd wince as her feet hit the floor and she felt the granules of dust beneath them, the remnants of what she had tracked in the night before. The fluorescents then popped on automatically, bright and angry, insisting that the day begin. Their ugly presence destroyed the illusion even further. And right then, that was when everything hit home at once and the feeling vanished like a startled deer. Caitlin wasn't living. She was just existing on the Moon.

This unpleasant routine, played out morning after morning for the past year, had become as familiar to Caitlin as the rhythms of a prison sentence. Which, if she were being honest with herself, is exactly what it was.

"Good morning, Caitlin."

"Good morning, Ava," she said, answering the AI that ran all the systems in her unit. "Any news from the world today?"

"Satellite communications with Earth have been restricted," Ava said in her gentle but detached voice. "All news and entertainment channels are temporarily offline. I can pull up the in-unit entertainment if you like."

"What have you got for me?" Caitlin asked.

"There are still two hundred and twenty-five unviewed Failvids for your amusement," said Ava.

"No thanks," said Caitlin, rolling her eyes. When she had inherited the unit that she now called home, Caitlin had also inherited whatever entertainment preferences the previous tenant had left behind. While scripted dramas and sitcoms remained just as popular as ever, this particular Hive resident had a predilection for Earth's other favorite form of entertainment, "Failvids." These were exactly what one would expect—thirty- to forty-minute reels of people damaging themselves in clumsy, painful, and often mortal ways. The hook for the viewer was watching each vid program with comprehensive virtual reality gear that allowed them to fully experience every fracture, bruise, and injury in vivid detail. Caitlin was not an elitist by any stretch of the imagination, but she did have to wonder what the extreme popularity of these kinds of programs said about humanity.

"What else have you got?" she asked Ava.

"A selection of random movies," Ava offered. "I can run through some titles if you like."

"I've seen everything before," she said. "Twice. Music?"

"Yes of course. The top forty songs are as follows . . ."

"Don't bother," Caitlin said. "What have you got under oldies?"

Despite having been born well into the twenty-first century, Caitlin possessed an unabashed love for classic rock from the 1960s and '70s. She had inherited the tastes of her father, who had always puttered around their house listening to Cream, Nazareth, and Deep Purple. "This is *real* music, Caity-did," he'd say. She hadn't always understood his words at the time, but she definitely did now. Listening to that music was like being able to reach out and hold on to a piece of her dad. And, given her present circumstances, she didn't have many pieces of anything or anyone to hold on to.

"I have Rush, Uriah Heep, Creedence Clearwat—"

"Stop right there, Ava," Caitlin said. "You had me at Creedence."

"As you wish," said Ava.

The screen in the unit flickered and *Bayou Country* began. As the swampy opening notes of "Born on the Bayou" poured out of the speakers, Caitlin climbed onto the treadmill and began her morning run. Exercise in space, even in the one-sixth gravity of the Moon, was vital to keeping muscles from atrophying and bones from growing brittle. This wasn't necessarily a problem in the Hive, or anywhere else indoors. Aldrin City had highly advanced artificial-gravity systems that simulated Earth's conditions, but the Hive still relied on more old-school methods of keeping one's feet on the ground. The entire structure was built on a slight slant, while underneath, gently rotating carousels turned in slow and steady revolutions until the gravity of Earth was replicated. It was a bit jarring at first, but eventually, one got used to the sensation. To Caitlin, it was almost like being on a cruise ship at sea. A little wobbly at times, but somewhat soothing.

Still, despite the gravity replication, the body was under constant and significant strain on the lunar surface. Not working your body enough could make returning to Earth incredibly difficult. And she had every intention of returning to her home planet as soon as humanly possible.

As Caitlin ran, her mind began to wander as she mulled over her situation and the circumstances that had led her here. She supposed, to people of a generation long since dead, the idea of living on the Moon would sound impossibly romantic. Enviable, even. Many times she'd thought about how much she'd love to bring those naive souls forward in time and give them a guided tour, just to smile wickedly at how fast their rose-colored glasses would come off. That wasn't to say there weren't places on the lunar surface that would inspire wonder. The shining glass-and-steel cylinders of Aldrin City, for example, were as pretty a picture as one could put on any postcard. In fact, those very cylinders *were* featured on many items in the gift shop on the commerce level, including postcards, which, even though no one sent physical mail anymore, still did brisk business. Chalk one up for kitsch.

But Aldrin City's unblemished magnificence was immaterial to Caitlin. She was about as far from there as one could get without crossing into the wasteland of the far side. A fully functioning replica of the best that Earth had to offer, the city represented the pinnacle of lunar colonization. New construction projects seemed to pop up daily, and most people figured that the entire surface would soon be covered in cities and towns.

The city's design was based on the ideas of Gerard K. O'Neill, consisting of a series of massive cylindrical structures built directly into the lunar regolith and stretching for more than twenty miles across the surface. O'Neill believed that a colony suspended above the Moon was more practical. He felt that, due to Earth's neighbor having a fourteen-day night as it rotates during orbit, the obtaining and maintaining of energy resources would present a problem. Additionally, he raised concerns about the expense of transit to and from the surface and the challenges of working and living in one-sixth Earth's gravity. But in the nearly one hundred years since he'd published *The High Frontier*, his treatise on the colonization of space, there had been a great many advances, particularly in the harvesting and distribution of both solar power and helium-3. The dream of Aldrin City could thus become a reality. After years of construction, the metropolis now stood proudly on the face of the Moon, easily visible from Earth with even the most economic telescope.

Inside the city's walls was a near-perfect mirror of the planet its builders had once called home—parks, lakes, forests, open fields, and sprawling urban locales. Much of the animal and plant life that had been endangered on Earth had been brought to Aldrin City, where they thrived. Through genetic engineering, some species now extinct on Earth, from tigers to lowland gorillas, had been bred and allowed a second chance at life in the lush preserves encompassing the ecological cylinders.

Transportation inside the city was equally advanced, with everything—from vehicles to the power grid itself—running on clean, sustainable electrical energy. Visitors traveled to and from the city via a single magnetic levitation train that ran on a loop from Aldrin City out to the mining colonies.

Of course, not all the cylinders were as luxurious as the largest ones at Aldrin's center, with the outskirts offering fewer amenities. The people there swam in concrete pools instead of lakes, lived in council estates instead of luxury condos. But even the most meager accommodations would be considered lavish by Earth standards. Put simply, Aldrin City was for tourists, executives, the elite, and all the other people who dwelled at the top of the food chain. The rest of the rabble, Caitlin included, ground out their days in Tranquillitatis, or as they preferred to call it, the Hive.

Caitlin imagined that, when it was first built, Tranquillitatis was conceived as a triumph of man over the forces of space, or at the very least a testament to the industry that would revolutionize life on the Moon and Earth. Signs to that effect hung all over the Hive, aging, covered in lunar dust and crud from the surface. They trumpeted the same slogans, promising a brilliant future: "Tomorrow Begins Today!" "Tranquillitatis: Where the Future Happens!" Or, her personal favorite, "Mine Your Future Today!" That one was hung right over one of the airlocks that led out to the surface. She was sure that the execs at the Guanghang Mining Company had visions of workers slapping it one by one as they walked out, like football players ready to take the field. If that had ever happened, it was well before she got there. Now if anyone acknowledged the sign, they just rolled their eyes. Besides, no one walked out of the airlocks anymore. The mining fields were much farther out, so everyone rode harvesters.

Caitlin finished her run and then worked her way through a series of core drills, crunches, kettlebell exercises, and yoga poses, all designed to keep her body protected from the diminishing effects of microgravity. She capped off her workout with a seven-minute plank, then stood up and stretched out, breathing heavily. Her body was sore and aching from the workout, but that was nothing new. Having spent the first six years of her life in the Moon's low gravity, her bones and muscles had never quite adapted when she went to Earth. She had always been taller than anyone in her grade and her skin was pale from being raised under artificial light. These features, combined with her blonde hair and aquamarine eyes, made Caitlin stand out from everyone else in the small Oregon town she'd been transplanted to, and not in a good way. So, in the absence of friends or dates in high school, she had thrown herself into training her body and mind as hard as she could. Eventually, her weakened bones and muscles bent to her will and her form became lean and strong, thriving under Earth's strong gravity and warming sun. But more than twenty years later, her joints still reminded her of her Moonborn heritage with a creak or howl of protest.

Still stretching, Caitlin shuffled her way into the shower stall. She hated showering on the Moon. Water conservation was a constant concern, with shipments coming in sporadically. You couldn't risk taking a long shower for fear of the water cutting off just as you had a head full of shampoo. So most people, Caitlin included, did things the navy way. She'd turn on the water long enough to get wet, then turn it off to lather up. Once she was soaped up from head to toe, she'd turn the water back on to rinse off. The process was unpleasant and clinical, robbing the showering experience of its inherent joy. When she made it back to Earth, Caitlin vowed that the first thing she was going to do was march into her shower at home and stand under the hot water until her skin scalded. Actually—she corrected herself—the first thing she was going to do was hug her daughter. In fact, sometimes Caitlin thought that was the only thing she was going to do if she ever got back. Just melt into her and never let her go again. Thinking of Emily sent a cold needle into Caitlin's heart, although in truth that needle never really left her. It simply flared up from time to time, a splinter agitated by errant missteps.

Caitlin hit the stall's center button to activate the water. Nothing. Offering a quick curse under her breath, she punched it again repeatedly, like an agitated office worker trying to summon a slow-moving elevator. She was about to hit the button again when Ava suddenly spoke up.

"By the way, Caitlin," the computer said, "this month's supply shipment from Aitken basin is running one day behind. All water will be rationed until further notice."

Caitlin hung her head with a sigh of resignation, leaning against the cool plastic wall. No shower this morning. And no coffee. Which meant that she would have to will herself into feeling like a human being. That would be no easy feat.

"Ava," she called out, her head still down, "what are you doing to me?"

"I'm sorry, Caitlin," answered Ava somewhat impassively, "but I believe this is a clear-cut case of not shooting the messenger."

"Don't be so sure."

Caitlin stepped out of the shower and toweled the perspiration off her body to give herself the illusion of *feeling* clean. She drew on laundered shorts and a T-shirt and checked the time. She had to continue getting ready for work, but there was one more task to complete, the most important one of the day.

"Ava," she said, "call home."

"Of course," the AI said. "Dialing now."

The main screen in the unit's living area flickered and glowed blue. After a moment's pause, Caitlin saw the words that always made her brighten up: "CALLING HOME." After a minute or so, the face she had been hoping to see filled the screen.

"Hi, Mom . . ."

"Hi, baby girl!" Caitlin said, reaching for the screen involuntarily and already feeling the tears in her eyes. "How are you doing, kiddo?"

"Fine," Emily said. Her blue eyes shone for a moment, then went briefly dark. A cloud passing over the sun. "You didn't call last night."

"I'm sorry, sweetie," Caitlin said. "They put me on a double shift at the mine again. You know how it goes. Mom's the only one who can get things done around here, right?"

Caitlin laughed weakly and threw up her hands in a gesture of mock surrender. Emily fixed her mother with a glare that made her look much older than her eight years.

"You could have at least texted, you know."

At this, Caitlin laughed again, and this time it was not weak, but hearty and full of bemusement. As the parent, wasn't *she* the one who should be correcting the behavior of her daughter?

"It's not funny," Emily scolded, although the sound of her mother's laughter had started to melt the ice. She tried to keep her face stern, but a slight smile insisted on peeking through. Caitlin saw the change in expression and leaped on it like a drowning woman to driftwood.

"You're right, you're right," she said, arms up. "Am I forgiven?"

A pause, and Emily nodded, the smile now in full bloom.

"I'm so glad," Caitlin said. "Are you having a good day?"

"Pretty good."

"Yeah?" Caitlin asked. "Did Dad take you out for pancakes?"

Emily's expression flickered a moment. The reaction was brief, but Caitlin could read it well.

"No," Emily said. "Ben did. Dad's still asleep."

"Asleep?" Caitlin asked, incredulous. "What time is it there? It's got to be after three, right?"

"Yeah," Emily said. "He came home late. He was yelling a lot when he did."

"I'm sorry, sweetie," Caitlin said, wishing that she could step through the screen, scoop her up, and keep her safe. Caitlin had made a lot of good decisions in her life, but marrying Eric Greene wasn't one of them. But she did get Emily out of the deal.

"It's OK," Emily said, and her voice dropped to a whisper. "I have more fun with Ben anyway."

At this, Caitlin couldn't help but agree. Ben Martin had been one of her closest friends since the campaign and one of the few she'd trust with her life or her daughter, which these days she considered to be pretty much the same thing.

"Ben is very fun, I'll give you that. He didn't spend all morning telling you war stories about your mom, did he?"

"Maybe a couple. Did you really save his life?"

"Well, we kind of saved each other's lives a few times over there," Caitlin replied. "It was a little crazy. But if he wants to tell you that, sure. I saved his life. Hey, did you get the package I sent?"

Emily's eyes went wide. "Oh yeah, I almost forgot!"

Caitlin was relieved when Emily held up the small wrapped parcel in her hands. With the travel ban in full effect, sending anything back to Earth from the Moon was a near-impossible task, doubly so if you were a lowly resident of the Hive. Luckily, Caitlin's vet status had earned her a few black market connections who were able to smuggle items off-Moon for her from time to time. Those connections weren't durable enough to get her home, but she could at least send an occasional gift to Emily.

Emily eagerly tore the wrapping off the package and turned it excitedly over in her hands.

"A book!" she said, and Caitlin took a moment to silently thank herself for getting her daughter interested in actual physical books as opposed to the electronic titles her friends read on their tablets, assuming any of them read at all, what with Failvids vying for their attention.

Looking at the cover, Emily read the title. "*Alice's Adventures in Wonderland*. Thank you! Will you read it with me?"

"Of course I will!" Caitlin said. Although Emily loved reading on her own, one of her and her mother's favorite pastimes before Caitlin had ended up on the Moon had been "pass-reading," where one of them read a chapter out loud and then passed the book to the other to read the next one. They'd managed to get through *The Hobbit* and *The Phantom Tollbooth* that way and had been starting on *A Wrinkle in Time* when everything had gone wrong.

"That's why I got it for you. I think you'll enjoy it," Caitlin said. "It's about a little girl who goes on a big adventure, just like you're going to."

"I know!" said Emily excitedly. "Just three more days."

"Just three days, kiddo." Caitlin nodded. "Then it's you and me."

"And you promised you're going to take me to Lake Armstrong, right?"

"Of course! Are you kidding? You think I'd break that promise? No way! I'd sooner die!"

Emily giggled slightly at her mother's remark, and in that instant Caitlin felt the distance between them shrink ever so slightly.

"Caitlin," Ava broke in, "I'm sorry to interrupt, but your shift at the mine is due to begin in just a few minutes."

"Yeah, yeah, thank you, Ava. Listen, I gotta get to work, kiddo," said Caitlin, even though the words were like broken glass in her mouth. "But I hope you have a great day, OK? And pretty soon, you're gonna fly up here, and it'll be like your birthday and Christmas all wrapped up together."

"I can't wait!" she said, and her smile grew wide, almost playful. "Mom?"

"Yes, sweetheart?"

"I love you to the Moon and back!"

"Well, I love you *from* the Moon and back, so there!"

For a few moments more, they chuckled and joked and blew kisses across the stars. Then the connection was gone and Caitlin was alone again. *Just in time too,* she thought.

She didn't want her daughter to see her crying.

Chapter Two

Back when the Moon was first colonized, life on the lunar surface was sold to the public as a glamorous, exotic experience. Something out of a movie or an Arthur C. Clarke novel, with glorious luxury liners majestically plying the stars and ferrying interstellar travelers from Earth to an orbiting landscape. Some of the posters advertising just that in their loud art deco style still hung, yellowing and faded, around the Hive. And maybe for those first pioneers, that was exactly what the journey was.

Caitlin had no clue, and frankly, she didn't care. For people currently living on Earth's closest neighbor, life was one thing: dirty. Moon dust got into everything. Every surface in Caitlin's unit was covered with a permanent gray film. The dust was smeared on the walls, coated the screens, got into her clothes, and if she wanted to take a drink of water, she had to rinse the glass beforehand or she'd have problems after the first swallow. This dust wasn't the harmless, innocuous matter that floated in the air on Earth, made up predominately of dirt, pollen, and dead skin. Lunar dust was hard and abrasive, scratching every surface it touched. Much of the Moon's regolith was made of silicon dioxide glass, the result of billions of years of meteoroid impacts, producing dust dangerous enough to shred lung tissue and scratch corneas. Most long-term Hive residents had what the locals called "Moon Lung," a persistent cough caused by silica particles being trapped in their airways.

Air scrubbers in the Hive took care of most of the more dangerous fragments, but sooner or later, everyone breathed in something they couldn't breathe back out.

Caitlin hoped she could get out of the Hive and off the Moon before that day came for her.

But, even if it were scoured every night by hand, the Hive would still make for a less than ideal place to live. Caitlin often thought how much she'd love to have sat down with the people who designed the place and asked them what their real calling in life was because they clearly had no concept of architecture. A series of geodesic domes spread out across the surface in no discernible order or pattern, the Hive dotted the Moon's face like ugly moles. They had been built in the middle of the century, with the domes inflated by robotic drones and covered with 3-D printed materials mined from the lunar surface itself. What had begun as a few small habitats to shelter the first mining pioneers had grown to more than a hundred domes connected by passageways and tunnels above and below the surface. The original builders had probably not imagined that the colony would last so long, which is why things were perpetually breaking down. Everything from water pipes to electricity went out with a fair amount of regularity. Thankfully, the oxygen suppliers had still never malfunctioned, but everyone living in the Hive shared the common belief it was only a matter of time before that particular calamity came to fruition.

There were no windows in the Hive because, really, what was there to see? In the early days there had been 3-D screens on some of the walls showing everything from interstellar vistas to lush images of Earth, including fish swimming lazily beneath an azure sunlit sea. However, all the screens had eventually shorted out, and no one had bothered to repair them. So they sat, dark and unused. Some of them still flickered aimlessly as if trying to will themselves back to life, but most just hung there, lonely, broken.

With no real or artificial sunlight inside the Hive, the entire complex was lit by dull, yellow-tinged fluorescents that made everything and everybody look jaundiced. Inside each dome, packed together in nondescript, anodyne rows, were the apartment units themselves. Utilitarian and basic, the spaces offered only the most austere of amenities. Caitlin had seen college dorms that were better appointed than the accommodations in the Hive. You had a few rudimentary pieces of furniture, an entertainment setup that was probably state of the art in the first days of colonization, and an AI unit to run everything. That was it, that was all. Thanks for playing, kids.

The Hive was also a noisy place, overstuffed with people from various walks of life. Some were immigrants looking to make a new life off-planet. Others were Moonborn but couldn't afford the high cost of living in Aldrin City. Then there were people like Caitlin Taggart, there because they had no other choice. Victims of hard luck or circumstance, they had all been thrown together into the Hive like animals in a strange, alien zoo and were now forced to coexist together.

This meant that the place had, over time, become a cauldron of conflicting cultures, ideologies, and daily rituals. Muezzin calls blended with Baptist hymns. Arguing couples were drowned out by crying babies, or vice versa. English, Chinese, Arabic, and Yiddish voices all tried to outshout each other, swirling together into a cacophony of sound rivaling the Tower of Babel. After a while, the outpouring became like white noise, or the dull roar of a seashell pressed against the ear. After a year of living in such perpetual dissonance, Caitlin, who had grown up in the countryside, sometimes wondered how she would ever be able to successfully return to the quiet of her old life.

Although she had spent the majority of her years on Earth, long enough to get married, have a daughter, and go off to serve her country in the Last Campaign, Caitlin Taggart had been born on the Moon, the daughter of a pair of would-be helium-3 miners. This was back in the gold rush days when everyone who had the capital and daring could stake a He-3 claim and try to strike it rich. Her father had mortgaged everything they had to be among the first to conquer the new lunar frontier. During this boom period of expansion, promise, and fortune-seeking, Caitlin had been born.

After the Taggarts' He-3 dreams had vanished in a fog of inexperience and poor decisions, they'd returned to Earth to start over again. For her parents, the homecoming bore the sting of defeat; for Caitlin, it came with the fear and apprehension of an alien setting foot on a strange, unwelcoming world. For years after arriving on Earth, Caitlin had faced a slew of anti-Moon prejudice. People seemed to think that anyone born on the Moon should stay there. Kids regarded her as a freak. Even though she was just as human as they were, she was still, for all intents and purposes, an extraterrestrial. And as such, she was by definition "different," prone to being peppered with questions like, "Is it true your bones break like glass?" And when questions ran out, children replaced them with insults.

The parents weren't much better, regarding her with suspicion and mistrust. Part of this was her general status as an off-worlder, which immediately put her in the "outsider" slot on everyone's scorecard, but there was also a general dislike of people who came from the Moon. If Earth wasn't a good enough place to be born, then why should it suddenly be a good place to live? Weren't Moon people happy where they were?

Many Terrans had a certain hysterical paranoia about Moonborns and their intentions for migrating to Earth. Even groups that had experienced oppression over the years had begun to pile on, grateful that, for the first time in centuries, the heat was off of them. In many ways, the arrival of Moonborns put an end to much of the racism and classism that had plagued the planet for generations. At last, everyone on Earth could unite against a common foe.

This hostility was made crystal clear to Caitlin when she overheard the mother of Jennie Thompson—the first and only real friend she'd made after arriving—chastising her daughter in the living room. "I don't want you bringing that Moon girl around anymore," she had said. The contempt she used when saying "Moon girl" was palpable and thick. "You know they're the reason your father lost his job, don't you?"

The hatred and uncertainty over the presence of lunar immigrants on Earth soil really took hold when America's most recent president was elected on the campaign slogan of "Earth for Terrans." The day he won, Caitlin felt like the writing was on the wall. Although she had long since shed her identity as "Moon girl," her passport and birth certificate still carried the truth about where she hailed from.

As the president continued to throw wood on the fire of the country's paranoia, people in the streets were already gleefully talking about mass deportation. However, for all the campaign bluster, no one believed such a deportation would happen, although there were many (including Jennie Thompson's mother, whose age had dulled her wits but not her all-consuming fear of Moon girls) who wanted it to happen, and fast. The president's rhetoric was met with resistance and didn't seem positioned to gain serious traction. The majority of the press and the public expected any bill proposing deportation to be stamped out by Congress. Of course, even if that happened, it was pretty much a given that life as a lunar immigrant would likely be unpleasant under the rule of the new administration. Because of this, Caitlin kept the truth about where she'd been born a closely guarded secret.

She might have succeeded in keeping her secret too, had, on the day of the new commander in chief's inauguration, some representatives of a radical pro-Moonborn group called Nightside not decided to set off a He-3 bomb at an American embassy in Senegal, citing the president's new policies. Luckily, the bomb wasn't a big one, but it was more than enough to cause a sizable death toll. Once the images made their way across the news platforms, that was all it took. While he couldn't get every Moonborn deported, the bombing was enough to enable the president to enact a travel ban barring anyone with a lunar passport from traveling to Earth. And, unfortunately for Caitlin, she happened to be on the Moon right when everything went bad. She had taken a brief trip to sort out her mother's affairs after her death and was just about to board a transport for home when she discovered that her passport had been frozen, along with all her travel privileges. And just like that, Emily had been left with a father who barely remembered that they lived in the same house and Caitlin was stuck on the Moon. She had tried working through legal channels, but the red tape was almost impossible to navigate.

"Just sit tight," her lawyer had told her. "With your veteran status, there's a good chance we can get you some kind of travel pass to get you back home. We're talking three, maybe six months, here."

"And what am I supposed to do in the meantime?" Caitlin had asked.

"Well," her lawyer said, "you could always get a job."

As crazy as that idea sounded, Caitlin decided that was exactly what she was going to do. She had never been one to sit around helplessly, preferring to be proactive and always moving forward.

Thanks to her parents' line of work, Caitlin still had a few contacts she could rely on enough to land a job hauling He-3 for Guanghang Mining. Sadly, her family, such as it was, had long since passed on. Emily was the only family she had left. Well, Emily and Caitlin's crew.

After struggling into her work clothes and zipping up her jumpsuit, Caitlin made her way out the door of her unit and into the dingy, cluttered hallway of the Hive's main complex. A few early-rising children streaked past, caught up in a raucous game, giggling and shrieking wildly as they ran. Caitlin shook her head, watching them dash up the corridor.

"Be careful!" she called as she made her way to the exit. But they were already gone.

◆ ◆ ◆

"Cutter Taggart is here, ladies and gentlemen! Now the day can begin!"

A round of exaggerated applause filled the Doghouse as Caitlin walked in. "Cutter" was her nickname at the mine, bestowed upon her by the old crew chief, Trigger, who became like a second father after she started at the mining company a year ago. He had worked with her dad on his failed bid at He-3 mining and, when the Taggarts had left for Earth, had stayed behind and made mining his life. He remembered Caitlin from when she was a baby and had immediately taken her under his wing. "No one cuts through rego the way you do, kid," he'd say in his gravelly voice at the end of a long day's work. Either that, or his other favorite compliment: "You've got the hot hand."

Much to Caitlin's shock, Trigger had passed away suddenly, just eight months after she'd come on board. Those who chose to live on the Moon generally didn't live as long as those on Earth, but Trigger had beaten the odds, making sixty-eight revolutions around the Sun before his heart gave out. While many people his age on the unforgiving lunar tundra would have retired long ago, Trigger remained a scraper right to the end. Mining rego was what he was born to do, he'd said, so Caitlin supposed it was only fitting that he had died doing it as well. But before he died, Trigger had taken care of two key pieces of business: he had given Caitlin her nickname and appointed her his successor as crew chief. Because of this, no one ever called Caitlin by her real name at the Doghouse, addressing her as "boss," "chief," or "Cutter."

She wasn't sure if any of the people she worked with outside of her crew even knew what her name was.

Miners congregated before and after their shifts at the Doghouse, which was as dirty, noisy, and crowded as the Hive, without the air of desperation. It was a lively, rowdy place where the crews bickered over who would harvest the most rego, commiserated about people they left behind on the world, and competed against each other in a one-sixth-gravity version of basketball someone had coined "g-ball." In the Doghouse, people were just as likely to break into a fight as they were into song. Music was always playing on a continuous loop, booming from a source deep within the Doghouse's bowels. As Caitlin made her entrance, she heard Joe Walsh's "Turn to Stone."

"Stow it, Diaz," she said. "We've got a lot of rego to move today."

"Where we headed, Boss?" asked Tony as he leaned casually against the lockers, his thick arms folded over his broad chest. Tony Parker was a mountain of a man, just muscle, sinew, and stoic intimidation. But Caitlin knew him well enough to know that it was all a front. Underneath, softhearted mush. She had watched him cry looking at an Earthrise, although she was sworn to secrecy.

"Bear Crater," Caitlin told him.

"Taurus-Littrow again?" asked Vee, another member of the crew, Tony's wife, and the closest thing to a sister Caitlin had ever had. And yet, she still didn't know her first name. Vee stood for something, but whether it was Violet, Veronica, or Victrola, Caitlin had no clue. She was just Vee, and she didn't like being asked about it.

"That's where the money is," Caitlin said. "The company thinks we can get a few more passes before we have to move southwest out to Fra Mauro. And that's not going to be a stroll in the park. So I'll take the easy money while we can still get it."

"You're the boss, Cutter," said Diaz, though his grin suggested teasing rather than deference. Caitlin shook her head. Freddy Diaz may have been a wiseass, but he was a good miner and a loyal crew member. Tall and wiry with thick black hair and brown eyes that were always in motion, he was born on the Moon and had never set foot on Earth or anywhere else. And chances were he probably never would. After more than a quarter century on the lunar surface, his body probably couldn't take the strain of Terran gravity. Not that it was much of an issue anyway these days. *Thank you, Mr. President,* Caitlin thought angrily.

"That's goddamn right," Caitlin said, giving him a wink. "Now suit up and move out. I want the rig ready to roll in twenty."

"All right, Diaz," said Tony. "You heard the lady. Let's get the *Invader* prepped. I don't want to carry your ass for another cycle."

"You know, Tony," Diaz said, "you keep going like this, you're going to give yourself a stroke. You need to relax."

"I'll relax when I don't have to babysit you out there on the crater," said Tony, but he was smiling as he spoke. "Which means I'll relax when I'm dead."

"Well, from the neck up, seems to me you already are, buddy!"

They headed out of the common area, jostling and trading insults. Vee and Caitlin watched them go and then made their way into the locker rooms to begin suiting up.

"Where's Shaw?" Caitlin asked, struggling into her counterpressure suit. A significant advancement from the cumbersome gas-pressurized outfits of old, these new suits acted almost like a second skin. Made from an interwoven network of shape-memory alloys, the suit contracted when heated, shrink-wrapping itself around the wearer's body. The "squeeze suits," as they were commonly known, made the kind of work Caitlin and her crew conducted daily that much easier. Plus they were laced with microencapsulated chemicals. In the event of a small rupture or tear, the agents would allow the suit to effectively heal itself. And in Caitlin's line of work, small ruptures happened all the time.

"Immigration," Vee said, working her own suit over her body. "Trying to get his wife here. He should be here before we roll."

"Still can't sort it all out, huh?"

"You know the drill," said Vee. "You're lucky you got your little girl a travel pass."

"Benefits of being a war hero," said Caitlin with a trace of bitterness.

"Don't knock it, girl," Vee said. Her green eyes, which always stood out from her bronzed skin, fixed themselves on Caitlin. "It's gonna get her here and away from that father of hers. Maybe then you might have a chance at getting her a residency."

"In the Hive?" Caitlin scoffed.

"Hey, beats living with her old man," said Vee. "What did you ever see in that waster anyway?"

"I . . . I don't know," Caitlin said. But deep down, she did. She had just come back from the war, a woman out of place. The Last Campaign, as it came to be known, was the most brutal and unforgiving of the three wars held in Iraq and its surrounding territories. Some people thought that the conflict's brutality stemmed from fundamentalist forces spending so much of the last century feeding on hatred of the West that they were desperate to continue acting on that hatred. Caitlin knew better. They weren't fighting because they despised America. They were fighting because they had nothing else left. These were the Dead Enders, to whom the only avenue left was violence.

The successful mining of He-3 had ended the world's dependency on fossil fuels. Twenty-five tons of the stuff could cleanly power the United States for a year. In the blink of an eye, the planet was suddenly freed from decades of dependence on Middle Eastern oil reserves to power their cities. One by one, the armies of the world began a steady drawdown, pulling out of the region and bringing home troops to nations of welcoming arms. Unfortunately, their absence left a void that was soon filled with blood.

Those left behind carved their nations into individual caliphates, twisted perversions of the term that ruled through fear, intimidation, and violence. And once again, the West was in the crosshairs. Those who had hated America for their presence on holy ground now hated them for their absence, telling their followers how the infidels had left their nation to burn and decay while they grew fatter on their newfound riches from the heavens. And, as the violence spread throughout the region, so too did the fear throughout the rest of the world. In an echo of the domino theory of the First Cold War, the consensus was that the bloody tide generated in the Middle East would soon wash up on American shores. Thus, no sooner had they stepped off the transports home, the troops were back on the ground with their boots in the sand, and among them was Caitlin Taggart.

Eventually, after years of conflict, an accord was reached, with the nations of the world agreeing to share in the wealth generated by the Moon's newfound energy source. And so, as it had been with many wars before, those in charge became rich and those who'd done the fighting got what was left. After the war, Caitlin came home a ghost, finding neither work nor peace. She wasn't "at home" in her own house, her own town, even her own skin. People at home could never understand how the return to civilian life was even more difficult than time in the military. With so much damage and senseless devastation happening overseas, much of it at their own hands, Caitlin and her fellow soldiers had turned to each other. They were surrounded by death on all sides, so they chose to embrace what life they could in their camaraderie and brotherhood. That last word was the most important to her, because it conveyed an unspoken trust. They weren't just friends who would do things for each other out of kindness or obligation. They were a family who would sweat, bleed, and die for each other because the code commanded it.

Caitlin remembered being holed up in a cave in Kurdistan as she and a small platoon held off wave after wave of Enders for sixteen hours. So many times before then, she had heard the phrase "Today is a good day to die," but had dismissed it as macho posturing, something wannabe soldiers tattooed on their biceps. But there, inside that cave alongside those men and women, she understood the term in all its forms. To die there in the sand with them, it *would* be a good day. Because she would have died for something. Not for what she was told she was fighting for, but rather for what was real, right in front of her. She would die in the company of others who would, if asked, do the same for her. And that was a good thing indeed.

But once she came back home, that feeling vanished, a fog burned off by midday sunlight. She felt as though she had nothing to live for and, even worse, nothing to die for. Caitlin felt like a curiosity, something to be studied from a distance, or perhaps, tiptoed around nervously. Every time someone said "Thank you for your service," her skin crawled. Caitlin knew they meant well, but she also felt like they were uttering the phrase out of obligation or guilt.

Even more unctuous were the people who tried to relate to her in some way, telling her about a family member who had fought in some other military conflict, as a means of establishing common ground. Or they'd come up to her and tell her about someone they knew who had died, as if that meant that they, too, could understand loss. She grew to dislike and mistrust civilians, finding comfort only in the company of other veterans. But then, as time went on, even they became difficult to socialize with. After all, she would say to herself, how could they tell horror stories about their old battles. Didn't they know that *her* war was the worst war?

This went on for months, until Caitlin felt alone and haunted. She would lie awake at night for hours as the wind howled outside and shadows formed long and terrible shapes on the wall. When the day came, all she felt was dread at the prospect of facing it.

Caitlin had known Eric back in high school, one of the few left in town who she thought knew her. Knew the real Caitlin Taggart before she'd gone off to the campaign, back when he was the quarterback with everything going for him and she was the cool gearhead chick who could keep his Challenger running every weekend. Coming back from all the horror and seeing him was like coming back to some semblance of the life she had known.

He'd suffered his own losses in her absence. A shattered knee had taken him from the gridiron to working with his brothers selling off-world real estate. He and Caitlin both seemed to be grieving for something—she for the lives she'd taken, he for the one taken from him. He was something for her to put her back up against, or so she'd thought. Another damn mistake. The marriage lasted less than a year, with much of that time spent either apologizing for or covering up Eric's alcohol- and drug-fueled mishaps.

"Anyway," Caitlin went on, "she'll be here for a time, but sooner or later she's going to have to go back."

"I know," Vee said, nodding.

Caitlin saw the look in Vee's eyes as she spoke and knew how well she understood her plight. Vee and Tony had also been unfortunate victims of the lunar travel ban. Like Caitlin, they'd both been born on the Moon and moved to Earth as children. Vee had barely qualified as a lunar resident, having come to Earth at less than a month old. Nevertheless, her passport labeled her as Moonborn, and when things had gone south on Earth, that label had come back to haunt her. She and Tony had been honeymooning at Lake Armstrong and planned on spending extra time cultivating new sites over in Aldrin City to expand their burgeoning contracting business. Then the Nightside bomb had gone off. Within a few months, they were out of business, money, and choices. Fast forward a few months more and they were riding a harvester with Caitlin and company, scraping up Moon dust for the betterment of a world where they were no longer welcome.

"I shouldn't complain," Caitlin said. "I know you've had your share of tough breaks. Although, whenever I hear your story, I just keep thinking about one thing."

"What's that?"

She tossed her friend a sly look, eyes glinting. "Who the hell honeymoons at Lake Armstrong?"

"Don't mess with me, Taggart. I'm not in the mood."

"Oh, you love it," Caitlin said. "Come on. Fire me up."

Caitlin turned around and Vee hit a patch on the back of her suit, sending forth an electric current. In an instant the suit sealed around her. She flexed and stretched, getting comfortable inside the garment she'd be wearing for the next eight hours.

"Whoo," she said, feeling the current pass through. "Tingles. Now you're up."

Vee turned around and Caitlin did the same for her. Vee gave her a nod.

The two walked out of the locker room and into the motor pool, where the harvester rigs were gearing up for the day's runs across the Moon's surface. Their rig, the *Space Invader*, was at the far end of the pool, and the two women began making their way to it.

"Gonna set the record today, Taggart?"

Caitlin turned around to see the grinning face of Tom Hudson looking down at her. She returned the grin with one of her own.

"Thinking about it," she said. "Figure someone's got to be bringing in rego around here. The way you run your crew, Earth might be blacked out by the end of the week."

"Cute," said Hudson. "Real cute. I'll have you know that the *Dun Ringill* has just come off a major overhaul. Best harvester in the fleet."

"It's not the harvester, my friend," said Caitlin. "It's the crew that runs her."

"If that's the case," Hudson said, "then you're *definitely* going down."

"Oh really?" said Caitlin. "Care to make a wager out of it?"

"Loser buys the round?"

"For a *month*," said Caitlin.

"Now you're talking," Hudson said. "You're on."

He put out his hand and Caitlin slapped it hard. Hudson grinned.

"See you back at the Doghouse, Taggart," he said. "I'll have my drink order ready."

He turned to go, and Vee cocked an eyebrow at Caitlin.

"My man has got eyes for you," she said.

"Please," said Caitlin, walking again.

"What?" said Vee. "What exactly is the problem here? He's young, handsome, and you both have . . . shared interests."

"What, mining rego?" asked Caitlin.

"Hey, it's a jumping-off point!"

"Look," said Caitlin, "he's a nice guy and all, but I'm not looking to get involved with anyone, OK? I'm trying to get home to my daughter. The last thing I need is to start making attachments."

"I'm just saying," said Vee, "it's cold up here. Might be nice to have something warm to wake up to."

"You're gross."

Finally, they reached the end of the motor pool where the *Space Invader* was prepped and waiting. She was a big, ungainly machine, designed to grind up regolith and convert it to He-3. A four-treaded vehicle, the *Invader* was fitted with a massive sawlike blade that jutted out from the front like an insect's proboscis. The blade, commonly called a "bucket wheel," was used for chopping and gathering rego before dumping it into an electrostatic separator. The process saved rocks more than fifty micrometers in size, since those were proven to have the highest He-3 content, and discarded the rest. In the center behind the cab, a giant dish, the solar collector, jutted upward. The collector gathered the Sun's energy and sent it through a piping system to the heater, which baked the regolith to seven hundred degrees Celsius, releasing the helium from inside the rock.

Now fully prepped, the *Invader* sat poised and ready in front of the airlock. On the other side was the vacuum of lunar space. Diaz and Tony scrabbled around, tools clattering and voices raised. Vee eyed the two of them with disdain.

"What was it you were saying?" she asked. "It's not the harvester, it's the crew?"

"Yeah," said Caitlin. "That was it."

"Care to revise your statement?"

"All right, you two," Caitlin barked. "Playtime's over. Let's get this thing on the surface."

"It's ready to roll, Boss," said Tony. "Just waiting for your go."

"You've got it," she said as she climbed into the *Invader*'s cab. Vee slid in next to her at the wheel as Tony and Diaz clambered into the back.

"Now," said Caitlin, "are we ready to head out?"

"Hell yes," said Diaz. "Let's move this mother!"

Caitlin looked around, doing a quick head count. Still no Shaw. Then she spotted him running across the motor pool, hastily pulling his suit up over his wiry frame as he did. He scrambled on board, running his hands through his brown tresses and offering an apologetic look.

"Nice of you to join us, buddy," Caitlin said.

"I'm sorry, Chief," Shaw said between deep breaths. "You know how Immigration is. It's worse than the goddamn DMV back on the world."

Caitlin winked at him to show that she understood. She ran a tight ship, but she also knew that you didn't earn your crew's respect by always riding them. "Everything OK?" she asked. "Can we expect a happy reunion between husband and wife?"

Shaw's face darkened. He looked at his boss squarely.

"Don't think so," he said. "She's leaving me. Said she can't wait around for me to come home, and even if she could, she never . . ."

"Never what?" asked Caitlin.

"Never could see herself married to a miner."

"We are a rare breed," Diaz piped up.

"Shut it," growled Tony.

"Forget it," said Shaw. "It's all good. Come on, we've got rego to move."

"Hey," said Diaz. "Forget her. All the family you need is right here, brother."

Diaz extended his fist and Shaw bumped it. Weakly, but it was enough for now.

"You sure you're good?" asked Caitlin.

"Yeah," Shaw said. "I'll be all right."

She decided not to probe further for the time being and nodded in compassion.

"Take a seat," she said. "Let's ride."

Shaw began stowing his gear. Vee started up the *Invader*'s massive engines and moved the rig toward the airlock. They slid forward until they were almost bumping against the exit. Behind them, the door to the motor pool slid shut, sealing them inside.

"Helmets on, people," said Caitlin.

Almost in sync, the crew snapped on their helmets, hearing the click as the locks slid into place. Unlike the older model helmets, which employed a layer of gold to shield astronauts' faces from the Sun's ultraviolet radiation, the newer helmets employed a visor made from a tinted high-density polycarbonate material that blocked the Sun's rays but allowed their faces to be seen. This was particularly helpful in their line of work. Facial expressions were often the first sign of distress, and when mining He-3, distress was something everyone encountered sooner or later. Being able to read it on a fellow miner's face could make the difference between reacting in time or being a second too late.

The crew looked at each other and nodded. Everyone was ready and everything was humming. They could all feel it. But before they could officially get moving, Caitlin had one last task to complete, already being met with a groan of protest from Diaz.

"No," he said, seeing Caitlin's gloved hands dancing over the dashboard. He shook his head. "Come on, Boss, not today."

Not bothering to answer, Caitlin hit the screen to activate the satellite radio. The Beach Boys' "I Get Around" filled the cabin as Diaz groaned.

"OK, fine," he said. "I get it. Music is a big deal in your rig. But does it have to be this . . . whatever this is? Stuff's like a hundred years old!"

"My rig, my radio," Caitlin said in a tone that conveyed how much pleasure she derived from torturing Diaz's eardrums. He merely shook his head. Reaching for the mic, Caitlin got on the comm to base control. "Control, this is Rego One, awaiting clearance," she said. A hiss of static and they received the OK to head out.

"Rego One, this is control. You are cleared for Bear Crater. Good hunting."

"All right, let's go make some money!" said Tony exuberantly over the music.

The amber warning lights surrounding the airlock entrance lit up and rotated slowly, accompanied by a Klaxon alarm that alerted anyone still in the vicinity to exit the area or be sucked out. The door slid open slowly as air rushed into space. Vee throttled the gearshift forward and the *Space Invader* headed out onto the Moon's surface.

As they rode toward Bear Crater, Caitlin gazed out the window at the scenery, such as it was. Buzz Aldrin, the second man to walk on the surface of this unwelcoming world, once described it as "magnificent desolation." Caitlin thought, in all the years that had passed since that fateful day in another century, no one had ever found a better way to capture the juxtaposition of awe and loneliness one felt when looking out over the Moon's terrain. The Sun shone almost white along the gray regolith, illuminating the younger patches that formed what were commonly called lunar swirls. Impact craters dotted the Moon's battered face, telling the story of countless asteroid and comet strikes. Along the plains, long-dead oceans of ancient lava rose and fell. And off in the distance, mountains protruded up from the surface like long-abandoned pyramids. In her time mining regolith, Caitlin had enjoyed views of the Moon no one else had ever seen. She supposed she should be grateful; maybe someday she would be. But for now, she couldn't stop thinking about what all of this had cost her.

Their sojourn across the Moonscape stopped along the rim of the massive crater. As large as the *Space Invader* was, out here, it looked like a child's toy set at the edge of an enormous sandbox. The men leaped out of the rig and began getting the gear ready. Caitlin gazed at the display on the dashboard, scoping out spots that looked the most promising, then climbed out of the cab and looked down into the crater before giving orders.

"Diaz!" she said. "You're on the bucket wheel. Keep the pivot arm loose and keep the blade moving. Watch out for anything large enough to jam it up. Tony, I want the collector flowing. I'm talking constant heat coming through those pipes. I'll run separator. And Shaw, once we've got the rock baked, you load the canisters. Everyone's got their assignments, so let's get it Bravo Zulu on the first try! Clear?"

"Hooah!" everyone said in unison before going to their respective stations.

With everyone in position, Vee hit the gas and the *Invader* made its way into the crater and down to the mining field. As the bucket wheel was dragged along the surface, it chopped up regolith in its wake. The small particles of rock and dust caught the sunlight as they were agitated, floating up and back down to the surface like mini shooting stars. It was almost hypnotic, Caitlin thought. She had heard rumors that new harvesters were being developed that would do the job automatically, lumbering over the surface like massive grain combines, chopping up the rego as automated droids handled the gathering and separating process. She supposed that was for the best, but she felt for the future generations of would-be miners being deprived of such beautiful sights.

About four hours into the shift, the *Invader*'s engine seized up and the rig sputtered to a halt in the middle of the crater.

"Dammit!" Caitlin said, and hauled herself out of the cab.

She climbed down to the surface. Tony was already working the problem.

"What've we got?" asked Caitlin.

"Damn rego's caught up in the drivetrain somewhere," he said.

Caitlin shook her head. Rego was a common problem everywhere on the Moon, especially when it came to machinery. The radiation that constantly bombarded the lunar surface gave the soil an electrical charge, which meant that it clung to everything. But the harvesters were supposed to be protected against such accidents.

"How the hell did that happen?" Caitlin asked.

Tony pointed to the engine covering and grimaced.

"Looks like we kicked up an iron fragment," he said. "Probably early in the scrape. Punched a hole right in the casing. Rego's been flowing into it ever since. Everything's gummed up pretty good."

By now, the rest of the crew had gathered around, assessing the problem. Caitlin was past assessment, only interested in solutions.

"How can we fix it?" she asked.

"Not sure," he said. "Back at the Doghouse, I'd just suck the stuff out with a vacuum. But vacuums don't work without an atmosphere. No air means no suck out here."

"There's plenty of suck out here if you know where to look," said Diaz.

"Can it," said Vee.

"So you're saying we're stuck?" Caitlin asked.

"Looks that way."

Caitlin considered their situation for a moment, then an idea struck her.

"Maybe not," she said. "I've got an idea. It's crazy, though . . ."

"Crazy can be good," said Tony. "What is it?"

"It's probably better if I show you rather than tell you."

"Fair enough. What do you need to get started?"

"I need a few of the canisters from the *Invader*," said Caitlin. "And we've got to bring them out to the crater wall. Over to the shadows."

"All the way out there?" said Diaz. "You'll probably lose an hour."

Caitlin looked out to the far edge of the crater and then back at her crew.

"Better than losing a day," she said, gathering up two canisters. "Let's get moving. Shaw? You're coming with me."

"Why me?" he asked.

"You've got the equipment I need," said Caitlin. "Plus, don't you think it's a lovely day for a walk?"

Having gathered their gear and the canisters, Caitlin and Shaw made their way farther into the crater, feeling impossibly small. As the temperature began to drop, Caitlin found herself grateful for the protection of her suit. While there was no heating system, the truth was the garment didn't need it. The vacuum seal trapped body heat, keeping miners warm.

"How are you holding up?" Caitlin asked Shaw.

"What do you mean?"

"You know," she said, "your wife and everything that's going on."

"Oh," Shaw replied. "If you're worried that my head's not on the job . . ."

"No. I'm worried because you're on my crew. And that means you're family to me."

Shaw allowed a small smile at this. In the time since Caitlin had taken over the *Invader* crew, she had taken on the role of den mother to the team. Making sure they got their physicals done, that they had eaten before work and stayed hydrated during and after a job. It had gotten so that the crew, in addition to Cutter, occasionally called her Mama Bear.

"I'm doing . . . surprisingly well, actually," Shaw said. "I mean, it sucks, but I think I knew this was coming for a long time."

"How so?"

"I don't think she was ever really in love with me," he said. "I think she loved the idea of me, if that makes sense. The idea of who she thought I was. Or, more to the point, who she thought she could turn me into."

Before Caitlin could ask more, they'd reached the crater wall. The Sun had dropped out of their sight, and with it, the temperature. They took a moment to look around. Shaw turned to Caitlin.

"All right," he said. "What's the plan?"

Caitlin dropped to one knee, placing a canister in a mini subcrater, the product of a micrometeorite strike.

"OK," said Shaw as Caitlin stood back up. "Now what?"

"Now we wait," Caitlin said. "It shouldn't take long . . ."

"For the water vapor inside to freeze!" Shaw said, finally picking up on what Caitlin was proposing.

"You got it," she said. "I'm just concerned that the other gases might freeze as well."

Shaw shook his head. "The temperature's not cold enough for the hydrogen, oxygen, or even He-3 to freeze. Just the water, which is all we need."

"See?" said Caitlin. "That's why I brought you with me."

As they waited for the cold to do its job, Caitlin returned to the previous conversation.

"What was her idea?"

"What?"

"Your wife," said Caitlin. "What was her idea of what you should be?"

"I don't know," said Shaw. "Work in an office. Ride an elevator every morning. Sit around with a bunch of dudes in ties saying stuff like, 'You don't have to be crazy to work here, but it helps!' and 'Is it beer o'clock yet?'"

"Sounds unpleasant," Caitlin agreed. "What did you want to do?"

"I wanted to teach," he said. "I loved science and thought maybe if I passed that excitement and enthusiasm to the kids, I could make some kind of difference. Problem was all I could get was sub work. And when that dried up, I knew I had to do something, so I came here. Figured I could put that science knowledge to good use and maybe still make a difference, even if it wasn't the one I'd intended to make."

"Well, if we pull this off, you're gonna help make a difference today," said Caitlin, nodding toward the canister.

"Yeah," said Shaw, looking around at the massive crater. "If she could only see me now."

Once she was convinced the Moon's temperature had turned the water vapor inside the first canister to ice, Caitlin picked up a second one. Dropping again to her knee, she opened the first canister, venting out all the gases, then looked up at Shaw, shaking it like a tumbler of scotch. Although no sound was produced in the airless void, Caitlin almost felt like she could hear the clinking of frozen cubes.

"Ice," she said, grinning. "Which we can then turn to steam."

"Great," said Shaw. "Only, if you're proposing what I think you're proposing, one gathering of ice isn't going to be enough. We need a heavier concentration."

"A good teacher always checks his students' work," Caitlin said. "That's why I proposed bringing extra canisters."

"So we've got to transfer the gases into the canister with the ice, freeze that water vapor, and do the whole process over again three more times."

"Sounds about right," said Caitlin.

Shaw reached into his equipment bag and extracted a high-pressure hose designed for transferring gases.

"Then let's get to work," he said.

◆ ◆ ◆

Once the job was complete, Caitlin and Shaw walked back to the *Invader*. Caitlin used the heating system on board the harvester to turn the water ice into steam. After Shaw fiddled with the tank's valve to reverse the flow, he brought the tank over to the hole in the rig's casing and handed it to Tony.

"What do I do?" Tony asked.

"Just point the canister at the drivetrain and open the valve."

Tony did as Shaw asked and a torrent of steam erupted from the end of the canister. He had to tighten his grip to avoid having it slip from his hands. The crew cheered in unison at the makeshift pressure washer as Tony cleaned out the collected grime from the Moon's surface. Within a few minutes, the drivetrain was cleared, Vee was able to turn the engine over, and Diaz had covered up the hole with foam sealant. They were underway again.

"Well done, crew," said Caitlin. "That's how we do it."

As everyone prepared to get back on board, Caitlin stopped Shaw for a moment.

"Your ex-wife might not think so," she said, "but I think the idea of you is pretty damn great."

She bumped her helmet against his and clapped him on the back before climbing the ladder to get on the *Invader* and back to work. By the expression on his face, Caitlin thought Shaw looked happier than she'd seen him in a long time.

When their shift was over, the crew walked back over to the rig, tired, aching, and covered in Moon dust. Diaz peered into the back of the *Invader*, marveling at the stacks of canisters, the spoils of a hard day out in the mining fields. From where they were on the crater, they would haul the canisters to a condensing station where the collected gases would be cooled in a cryogenator. The He-3 would be drained off, and excess gases produced by the cooling process—like hydrogen, methane, and oxygen—would be collected separately and used to sustain life-support systems in the colonies. As for the He-3, it would be loaded onto industrial transports at the Ponca City docks and sent back to Earth. But as far as the *Invader* crew was concerned, all of that was someone else's problem. By the time the gas was on a transport back to Earth, they would be on to another crater, mining the next helium batch to build a better future for everyone else.

"All right," said Caitlin, "let's head home. Think we've made the company rich enough for one day."

Everyone nodded and piled back into the *Invader*, still chatting, bickering, and bantering. The radio blasted the Kings' "Switchin' to Glide." Caitlin's body felt sore but exercised, the way it should feel after a day of exertion and hard work. Her father would have simply called the feeling a "good tired."

"Who's buying tonight?" asked Diaz.

"Every day you ask that question," said Shaw. "Is the answer ever going to be you?"

"I told you," Diaz said, "I'm waiting on my chits."

At the mention of chits, Caitlin felt herself bristle. It was a particular point of irritation for her that they didn't actually get paid for their work. For miners like her, with family back on the world, the company had arranged for a stipend to be transmitted to Earth each month, but otherwise, execs thought room and board were sufficient compensation. Or maybe they thought the privilege of pushing Moon dust back and forth was its own reward. Caitlin didn't know.

In lieu of pay, what was offered were "chits," small plastic tokens that acted as currency around the Hive to buy anything extra that the company didn't provide. Generally speaking, that meant booze. A makeshift bar called the Dark Side served what passed for alcohol on the Moon. Basically, they were just processed cubes that, when mixed with water, liquefied and became something approximating a drink. The venue had whiskey cubes, vodka cubes, Jaeger cubes . . . there was even a beer cube, although no one among Caitlin's crew had ever felt brave enough to try it.

So the crews used chits to get skunked after a day of mining, but Diaz was always giving his chits away to anyone who was short, with the promise that he would one day get them all back with interest. The rest of the crew considered his gestures to be noble, but the paybacks never seemed to materialize. As such, they were always stuck picking up the tab for him, not that any of them really minded.

"Trust me," said Diaz, even as everyone chided him. They had heard it all before. "Trust me. Any day now. Mrs. Huang's gonna pay me back. Jimmy Egan. The Frenes in 2205. It's all gonna come through and I'll be hip-deep in chits."

"You can replace that *ch* with an *sh*, and you'll be closer to the mark," said Tony.

More laughter. Driving over the surface of the Moon, teasing and joking with these disparate people, Caitlin felt that, just for a moment, she might be OK. That maybe things weren't as dire as she usually thought they were. Then she caught a glance of Earth rising high in obsidian firmament and her heart broke once again.

Caitlin got back to the Hive, wanting only to crawl into bed. She had gone to the Dark Side long enough to collect the free round for her and her crew for outpacing Tom Hudson in mining rego. Hudson took the loss gracefully, promising that the next time he paid for a drink it would just be the two of them, but she brushed him off gently with a promise that, if he kept making bets, he'd be paying for her drinks for a long time. For all the merriment, she took the moment when Tony decided it was time to stand on the bar and sing Otis Redding's "These Arms of Mine" as her cue to leave. As she got to the door, she fumbled in her jumpsuit pocket for the plastic card that unlocked her unit. She sighed, assessing her situation. A shower was out of the question thanks to the rationing, so she knew she was going to have to sleep dirty and grime-ridden. But, she told herself, at least she would sleep. She was working a double tomorrow, so she intended to get as much shut-eye as she could. She pressed her thumb to the plate in front of her unit, allowing the door to slide open. She was just about to walk in when she spotted the man waiting for her.

"Taggart?" he said. "Caitlin Taggart?"

"Jesus!" Caitlin said, jumping back. "You can't sneak up on people like that!"

"I'm sorry," the man said. "Very sorry. But you are Caitlin Taggart, yes? Captain Caitlin Taggart?"

"Yes," she said. "Retired. Who wants to know?"

The man extended his hand and pumped hers up and down excitedly. "David Richards," he said. "I work with Lyman Ross."

"OK . . . and he is?"

"Sorry, sorry," Richards said, waving his arms. "Son of Senator Hamer Ross from Texas and the head of Core One Mining? The mining company? He is very interested in meeting with you!"

"I appreciate that," Caitlin said. "But can it wait until tomorrow? As you can see, I've had a long day and—"

"I'm afraid it's somewhat of an urgent matter. Time is of the essence."

"Well, then, I'm going to have to decline," said Caitlin. "I don't just meet with strange men because they're on a schedule."

Caitlin turned to go and Richards piped up again.

"Mr. Ross knows he's inconveniencing you," he said, "but he wouldn't do so if it wasn't extremely pressing."

She stopped and looked back. Something in his voice had gotten her attention. "How pressing?"

Richards looked at Caitlin and she could tell by the glint in his eye that he knew he had her on the hook. All he had to do was reel her in.

"What if I told you that he can get you home to your daughter?"

Chapter Three

Looking around at Lyman Ross's private office in Aldrin City's Hotel Cernan, Caitlin Taggart had only one continuous thought: *I am in the wrong business.* Compared to the bland, filthy lodgings at the Hive, the opulence on display was extreme. Everything seemed to be coated in oak and enhanced by the tawny light coming from elegant wall fixtures. The desk she was sitting in front of was equally ostentatious and, in a place like the Moon, pointless. Life in a harsh, unforgiving environment such as the Moon was supposed to be about function. Here, the furniture was nothing but form. Lyman Ross was obviously a man who cared a great deal about impressions.

"There she is!" a Texas-accented voice bellowed.

Ross crossed the distance between himself and Caitlin with loud, heavy footfalls designed to announce his presence to anyone within earshot. His suit was immaculate and probably cost more than she could make in a year of moving rego, chits or no chits. Equally immaculate were his teeth, white, gleaming, and gigantic. Caitlin found herself wondering if, at the right angle, they might be visible from Earth. He finally reached her and shook her hand vigorously, smiling excitedly. During the brief but spirited handshake, Caitlin noticed rope bracelets on his wrist and a brief flash of tattoo. That, plus the shaggy blond hair that poked out beneath his rather large cowboy hat, told her that the suit was little more than a costume, just as the office was a stage. And the play that was about to begin was titled "Daddy's Boy Tries to Make Good." The only question she had now was what her role would be.

"Man oh man, is it a pleasure to meet you, Captain," Ross said. "My brother was at Samarra. He was a reporter for the *Newsfeed*. He saw what you and your platoon did there."

He pointed to the nearby wall on which hung a tattered American flag, no doubt recovered from the battlefield. Ross eyed the flag a moment. Caitlin wondered if he was about to salute.

"A great day," he said. "Great day."

"Only if you read about it on the *Newsfeed*."

At that remark, he didn't flinch at all. He just pointed at Caitlin, smile still intact. "I heard that," he said. "I heard it!"

Ross moved around to the other side of the desk and produced a large bottle of amber liquid. He poured two drinks and handed a glass to Caitlin.

"Bourbon?" he asked. "We've got the real stuff here. Not that cubed shit y'all drink back at the mining camp."

Caitlin took the drink, though a part of her felt just a little wrong for doing so. But with just one sip, regrets washed away. She hadn't had a real drink in a year. The taste was sharp, smoky, and rich, and every dormant sense in her mouth was suddenly shaken awake. Ross immediately read her reaction, and instead of one pointed finger, Caitlin now got two, one from each hand. His smile grew to an almost impossible width, followed by a boisterous guffaw.

"Ah?" Ross said as he nodded. "Ah? Do we have a winner? Yes, I think she likes it!"

"It's good, thank you," Caitlin admitted, setting the drink down. "Now, can you tell me why I'm here?"

Ross slapped the desk almost gleefully. "Right to the point!" he said. "I like it! I really, really like it! OK, Captain—"

"You can just call me Caitlin."

"All right then, Caitlin," he said. "I will tell you why you're here. I'm about to make you absolutely filthy rich. Davey boy!"

Richards scuttled over and pointed a remote at a holoprojector on the desk. There was a quick flash and a 3-D image of what looked to be an asteroid appeared, rotating slowly on its axis.

"Asteroid 1222 Thresher," said Ross. "It's packed with more platinum than any other near-Earth asteroid we've tracked. To put a number to it, we're looking at about five trillion dollars' worth of platinum. We think it came out of the asteroid belt between Jupiter and Mars. Probably got knocked out by Jupiter's gravity or something. Whatever the case may be, it's presently on a flyby course with Earth. Once it passes by our geo-sats, it won't come back for another hundred and fifty years."

He leaned forward on the desk. The 3-D image cast his face in an eerie blue glow.

"What do you know about asteroid mining, Caitlin?"

"That it's dangerous," she said, "which is why no one does it. It's also not entirely legal yet."

"Right, right," said Ross. "It is dangerous. You know what else people thought was dangerous? Building a machine that could fly. Or a rocket that went to the Moon. Hell, if we avoided something just because it was dangerous, we never would have left Earth at all."

"That would have been fine with me," Caitlin said. She noticed that his answer had deftly skirted the issue of asteroid mining's shaky legality.

Ross's eyes narrowed and his voice lowered to an almost conspiratorial whisper, but the smirk remained. "I know it would," he said. "And that's why we need to talk!"

Ross stood up and began pacing the room excitedly. This was the pitch, Caitlin realized, what he had been building toward since he first got the idea to summon her here.

"Asteroid mining *is* dangerous," he said. "But it's also the wave of the future. There are countless asteroids floating around out there between

Mars and Jupiter, and thousands more between Earth and Mars. And nearly all of them are filled with materials we can use. Water, minerals, alloys. Come on, Caitlin, you read the papers. Tensions between Earth and the Moon are at an all-time high. People on both sides of the belt aren't too happy with our commander in chief's little cleanup proposal. Word has it that the lunar government is considering leaving the New Coalition. Becoming a sovereign state. This is a pressure cooker, and it's just about ready to go bust. The time has come for bold choices. What I like to call a zero-limit option."

"Zero-limit option?"

"Something my dad used to say," said Ross. "It's like the point where you've run out of choices. The zero limit."

"I think that's zero sum."

"No," said Richards, piping up from the back of the room, "that's when the gains of the winner balance out with the losses of the loser."

"It doesn't matter!" said Ross, his tone growing exasperated. "Jeez. It's just a turn of phrase. The point is, it's the Wild West up here right now. And you want to know what the crazy thing is?"

"What's the crazy thing?" Caitlin asked.

"Everything they're fighting about down on Earth, in fact, everything we've been starting wars over since we first crawled up out of the sea," said Lyman, "water, minerals, fuel, all the silly little things we've been so busy killing each other for, it's here in abundance in space. Hell, forget about getting rich. This is really about saving the world, you know what I mean?"

"Sure," said Caitlin, "but it's also about getting rich."

Lyman shrugged. "If the fruits of my efforts turn out to be presented in gold, then who am I to complain?" he said. "And remember, you're a partner in this, so some of that fruit can be yours."

Caitlin remained unsure. Something about Ross . . . well, everything actually, set off alarm bells in her brain. Ross seemed to sense her apprehension and tried a different tactic.

"During the nineteenth century, do you know what the most valuable metal in the United States was?" he asked. "Aluminum. It was more precious than gold. Napoleon had even saved his aluminum cutlery for his best guests. And when they finished the Washington Monument in 1884, they made the capstone out of a six-pound pyramid of aluminum. But it didn't take long for some enterprising souls to figure out how to separate aluminum from rock cheaply. Before too long, factories were producing fifty pounds of aluminum a day and that same stuff Napoleon saved for his best guests came in a seventy-five-foot sheet you could buy at your supermarket. And the company that capitalized on it, Alcoa? It's worth more than thirty billion dollars today. It just takes one visionary mind to shift the balance of power or economics, Caitlin. And these asteroids? They represent the next gold rush. It's all out there. Just waiting for some enterprising soul to reach out and take it."

"And I gather that enterprising soul is you?"

"It's going to be someone," he said. "And why not me? Core One has the tools and the resources to become the premier asteroid mining company of the next decade. All we need to do is prove that it can work."

"That's where I come in," Caitlin said.

"That's where you come in," Ross agreed.

Richards hit another button on his remote and the asteroid image flickered out, replaced by a rotating image of a compact and rather ugly-looking spacecraft.

"The *Tamarisk*," Ross said with all the gusto of a proud papa. "She's an older model cargo hauler, class 627, but we've given her a refit and a total overhaul. Now she's a rock grabber."

"Rock grabber?"

"An asteroid retrieval craft," said Ross. "The first of her kind. It's simple, really. You and your crew take her out to the Thresher and latch on to the rock itself. Then you deploy a series of robotic probes, each one equipped with its own electric propulsion system. Once the probes are on the surface, you and your crew detach and head home. Those little suckers will take over and steer that thing into lunar orbit. And that's when the real work starts."

"So if your little droids are going to do the work," Caitlin asked, "what do you need a crew for?"

"Come on, Caitlin," Ross said. "You know better than anyone that certain ops call for a human touch. You can't trust a machine to get all the details right. From where I sit, the whole thing should be as easy as sliding off a barn. You ever work one of them prize-snatching machines at a diner? Same idea."

"I never got the prize once," Caitlin said.

"Oh, you will this time," said Ross. "I guarantee it. Word has it you and your crew are the best miners on the surface."

"Mining rego's a little different than slowing an asteroid down in the middle of space," Caitlin told him. "There're a lot more factors to consider and a lot more that can go wrong. And all of that's before we even set down on the surface. But the bigger question—why us? Why not use a crew from your own company? Surely you have to have people trained for this kind of thing."

"Well," said Ross, settling back into his chair and putting his feet up on his desk. As he did this, Caitlin took note of his rather loud—and presumably expensive—boots. "Now there's the bitch of it. You see, all the legalities about mining an asteroid haven't really been sorted out yet. As you probably know, there were a number of asteroid mining companies starting up in the early twenty-first century. However, most of 'em stalled out because of lack of funding or drowned in a sea of corporate red tape about who really owned the rights to mine space. Things haven't changed much over the last fifty years or so. But I'll let you in on a little secret. Most of the He-3 mining companies, yours included, have been working in secret on asteroid mining procedures. Sooner or later, the floodgates are going to open, and every rock out there's going to be up for grabs. The thing is, no one can make a move until the Interstellar Commerce Commission rules that asteroids are officially cleared to be mined. But, if say a group of privateers went out and snagged themselves a rock, proved it was viable, and acquired our services to mine it further? Well now, that's just capitalism at work."

"And if those privateers were to have an accident while snagging this rock, Core One would have no responsibility, correct?"

There was no answer to this query, simply another shrug and that omnipresent grin. Caitlin sipped her drink and pressed on.

"What about my job?"

Ross waved a dismissive hand. "Taken care of," he said. "Mr. Chen at Guanghang is a good friend of the family. He's quite interested in the proposal."

"And what does he stand to gain from it?" asked Caitlin.

"With five trillion dollars, there's plenty to go around," he said.

"Tell me again why I'd ever consider this?"

Ross swept his feet off the desk and sat up, hands folded on the desk surface. "You know who my father is, yes? Well, he's one of the stockholders of Core One. And, between you, me, and the lamppost, he stands to gain quite a bit from this little endeavor. To that end, he's prepared to compensate those responsible in whatever way they wish. I know you've been applying for a travel pass to get back on planet, using your veteran's status to help your case. And I also know it's been getting stuck in the wheels of bureaucracy. Now I ask you, Caitlin, who better to grease those wheels than a United States senator?"

"And if we fail?"

Ross leaned back again, placing his hands behind his head. "This is the free market, Caitlin. We don't reward failure. Only success."

Caitlin turned Ross's entire proposal over in her head before standing up. "I can't do it," she said.

Ross's expression remained, but something in his eyes changed slightly. "You're joking," he said.

"I don't have time to joke," she told him. "You're right. I have been applying for a visa, and if I play my cards right, it might go through in a year. Maybe eighteen months. If I take the shortcut you're offering, I could be home sooner, sure. But I could also get myself killed. Worse yet, without the protection of your company, I could also get caught by the ICC. Which means that not only would I lose my job, but the only way I'd be seeing my daughter is on the other side of a plate-glass window."

"ICC won't be a problem," said Ross. "They've got far bigger fires to put out these days, believe you me."

"Are you willing to bail me out if you're wrong?"

His silence was answer enough for Caitlin. She reached over to shake his hand.

"Thank you for the drink, Mr. Ross," she said, "but I'm afraid you've wasted your time."

Before Caitlin made for the door, Ross quickly handed her a small card made from clear plastic.

"Now that's my private line," he said. "The *Tamarisk* leaves Ponca City docks in three days with your crew or someone else's. You have a change of heart, that's how you can tell me."

Richards showed Caitlin out. Ross's smile trailed her as the door closed.

The maglev train ride back to the Hive from Aldrin City passed in a blur. Caitlin's thoughts were spinning and turning wildly, like leaves in a fall storm. Part of her wondered if she was crazy to turn Ross down. She had more than enough confidence in her crew. In the year she'd spent working with them, she'd seen the team rise to multiple challenges, conquering each one and effortlessly moving on. She believed that together they might be able to pull off the job without losing a drop of sweat and that, with a little luck, she'd be home in time for Christmas with Emily. But the question that ate at her was whether she was confident enough in her crew, in Ross, and in herself to risk her entire future with her daughter, not to mention her life?

She leaned back against her seat and exhaled. *In war it was so much easier,* she thought. You didn't have time to weigh the options. You just reacted and trusted in your training and instincts. "Move from your *hara*," her drill sergeant used to say back in basic. The Chinese called it the *dantian*, but in Japan it was the *hara*, your lower abdomen and a center of tremendous energy and qi. The idea was that all movement, whether physical or emotional, should be focused on that area. If you focused your energy on your *hara*, it was almost impossible to be knocked down. The same was true when it came to making decisions. "Listen to the energy coming from the *hara*," he would say. "Whatever it is telling you is always correct." The idea existed in many cultures, from China to Japan to the *kath* of the Sufi. But in the end, it all came down to the same thing: gut instinct. In the Last Campaign, Caitlin had always trusted her instincts to see her through. But now she didn't know.

When Caitlin got back home, she was shocked when Ava informed her that she had fifteen missed transmissions, all from Ben.

Emily.

She raced across the room, her legs watery and unresponsive, and told Ava to contact Ben. After what felt like hours, his bleary, panicked face finally filled the screen.

"Ben?" Caitlin asked. "What is it? What—"

"He finally did it," Ben said. "He finally screwed everything up."

"Who?" she asked, wanting to choke him for being so cryptic. "Who screwed what up?"

"Eric," he said. "He's been arrested."

Caitlin's stomach felt like it had just collided with an angry fist. "How?"

"Apparently he was trying to move trank across the border," he said. "Drug deal gone bad. Patrol nailed him near Los Ebanos."

Goddammit, Eric. Caitlin felt the anger surge.

"Which side of the fence?" she asked, trying to figure out the best-case scenario. He was screwed either way, but if he was still in Mexico, chances are he'd never come back.

Ben shook his head. "They've got him in Tamaulipas, for processing," he said. "Who knows when—"

"Emily?" Caitlin asked. She really didn't give a shit what they did with Eric.

"I've got her," Ben said. "Thank God she called me when she did. Eric left sometime last evening and never came back. She was all alone in that apartment, Cait."

Caitlin closed her eyes. *That son of a bitch*. Ben looked at her through the screen, his expression serious.

"Cait," he said, "I've got her for now. But you and I both know I can't keep her for long. Not the way things work these days. Both your parents and Eric's parents are gone. That means she's going to be systemized."

Caitlin's heart began to pound and the room swam as she processed the word. *Systemized*. As painful as it was to process, she knew Ben was right. With no next of kin, Emily would go into the system, which meant that, unless Caitlin got to her first, she would be subjected to standardized housing in the foster block until she was eighteen and then jettisoned out into the world without a second glance. There was a time when kids could go through the system and come out healthy, well-adjusted members of society. Now, however, with exponential population growth straining an already-overcrowded Earth, the system was little more than a conveyor belt, with lost and confused kids going in on one end and ghosts coming out on the other.

"What if I transmit authorization to name you her temporary legal guardian?"

"Yeah, we can do that," said Ben. "She'll have to stay on Earth until this is sorted out, which means her trip to see you is off. But, more importantly, it'll still only buy you thirty days. With my vet status, I can maybe stretch that to forty-five."

"I won't need that long," she said.

"Cait?" said Ben. "I've seen that look before. You're not planning anything stupid, are you?"

"Don't worry about me," she replied firmly. "I'll send whatever authorization you need. You just take care of her, you understand me?"

"You got it, Cait," Ben said. "But unless you can sort this out in a month—"

"Leave that to me, Ben," Caitlin said. Now the tears were starting and her voice had grown unsteady. "Where is she? Can I see her?"

"She's asleep," Ben said. "It's still early here and she had a long night. I can wake her if you—"

"No! Let her sleep. But you look out for her, you hear me? You look out for her."

"With my life, Cait," said Ben, and she knew he meant it. "With my life."

The connection was broken, and Caitlin felt the anger well up like a geyser. She let it come. She looked at the blank screen and wanted desperately to put her fist through it again and again. But she wouldn't.

There was a call she had to make.

Chapter Four

"So that's the deal."

Vee, Tony, Diaz, and Shaw were all seated around the kitchen table in Caitlin's unit. The fluorescents cast the room and their faces in a sickly yellow-green hue. But even in the dull, alien light, Caitlin could clearly read their concern. Tony spoke up first.

"You sure you can trust this guy Ross?" he asked.

"No," Caitlin told him honestly. "But taking this job is the best chance I've got of getting to Emily before the system does. I've got to take it, no matter what the risks."

"*You've* got to take it," said Tony. "What about the rest of us?"

"Of course not," Caitlin told them. "No one here has to come, and I'm not going to force you to. I can go down to the docks and hire a crew if I need to."

"A crew of greenhorns, you mean," Vee said, snorting. "People who don't know your timing, your rhythm, or the first thing about what they're doing."

"Let's be honest, honey," Tony said to Vee. "It's not like we know a whole lot more. We're rego miners, not asteroid wranglers."

"We all have spaceflight training," Caitlin reminded him. "And the company has had us running asteroid redirect sims for a year now, just in case we ever get clearance to start trying to mine the damn things."

"Exactly," Tony said. "Sims. Are you willing to risk everything based on what you've only done in a simulation?"

"For me, it's worth the risk," said Caitlin. "And think of what we all have to gain. I'm not the only one who gets a pass home, remember. Even you, Diaz. I know you can't necessarily come to Earth, but Ross said he'll give you your pick of jobs, maybe even your own crew."

The room was silent a moment as everyone took in what Caitlin was proposing, weighing out the risks versus the reward in their minds.

"The bottom line is," Caitlin continued, "I can't do this without you. I mean, I will if I have to, but this is my chance to get home, and the only way I know how to make that work is if I have you all with me. I know it's a lot, asking you to risk everything for me and my kid, and I wouldn't blame you if you all walked out that door. But this is me with my hat in my hand."

Diaz shrugged his shoulders in a relaxed, convivial gesture. "You don't have to sell me," he said. "I roll with you, Mama Bear. No matter what."

"You know I've got my reservations," said Tony, "but I think a ticket to Earth for Vee and me is just too good of an opportunity to pass up. Besides, if you do pull this off and make a killing without me, Diaz will never let me live it down."

"You're smarter than you look, Big Tone," said Diaz. Tony gave him a wink and a nod, then he looked over at Vee, who turned her eyes to the ceiling.

"I'm with Tony," she said. "I've got reservations too, but we're a family. We take care of our own, so if you need us to get your back, then you've got us."

Caitlin smiled, quietly emotional, grateful for this crew, these people. They were *her* crew and they'd just proved it to her. She looked at Shaw.

"What about you?"

"It's cool with me," said Shaw. "I don't have much to live for these days anyway."

"All right then," Caitlin said drily, worried about Shaw's state of mind. "We ship out in three days. I checked, and Ross has already gotten everything squared away with Guanghang. So get home, get organized, and get some rack time. You're gonna need it."

Everyone stood up and headed for the door. Before she left, Vee turned back and gave Caitlin a hug.

"We're gonna get you home to that girl," she said. "Don't worry."

"I'm not worried," Caitlin said, hoping that she sounded at least somewhat convincing. "I've got you with me. You're the angel on my shoulder."

Vee gave her a wink and headed out the door. "You keep thinking like that, and we just might make it through this."

She walked out into the hallway, and Caitlin closed the door, resting her head against the surface, feeling the coolness of the aluminum on her skin. She was worried about what lay ahead, terrified. But she had no other option. Her father used to say that, to a brave man's eyes, danger shines like the Sun. Caitlin didn't know if he said such words because he believed them or because he wanted her to believe. God knows she wanted to feel brave right now, but she couldn't escape the feeling that the danger in front of her wasn't bright or shining. It was dark and hulking. A dead star in space.

◆ ◆ ◆

"Caity-did? Where are my glasses?"

"I saw them on the kitchen table, Dad."

"No," Brandon Taggart says. "I just looked and they weren't there."

"Keep looking . . ."

A few minutes later, Caitlin's father comes into his room, his glasses in hand.

"Found them!" he says. "They were next to my keys. You know why I put them there, don't you?"

"So you'd remember where they were," says Caitlin, giggling. Her father is always misplacing something: his wallet, his keys, his glasses. She is often tasked with finding whatever has disappeared, with the looming promise of monetary reward. But usually her mother finds the lost items. Her dad is always in awe of his wife's ability to find even the most hopelessly misplaced object. "She could find a haystack in a stack of needles," he says. Years later she will learn this is just "Dad humor," the desire for leaden one-liners and puns that infects every man within five years of reproducing.

"That's right, kiddo," he says. He walks to the closet and withdraws a suitcase. Unfolding it on the bed where Caitlin sits cross-legged, he begins to pack. Caitlin watches him work.

"Will I like it there?" she asks finally. "On Earth?"

"Of course," says Brandon. "You'll love it. I've got a nice place picked out for us in Oregon. You'll be able to run on the beach, swim in the ocean. Maybe we'll even get a dog."

"But it's going to hurt, right?" she asks. "My bones and everything? I'm not used to the gravity down there."

"It'll be an adjustment, sure," he says. "But you're only six. You'll adapt quickly. And you've been taking your vitamins, right? Following all the exercises the doctor showed you?"

"Yeah," says Caitlin, then her mind shifts gears to a topic that she has been scared to broach, worried about what her father will tell her.

"Will I have to get glasses?"

"It's possible," her dad says. He was never one to fence with the truth, a trait she herself will one day inherit. "Some people's eyes don't adjust to the change in pressure. But you're strong, Caity-did. I bet you're going to surprise us all. Besides, even if you do need specs, I'm sure you'll look great in them. Here, try 'em on."

He puts his own glasses on her face with a boop *sound, and the world immediately goes fuzzy, everything becoming just a ruddy smear on the lenses. She takes them off, squealing, then thinks a moment, watching her dad put his life into the case, one article at a time.*

"What about you?" she asks. "Will you like it there?"

He stops packing and walks over to her, kneeling so they are eye to eye.

"That depends," he says. "Are you gonna be there?"

"Well, yeah," she says. "Of course."

"Then I think I'm gonna like it just fine."

He smiles at her and she smiles back.

"But it's not going to be like here, though," she says. "You won't be the boss."

He looks at her, and she can feel the warmth in his gaze.

"You don't miss anything, do you?" he says, then stands up to continue packing. "You're right. I won't be running the show down there, but maybe that's not such a bad thing. Helium-3 might be the wave of the future, kiddo, but right now, it's too expensive to make it worth a damn to most of the world. Down there, everything's still running on that dirty old black stuff. That's just the way that it is. Besides, it won't be so bad. I'm not the boss around here, am I? And we get along just jake."

The thought of Caitlin's mother, lovingly considered the true boss of the household, pleases her. But another thought crosses her mind, and her expression changes to one of worried thoughtfulness.

"I heard you and Mr. Terrell fighting last night," she says. "I heard what he said."

"Is that a fact?" her dad says. "And what did you hear him say?"

Caitlin looks down. "That you were climbing your way down the ladder of success."

"Well, Jason Terrell and I are climbing different ladders, sweetheart." He picks up a picture and tosses it into the suitcase. Caitlin sees that it is a photo of herself with her parents during their last vacation to Lake Armstrong. "And, as far as I'm concerned, I'm sitting pretty, right at the top."

Her dad reaches down and scoops her up in his arms.

"Family first, kiddo," he says. "Always. Now come on. Let's go see what the boss has planned for dinner . . ."

◆ ◆ ◆

Caitlin's eyes snapped open, and for a moment she wondered if she'd even shut them to begin with. Sitting up, she grabbed her tablet and checked the time. Two hours until she had to be at the docks. With a sigh, knowing that sleep was no longer an option, she got up and tried to run, hoping the adrenaline would push the fear out of her system. After logging a few miles, she hopped off and hailed Ava, asking her to try to call Ben.

"Hey, Cait," he said. "It's early up there. Something on your mind?"

Since her meeting with Ross and her subsequent decision to take on the Thresher mission, Caitlin hadn't had a moment to call and tell Ben and, more importantly, Emily, what was happening. Although, if she really were going to level with herself, she supposed that wasn't entirely true. She'd had moments here and there, but she had simply been too terrified to take advantage of them. What would she say to her daughter?

"Hi, honey! I'm about to risk my life doing something that's possibly stupid and definitely dangerous and illegal. But the good news is, I'm coming home! Whether it's on a luxury transport or in a plastic bag, I'm coming home! Now, do you want to read The Runaway Bunny *before bedtime?"*

So she'd held off calling. But now, with the mission's departure so close, she felt like she had to tell her.

"Is Emily there?"

"No, sorry, Cait, she's at school. What's up?"

Everything came out in a rush of words. The asteroid, Lyman Ross, the mission, the chance to come home—Caitlin told him everything. As she talked, Ben tried to take it in, a man gathering spilled ball bearings. When she was done, Ben pursed his lips, considering everything.

"Lot to process there," he said at last. "But you know what it sounds like to me?"

"What's that?"

"Sounds like something that Caitlin Taggart was made for."

Caitlin scoffed at the idea and shook her head. "No," she said. "I don't think so. Not this time."

"I remember the first day we were on the ground in Iraq," Ben said. "We were somewhere on Highway 1 on patrol to Mosul, I think, and some goddamn Enders pop up out of nowhere, just light us up like it's a damn shooting gallery. And right away, the man standing next to me gets his arm blown away by an M14, just taken clean off like a branch being snapped from a tree. Now remember, this is my first deployment, so I do what any non-com puke would do and I freak out."

"Not the first time, and not the last time," Caitlin teased.

"Fair enough," said Ben. "Fair enough. But then, out of all the smoke and the blood and the noise, there comes this woman. This fierce, wild-eyed . . . hell, I'll just say it, Amazon, coming like a bat out of hell. And she takes the wounded man, ties off his arm and gets on the M240 and pushes back the Enders almost singlehandedly until the helos come in and airlift us out of there. And the best part?"

"They managed to save the arm," said Caitlin, lost in her own memories of that day.

"That's right," Ben said. "That was the day I knew that when Caitlin Taggart decides she's going to take something on, she latches on and doesn't let go. And, if anyone tries to tell her different, well, then God help them."

He paused.

"Now you go and you kick that big rock's ass, then you come home to your girl, you hear?"

Somewhere in Caitlin's belly, invisible hands stirred up fear and anxiety. Was she going to cry? Throw up? The next words were almost impossible to utter.

"Emily," she finally managed. "If I . . . then you have to . . . you have to tell her—"

"You're gonna tell her yourself," Ben said. "I'm not taking any deathbed confession from you, Taggart."

"OK," Caitlin said. "But if I die, and I don't get to tell her, I'm going to make it my mission to come back and haunt you for eternity."

"I'd rather you didn't," said Ben. "I had you living in my head for four years during the campaign. That was enough."

They shared a brief laugh, and Ben fixed his gaze on her.

"Your dad would be proud of you, you know."

"Oh please," said Caitlin, waving a hand at him. "What do you know about it? You never met him."

"You sure about that?"

He winked, leaned forward, and severed the connection. Caitlin was alone again, but his words stayed with her.

Your dad would be proud of you.

Then, almost as an echo, her own father's words bounced back in answer.

Family first, kiddo. Always.

"Ava?" she said suddenly.

"Yes, Caitlin?"

"I have to go away for a while," she said. "Maybe for good. And, if that's the case, I just wanted to let you know that . . . it's been nice having you to talk to."

"Thank you, Caitlin," said Ava. "I have to admit, I'm surprised at this outpouring of emotion. It's not like you."

"Well, what can I say? You're one of the only friends I've got up here."

With that, Caitlin stood up, pushed back her hair, and breathed deeply.

Time to get to work.

Chapter Five

The last time Caitlin had seen the Ponca City docks, she had been inbound to the Moon to settle her mother's estate. Back then, she had expected to be back in less than a week and on board a transport home to Emily without so much as a glance out the window. That had been a year ago. Seeing the area again now, Caitlin didn't feel that the docks looked all that different. Still the same busy, bustling place. Voices shouted instructions, orders, and demands in equal volume. Sparks rained down as hull plates were patched. Ground personnel waved hand beacons to direct docked ships to their maintenance and refueling positions. Thanks to the embargo, there was a lot less civilian traffic, but the luxury liners still did brisk business. Embargo or no embargo, money always granted people access. Passengers disembarked from various ships, scanning around for signs to point them in the right direction. As Caitlin walked in, she saw the *Ecliptic* sliding into her moorings overhead, sleek, black, and cigar-shaped, like a finger slipping into a wedding ring. She shook her head as she watched the liner dock. With all the places to go to on Earth, she would never understand why anyone would pay to vacation here.

She kept walking, looking up at the rego transports firing up and beginning their transit back to Earth, the worker tugs buzzing around them like mayflies. She watched as the *Iron Horse* cleared the dock and burned its escape thrusters, heading starward. She thought about the men and women on board and where they were headed, and something stabbed her deep inside her chest.

Above the roar of thrusters, the hiss of mooring clamps, and the beeping of cargo loaders, an automated voice droned over the speaker system, welcoming disembarking passengers with cheerful dispassion.

"Hello, and welcome to the Moon. Visitors, please follow the yellow line to customs. If you are here on a work visa, please follow the red line to the labor division to receive your assignment. Outbound travelers follow the blue line to your designated transport. Thank you; and whatever your destination may be, may the stars always be visible."

Caitlin rolled her eyes and looked down at the concrete floor. Her line wasn't yellow, red, or blue. There were no maps to her destination, which, she supposed, was exactly how her employer wanted it. She looked around, trying to figure out which direction to take.

As she searched the area, Caitlin noticed the one thing that had changed about the docks since her last visit, namely, the increased presence of ICC enforcement. Shock troops were everywhere, their faces sheathed in black, eyes covered by goggles, and bodies encased in Kevlar. They scanned the docks slowly and purposefully. Caitlin noted the machine guns resting on their hips. Some people believed the guns were just for show, that a weapon couldn't fire in space. But Caitlin knew better. The ammunition contained its own oxidizer, and thus no atmospheric oxygen was required to fire a bullet. So, if the shock troops wanted to use their weapons, there'd be nothing to stop them. Keeping that firmly in mind, Caitlin tried her best to avoid eye contact, hoping not to be noticed. Unfortunately, she was too late and one of the troopers approached her. He stuck out a gloved hand and spoke to her in an authoritative tone, his voice modulated by his mask.

"Travel pass and destination, please."

Inside Caitlin's mind everything suddenly turned to static, white noise hissing insistently. The trooper didn't seem pleased with her lack of response and repeated the question with greater insistence.

"Travel pass and destination, *please*. Now, ma'am."

Caitlin realized now that some form of a response would have to be forthcoming, so she opened her mouth, prepared to bluff.

"Hold up! Hold up!" A voice came from behind. Caitlin turned to see Tony running up to meet them, waving a plastic card for the trooper to see.

"Crew pass," he said. "The *Tamarisk*. Work tug out of bay 815."

The trooper took the pass and scanned it, eyeing Tony with suspicion.

"Destination?"

"Crisium Sea," Tony said. "Scanning survey of Dorsa Tetyaev."

Another inspection of the card, then the trooper's masked face turned from Tony to Caitlin and back again. Finally, he passed the card back.

"Proceed."

"Thank you, sir," said Tony, giving a two-finger salute. They began walking away, and he tipped Caitlin a wink.

"Helps to have friends in high places," he said. "You ready to see the old girl?"

"I don't know," she said. "Am I going to be happy?"

"Try not to think about it in terms like 'happy' or 'sad,'" Tony responded. "Instead, I want you to try to find a place that's a little more in between."

Caitlin turned the corner to the docking bay and set her eyes on what Tony was attempting to prepare her for. Little more than a set of connected cylinders with a pair of solar panels poking out from the bow section at awkward angles, the *Tamarisk* looked old, ungainly, and obviously repurposed. As Ross had noted, the craft was obviously designed for a much more mundane function—a cargo tug or even satellite repair—and was now reaching well beyond its station in life. Caitlin couldn't help but think about one of her dad's favorite classic movies and the main character's reaction when he first laid eyes on the *Millennium Falcon*. Almost reflexively, she echoed the words of the character.

"What a piece of junk!"

"She is an ugly one, I'll give you that," Tony agreed. "But we've been working her over all night, and we think she'll get the job done."

"What are the solar panels for?" Caitlin asked. "Solar-electric propulsion?"

"I wish," said Tony. "Sensors, heating, and telemetry are all solar powered. The propulsion system? Old-school hypergolic. Nitric acid and hydrazine."

"Devil's Venom?" Caitlin asked, concerned. "I thought no one even used that stuff anymore."

"There are a few things on board that people don't use anymore. That's part of her charm."

"Wonderful," Caitlin said. "So we're riding out to an asteroid on a mission that no one has yet to successfully attempt, let alone complete. And we're doing it on something that Wile E. Coyote himself might have second thoughts about boarding. What could possibly go wrong?"

"I learned a long time ago never to ask that question," Tony said.

"Why is that?"

He draped an arm around Caitlin's shoulder and gave her a wry look as they prepared to go aboard the ship.

"Because God might be listening," he said. "And he just might decide to answer."

◆ ◆ ◆

As Tony and Caitlin walked over to the *Tamarisk*, they saw the rest of the crew milling around, attending to various chores. Diaz was clambering up and over the hull, looking for cracks and imperfections and chattering madly. Vee was in the cockpit, making final adjustments, and Shaw was stowing equipment in the cargo hold. He seemed detached, almost robotic, as he went about his work. Caitlin contemplated going over to him and then, somewhat selfishly, decided to move on instead. She was concerned and felt guilty over his involvement in the mission, but she had her own drama playing out in her mind and wasn't ready to get sucked into someone else's narrative.

Caitlin slowly made her way on board the *Tamarisk* and into the cockpit, where Vee was busy flipping switches and running last-minute checks.

"How are we looking?" she asked. "Good?"

"Oh yeah," said Vee. "She's an old bucket, but she'll fly true enough."

"Good," Caitlin said. "Then let's get moving. I don't want to give ICC the chance to ask any more questions."

"Let's do it," Vee said.

Caitlin headed aft and marshaled the remaining crew on board, diffusing another argument between Tony and Diaz over stowing exosuits in the escape lander, the *Alley Oop*. The suits were fitted with an internal reaction-control system that would enable them to stay grounded on the asteroid—in theory, at least. She fervently hoped they wouldn't have to find out until they'd towed the asteroid safely into orbit above the Moon.

"Take care of those," she told them. "Gravity on the asteroid is a tricky thing. You jump high enough, and you can reach escape velocity. When we're on the surface, those suits are going to be the only thing keeping us grounded."

"Tell this guy," said Diaz. "He's tossing them around like golf clubs."

"You keep it up," Tony said, brandishing his fist, "and you're going to reach escape velocity right now."

"Please, ladies," Caitlin said, "we haven't even left the dock yet. What's that?"

She pointed to the small, ungainly-looking thing on wheels folded up in the corner of the hold of the *Alley Oop*.

"Looks like a rover of some kind," said Diaz.

"Yeah, that's exactly what she is," said Tony. "She's what they call a lunar truck. Six wheels, each one with two tires that can be steered independently in a three-hundred-sixty-degree rotation. She can go forward, backward, side to side. Just about any way you need to go. Electric motors, two-speed transmission, lifting force of up to four thousand pounds. And, the best part, she's fully customizable. She can be fitted with a scoop, a backhoe, crane, whatever you want."

He motioned to the side of the rover, noting the name: Noser. He grinned at Caitlin.

"Cute, huh?" he said.

"Adorable," she told him. "It's not going to affect the weight, is it?"

"Nah," said Tony. "It's light. Ferrous aluminum, same as the *Invader*. Might come in handy if we end up on the surface."

"I don't want to think about that," Caitlin said.

"What about these babies?" asked Diaz.

He jerked his thumb over to a rack of smaller, more compact suits and wiggled his eyebrows.

"Are those . . . ?"

"Drop suits!" said Diaz, almost unable to contain his excitement. "Designed to bail out in the atmosphere. Four-layer pressure suit, heated sun visor, onboard pressure control system, HD cameras on all four limbs. Man, I'd risk a trip back to Earth just to try out this baby!"

"You're welcome to it," said Caitlin. "As for me, I will pass. In fact, all this stuff . . ."

She gestured to everything in the hold related to landing on the asteroid. The suits, the rover, even the lander itself.

"All of this stuff can go in a little box marked, 'Things Caitlin Doesn't Want to Talk About on This Trip.'"

"You got it," said Diaz.

"All right then, as you were."

Walking back to the cockpit, she passed Shaw, who was securing gear in the hold.

"How are you holding up?" she asked him.

"Right as rain," he said, not taking his eyes off his work. "Don't worry about me."

"If I did that, I wouldn't be much of a crew chief, would I?"

Shaw managed a small grin and Caitlin returned it, giving him a pat on the back as she continued to the cockpit.

"Get that gear stowed," she said over her shoulder. "And then let's get moving!"

"Yes ma'am," said Shaw, returning to his task with slightly renewed vigor.

After twenty more minutes and a lot more bickering, they were all strapped in and ready to depart. Vee fired up the thrusters and gently steered the craft out of its moorings. Caitlin felt weird being on a spaceship again. The sense of motion was completely different from being on the surface, with the feeling of standing on a wooden dock in the middle of slightly choppy water. She closed her eyes and tried to adjust, but it wasn't helping.

"Lost your space legs?" Vee asked.

"Might be losing a lot more than that if we keep going like this."

"Don't worry, girl," said Vee. "You leave the driving to me. At least until we get out of the docks."

Caitlin managed a nod and put her head between her knees.

The *Tamarisk* drifted upward above the docks and the mood became tense. Ross had promised that the clearance code he supplied would allow them to leave lunar space without issue. But the cowboy also struck Caitlin as a guy who was good at making promises but tended to come up short when time to deliver. According to their work permit, they were supposed to be headed for the Crisium Sea. But in order to reach the Thresher, they would have to break orbit. And once they deviated from their course, everyone on board knew that ICC traffic control was going to be all over them.

The potential dilemma quickly became reality.

"Unidentified transport, you are off course," a stern voice crackled over the comm.

Here we go, Caitlin thought.

"That didn't take long," said Tony.

"Nope. Not at all," Caitlin said before speaking into the comm. "ICC tower, this is the *Tamarisk*. We've received new orders and are acting in accordance."

A pause as Caitlin's transmission was processed. Then, after a long wait, a response.

"Clearance code?"

The crew all looked at each other, their eyes darting back and forth, before Caitlin took a breath and answered.

"Clearance code AEV-WJ 083177," she said, hoping that the nerves in her voice were inaudible.

Silence. Everyone froze, awaiting either clearance to leave or a swarm of patrol skiffs to surround them and force the vessel back down to the surface. Caitlin had a dreadful flash of Emily and what would happen to her if they were caught. A coal burned in her stomach as she realized that she might have made a terrible, irrevocable mistake, and in doing so had jeopardized everyone on this ship.

The tower came back on the line.

"*Tamarisk*, you are cleared for transit."

The crew exhaled collectively as Caitlin acknowledged receipt of the message, and Vee began to move the ship up and out of orbit.

"We made it!" said Diaz.

"I'd prefer you say that when we're on our way back," Tony said.

"You know what this means," Caitlin said to Diaz.

"No," said Diaz. "Please. Don't do it."

"I've got to," Caitlin told him. "It's tradition."

A few pushes of assorted buttons and music filled the cabin. Montrose, "Space Station #5." Diaz looked defeated.

"This is going to be a long-ass mission," he said.

The music rising, they moved up and out over the Moon, headed on an intercept course with the asteroid. Diaz's mood changed as he looked out the starboard portal, his eyes wide like a child. He looked back at Caitlin.

"It's the Moon," he said. "I've never seen it from space before."

Caitlin and Diaz peered out the window together, marveling at the mottled gray surface, its ridges and rills rising like currents on a dark and lonely ocean. They could make out the Hive to the east, splayed haphazardly across the landscape and, far to the west, the lights of Aldrin City, standing out against the dark like Oz's emerald counterpart. Diaz looked as if his eyes couldn't drink it all in. Caitlin patted him on the shoulder.

"Doesn't seem so bad from up here," she said.

Caitlin sat back in the copilot's seat as a beaming Tony looked over at Vee.

"You thinking what I'm thinking?" she asked, unable to hold back her own joyful expression.

"Oh yeah," Tony said.

"What is it?" Caitlin asked.

"We just had a funny thought," Vee said. "This is the first time Tony and I have been anywhere since our honeymoon."

Tony slid his arm around Vee's shoulder.

"Remember that place we stayed in?" he asked. "On Lake Armstrong?"

"I do indeed," said Vee. "And I remember how you had the whole trip planned with an itinerary and everything. Morning massage, diving, solar sailing . . ."

"But we didn't get to any of them, did we?" Tony said with a sly look.

Vee elbowed him in the ribs. "Stop it," she said. "You're so nasty."

"Is it wrong for a man to say he enjoyed his honeymoon with his new bride?"

Vee just shook her head. "So if this job pays out," she asked him, "are you finally going to take me on another vacation?"

"Babe," said Tony, "why else do you think I took this job?"

◆ ◆ ◆

They broke free of lunar orbit with relative ease, slingshotting around the far side and using the Moon's gravity to direct themselves onto the path toward the asteroid. As the ship made its way away from the Moon, Earth loomed ahead through the window, a blue-and-white thumbtack stuck in the dark curtain of space. As they had when departing the Moon, the crew stopped what they were doing and enjoyed the view.

"Think we should just keep going?" said Vee, looking at Earth and no doubt feeling its pull.

"Sure, why not?" Caitlin said. "We'll just tell them we got lost."

"Works for me," Tony said. "Almost feels like the truth, doesn't it?"

◆ ◆ ◆

Given the asteroid's current location, the crew deduced it would take several days to reach it. While en route they spent time getting acquainted with the Thresher. According to the file Ross had supplied, it was an M-type. Asteroids were classified based on their composition. C-type asteroids, the most common, were more carbonaceous in their makeup and primarily rich in water, metals, and various organic compounds. Those who had their eye on mining C-types saw them as potential sources for rocket propellants or rubber and plastics for living in space. The second most common asteroids after C-types were the S-types, so named for their stony composition. These bodies had a relatively low metal content, but some had been found to be high in platinum. Prospective miners could potentially sell their metals on the terrestrial market to fund future mining missions. Then came the M-types, the category into which the Thresher fell. Originally the "M" was for "metallic," although that had since been in dispute, as many supposedly metallic asteroids were found to contain silicate deposits. The Thresher seemed to have a stony surface but a solid platinum core, which was what had Ross's ears pricked up.

The Thresher also had an unusually slow rotation, taking almost a full eighteen days to turn fully on its axis. This would prove advantageous should the *Tamarisk* crew be forced to land on the surface. Since the asteroid lacked a magnetic field, there would be very little protection from the Sun. Having eighteen days of continuous dark in which to think of a way out of their predicament would be very welcome indeed.

"Contact!" Shaw said suddenly, looking intently at the infrared scanner.

"You see her?" asked Diaz, floating over to look down at the readout.

"Oh yeah," Shaw said, nodding quickly. "She's reading loud and clear."

Caitlin scanned the windows, looking for any sign of the asteroid, but saw nothing. This wasn't surprising, as asteroids tended to reflect only about a tenth of the sunlight that fell on them. That was why they were generally hard to spot, even with advanced telescopes. However, the volume of sunlight they absorbed heated them up and made them positively glow with infrared radiation. As a result, it fell to Shaw to spot her on the scanner.

"Let me know when anyone's got a visual," Caitlin said.

After a moment where the crew scanned the stars and onboard displays, Tony called out.

"Got her!" he said.

Everyone looked at once to where Tony's eyes were fixed. Caitlin spotted the Thresher, pitch-black and reflecting only a fraction of the Sun's light. It hung suspended in the blackness, floating in a slow and steady orbit. Looking at the asteroid, Caitlin felt fear wash through her. To her, the Thresher looked dark and unwelcoming. A cold, dead thing lurking on the outskirts of space, seeming to regard them with something akin to menace. After a moment, she turned away and focused on the instrument panel. Even though she couldn't look at the asteroid anymore, Caitlin still felt as though it continued to hold her in its gaze.

Chapter Six

With the Thresher now hulking just outside the *Tamarisk*'s windows, time was running short. They had to get moving.

"All right," she said. "This should be pretty easy. First, we need to move close to the rock so we can tag it on the first pass. That means a five-minute burn to put us in orbit. After that, we're going to circle around a second time and then use the ship's capture unit to stabilize the asteroid. Once it's stable, we'll be able to deploy the robots. If all goes according to plan, they'll attach themselves to the Thresher and simply steer this thing into lunar orbit or wherever the hell Ross wants it to go."

"Walk in the park," said Diaz, clapping his hands and rubbing them together.

"Walk in the park, huh?" said Tony. "Like that time in the Sea of Serenity?"

"The boulder again?" said Diaz. "You're not going to let that go, are you?"

"You know, when someone decides to blow a seismic charge in a spot way off the grid and then sends a boulder rolling right in your direction, that's the kind of thing that's hard to let go."

"I thought we could widen the harvest field," said Diaz. "Which, I should point out, we did."

Tony shook his head. "When I was a kid, I always prayed that God would send me a kid brother," he said. "I should have known to be careful what I wished for."

"Can it, both of you," Caitlin said. "We're on approach. Let's get to work. Shaw will be manning the infrared. Diaz and Tony, you're going to fire the tag when we get close enough."

"We're on it, Boss," said Diaz.

Tony and Diaz floated up the tunnel, heading aft, while Shaw kept his eyes fixed on the screen.

"We've got to make another pass before we're in range," he said, his face bathed in the reddish-green light from the board. "Just keep it level and bring us around."

"You got it," said Vee. "Bravo Zulu."

Behind them, Caitlin could hear Tony and Diaz squabbling over their assignment. She looked over at Vee.

"You ever feel like a den mother?"

"Or a preschool teacher?" she replied.

"How's it feel being back on a stick?" Caitlin asked. "Like riding a bike?"

"Hell yeah," said Vee. "It's been a while since I've done any real flying. Not since our first year in the Hive."

"That's right," Caitlin said. "You told me. You and Tony ran a worker tug at the docks, right?"

"Sure did," said Vee. "Six months training, then three months' work before they made us redundant. We liked it, though, being up there above the surface. Just the quiet of it, you know. You could almost forget about your station in life. What about you?"

"Me?"

"Yeah, when's the last time you flew anywhere?"

"Well, outside of my one-way trip to the Moon, I haven't left the ground since the Last Campaign."

"You flew in the campaign?"

"Me? No." Caitlin shook her head. "I mean, I have flight training, but it's rudimentary stuff. And when it came to the war, I was just a passenger. I rode in 'em all, though, at one time or another. VTOLs, stealth choppers, tiltrotors, the works."

"Man," said Vee, "must have been something."

"Oh yeah," Caitlin said, "Something . . ."

◆ ◆ ◆

The helicopters pass over the desert sand almost silently, their shadows sliding across the dunes like black dolphins breaching on a sun-baked sea. In the distance, the Great Mosque of Samarra rises from the city, a curving tower spiraling up in a graceful ascent toward the heavens. Caitlin sees it and marvels at the splendor of its architecture. She wonders if the hands that built this tower could ever have imagined the abominations it would eventually bear witness to. She turns away and addresses the soldiers seated in the helo.

"Check your pads," she says, pointing to the holoprojector on her wrist. She punches a few keys and a face appears, hovering above the glass and flickering slightly.

"Hamza Mahmood," she says, getting ready to resummarize the mission. "Murder of US nationals, conspiracy, bombings, the list goes on. We bring him in, and we deal a serious blow to the insurgency. We have intel that says he's hiding in a safe house off of Al Bank Street. We're going to fast-rope in, take down the house, and bring him in, alive if possible. All right?"

"Yes ma'am!" they all respond as one. Caitlin walks up and down the rows, slapping each soldier's helmet, wishing them luck, and telling them to be careful. One of the men, a cocksure noob named Evers, grins at her.

"I don't need luck, Captain," he says. "I'm invincible."

"Well, I'll tell you what," Caitlin says, "if that's the case, once we hit the street, I'm going to stand behind you the entire time. Let the Enders' bullets bounce off your invincible ass so I can get back home."

Everyone laughs, but Evers's feelings are shared by much of the team. They do feel invincible. Strong, powerful, armed with the most advanced weapons and technology available on Earth. Technology at least fifty years ahead of anything anyone else has access to. They are the war hammer of the Allied military machine and they've come to strike a killing blow.

"All right," says Caitlin, "thirty seconds out. Are you ready?"

"Yes ma'am!"

"Are you mean?"

"Yes ma'am!"

"Are you hungry?"

"YES MA'AM!"

"Then let's get so—"

Before she can finish her thought, the RPG hits the tail rotor.

◆ ◆ ◆

"Cutter!"

Diaz's crackling voice over the comm shook Caitlin back.

"What is it?" she asked.

"This baby's getting closer," he said. "We gonna tag it or just enjoy the view?"

Caitlin looked out the window and saw that Thresher was indeed drawing nearer. She could make out the massive number of impact craters on its surface.

"Man," she said, "this thing has taken one hell of a beating. It's almost more crater than asteroid."

"That could explain why the rotation's so slow," Shaw said, looking at the Thresher's punched and broken face, the evidence of its hard-fought journey through the solar system. "Large enough impacts could have despun the asteroid and slowed it down."

"All right, let's get to it," Caitlin said. "Shaw? How are we looking?"

His face was a mask of concentration. "Just about there. A few more meters."

"Vee?"

"She's holding steady," she said, working the thrusters delicately, keeping the *Tamarisk* on a level course.

"All right then," Caitlin said. "Let's do this. Shaw?"

"Now's as good a time as any," he said. "Punch it."

"Diaz, Tony," said Caitlin, "you heard the man."

"Roger that, Boss," said Tony. "Punch it!"

There was a slight jolt as the rocket-powered probe was launched from the *Tamarisk*. Caitlin looked out the viewport as the projectile made its way down to the asteroid's surface. Ungainly-looking, the probe was little more than a cylindrical beacon placed on top of a set of three spidery-looking legs. Still, it was built with a sophisticated set of thrusters designed to keep the beacon from bouncing off into space in the asteroid's low gravity. Upon touchdown, the craft's legs would drive massive screws into the surface while, at the same time, two pitons would fire to firmly secure the probe onto the Thresher.

If all went well with the landing, the probe would then begin sending out a constantly cycling tracking signal that would, in theory, officially claim the asteroid for Core One Mining.

Shaw studied the scope intently, watching the probe's descent. Finally, it struck the asteroid's surface, gently kicking up debris.

"We've got hard contact!" he said at last. "The probe is down and locked."

"Phase one complete," Caitlin said, allowing herself a brief sigh of relief. "The flag has been planted. Nice work, team."

Diaz and Tony floated their way back up the tunnel to the cockpit.

"Man, if only the whole mission was that easy," Diaz said.

"Why isn't it?" Vee asked. "If we can send a probe down to this damn thing, why can't we just send these little robots down the same way?"

"I asked Ross the same question," said Caitlin. "He gave me some line of crap about how the guidance systems on these things aren't sophisticated enough to compensate for the asteroid's rotation."

"Sounds like someone went with the lowest bidder," Tony muttered.

"Does this surprise you?" Caitlin asked.

"OK, OK," said Diaz. "Are we gonna stand around and bitch all day, or are you gonna have some real work for us?"

"Don't you worry about it, Diaz," Caitlin said. "Here's where the fun begins."

"What's the plan?" Tony asked.

"On paper it sounds pretty straightforward," Caitlin told him. "We circle around for another pass, deploy the claw, launch the robots, and get the hell out of Dodge."

"I like it," said Tony. "Especially that last part."

Caitlin nodded in agreement, although she couldn't help but dwell on the subtle difference between theory and practice. The plan was to use the *Tamarisk* as a gravity tug. Since the gravity of one object affected the gravity of another, theoretically, if they moved the *Tamarisk* near the asteroid, the asteroid should move closer to the *Tamarisk*, almost like a dog sniffing out an open hand. Once they had it in their influence, they would deploy the advanced retrieval mechanism and the asteroid would be theirs. It all sounded so simple, but as Caitlin looked out the viewport at the asteroid, hanging there menacingly against the stars, she started to think about what could go awry. As she did, Tony's reminder once again passed through her mind.

"Because God might be listening . . ."

Chapter Seven

After a few passes around the Thresher to get their bearings, the crew began their preparations to line up the *Tamarisk* to capture the asteroid.

"OK, it's showtime," said Caitlin. "Everyone ready?"

"Oh yeah," yelled Diaz triumphantly. "Drop your linen and start your grinnin'! Ladies and gentlemen, it is time to dock with the rock!"

"I would give every chit I ever earn from this day forward if he would just shut up," Shaw said under his breath.

"Amen to that, brother," said Vee. She looked over at Caitlin. "We good?"

Caitlin gave her a nod and a slight shrug. It was the best she could manage at the moment. She hoped they were good. They'd all been trained in spaceflight and docking procedures, Vee in particular. But this was something entirely different. When two spacecraft docked, they were both moving in a controlled fashion and they had both been designed to fit together, with locks and clamps made to form a perfect seal. Asteroids offered no such amenities, and their asymmetrical, unbalanced shape meant that finding the perfect spot to link up with involved a lot of guesswork and even more luck. If the wrong area was chosen, you could latch on to a smooth patch of platinum. Go somewhere else and you were scraping at dust and rocks with no purchase. And, Caitlin thought, just to add a cherry to the top of the parfait of awful Lyman

Ross had served them, asteroids tended to rotate of their own free will, unlike a spacecraft, which could be controlled with thrusters.

So there was no real way of telling whether they were good. There was only guessing as to the least likely moment for catastrophe.

"OK," Caitlin said at last. "Let's do this. Vee, thrusters at station keeping."

"You got it."

"Bring us in nice and steady. Shaw, how are we looking?"

"Thirty meters out," he said. "I'd throttle back a little bit."

"All right. Vee, ease up on the stick."

Vee complied and Caitlin called back to Diaz and Tony.

"Get ready to deploy the ARM," she said.

The advanced retrieval mechanism was a clawlike device that extended from the nose of the craft and could be used to dock with other ships or grab something floating loose in space. In this case, that something happened to be a giant hunk of asteroid.

"We're in range," said Shaw.

"Deploy," Caitlin told Diaz and Tony.

The ARM slowly extended out from the *Tamarisk*, looking like the giant steel talons of an eagle as it reached out for the Thresher. Caitlin watched as the asteroid grew closer, paying close attention to their speed. She knew that if they came in too fast, the ARM would crumple up against the Thresher like a soda can.

"Slow and steady, Vee," she whispered.

"I've got it," she said. "I've got it."

"All right," said Shaw. "Three, two, one . . . capture."

Caitlin felt a nudge as the ARM made contact, reminding her of the bumper boats at Mountain Waters when she was a kid. Like the probe, the ARM was fitted with harpoons, which gripped the asteroid and held it in place. She smiled at Vee, squeezing her shoulders.

"We got her!" she said. "Now fire the RCS!"

Tony did as instructed, activating the reaction control system to stabilize the ship and match its rotation to the asteroid's. The *Tamarisk* was juked left and right a few times before the jets finally began to do their jobs. Eventually, they were able to slow themselves down into a controlled glide.

"Damn!" said Diaz. "Now that is how we do that!"

A smattering of applause broke out on board as the crew collectively released their breath.

"Nice work, everyone," said Caitlin. "Let's get ready to deploy the bots."

She took another deep breath to center herself before starting on the next task.

Almost home, she told herself.

That was when the fire broke out.

Chapter Eight

"Everyone here is going to die."

Alex Sutter looked out at the half-empty conference room in the Embassy Suites in downtown DC. He had hoped for a better turnout, but he also knew that what you hoped for and what you actually got were often not the same thing. As a member of the Federal Emergency Management Agency, Alex's job was to work with the Planetary Defense Coordination Office on monitoring and preventing potential asteroid strikes. The problem was the current budget allotted to both agencies was just about enough to allow them to monitor one-fifth of the solar system, which meant a lot was going on up there that no one knew about. But, in the current political climate, and with tensions rising on the Moon, scraping up more money to pay for bigger telescopes wasn't a priority. There were too many actual problems to address. Theoretical ones weren't on the docket. Hence his current predicament, giving a presentation (which, if he was being honest, was a thinly veiled plea for more money) to a lackluster group of people, all of whom looked like they'd rather be anywhere but there. In fact, if Alex were a betting man, he would have wagered that a lot of the people who were on hand had only come out of sheer morbid curiosity. Nevertheless, they were here, and as such, he was obligated to present to them. He adjusted his glasses and pressed on.

"Everyone is going to die," he repeated. "The question is, how long do you want to wait before you buy the insurance policy? Every single day, approximately one hundred tons of debris from space strikes the surface of this planet. Barely any of it is noticeable, mostly just dust and pebbles from nearby comets. But every once in a while, something bigger gets through."

He clicked the tiny remote in his hand, and the screen behind him changed to a grainy black-and-white image of three people standing in a room. Above their heads, a hole had been blasted through the ceiling. One of the people, a man in a suit, was holding a black rock in his hands. Looking at the rock was a policeman and, standing in between both men, a middle-aged woman with a distressed look on her face. It was this woman that Alex wanted the attendees to pay particular attention to. He was always excited about this part of the presentation, believing for certain that her story was guaranteed to get them hooked. It had worked in the past—usually with kids during school presentations, admittedly—and he hoped that it would tonight as well.

"Meet Ann Hodges," he said. "On November 30, 1954, she was taking a nap in her home in Sylacauga, Alabama, when a rock the size of a grapefruit smashed through the roof of her house, bounced off her radio, and landed on her. Her arm and hip were badly bruised, but she managed to walk away from the impact relatively unharmed. What struck her was this . . ."

Another click of the remote and the image changed to a close-up of the rock, now on display at the Alabama Museum of Natural History at the University of Alabama.

"A chondrite," Alex said. "A meteorite that broke off from a larger asteroid and made its way to Earth. Now, as I said, this piece was no larger than a grapefruit, and yet when it entered our atmosphere, it made a fireball large enough to be seen from three states. Had its descent not been slowed by the roof and the furniture in Mrs. Hodges's house, she most likely would have been killed. So if something the size of a grapefruit can do that, imagine something larger? Maybe the size of a small house?"

Alex paused for dramatic effect and was greeted only by the sound of rustling papers, weight shifting in seats, and an errant cough or two emanating from the semidarkness. He sighed, cleared his throat, and went on.

"October 9, 1992, witnesses in Pittsburgh, Philadelphia, and Washington, DC, all report a green fireball streaking toward Earth. It's captured by no less than sixteen independent video cameras. And this is in 1992, in the days before everyone had a video camera in their pocket. Those who saw it reported it as being brighter than the Moon, which was almost full at the time. It crossed several states in forty seconds before coming down over Peekskill, New York, and striking Earth. Or, more accurately . . ."

Alex tapped the remote again, and the image changed to a red car sitting in a driveway. The rear of the vehicle on the passenger side was completely pulverized. On the ground beside the bumper was a black lump of rock. The image brought a slight ripple from the group, which Alex took as a good sign. He continued.

". . . striking Michelle Knapp's Chevy Malibu, where it almost hit the gas tank. Experts from the American Museum of Natural History confirmed that the object was a meteorite. A twenty-eight-pound meteorite about the size of a bowling ball, to be exact."

Another touch of the remote and a video rolled, showing a bright-white object streaking through a dusky winter sky captured from different angles.

"February 15, 2013," Alex said. "Chelyabinsk Oblast in the Ural Mountains of Russia. A meteor enters the atmosphere at a shallow angle. This angle, combined with the fact that its most likely point of origin was close to the Sun, meant that the object entered our atmosphere undetected. It streaked overhead until, approximately twelve miles from the surface, heat and pressure caused it to explode in an airburst over

Chelyabinsk. The amount of energy released was five hundred kilotons. That's thirty times more powerful than the atomic bomb that destroyed Hiroshima. More than fifteen hundred people were injured as a result, mostly from broken glass due to the number of windows shattered. Additionally, the force of the explosion sent out a shock wave that made its way around the planet twice. The Chelyabinsk meteor is the largest natural object to enter our atmosphere since the Tunguska blast of 1908 and proof positive that humankind is vulnerable to objects from space. At the time, Dmitry Medvedev, the then-prime minister of Russia, as well as representatives from many other countries, called for an organized, interconnected global system to be put in place to safeguard the planet from impending strikes. To date, despite many valiant tries from various agencies, including NASA, no such system is in place."

He scanned the room again, taking a pause before starting to conclude his speech. Much to his dismay, he noticed that, during the course of his talk, several seats had lost their occupants. This was the ongoing battle scientists faced when trying to raise awareness about the threats posed by near-Earth objects, the so-called giggle factor. For most people, the idea of an asteroid striking Earth with life-altering results ranged from impossible to downright laughable. During the twentieth century, interest in asteroid impacts spiked when scientists discovered the Chicxulub Crater in the Yucatán Peninsula, the crater thought to be caused by the impact that wiped out the dinosaurs. After that fervor died off, the public's interest was briefly rekindled when, in 1994, a comet known as Shoemaker-Levy 9 collided with Jupiter. Named for Carolyn and Eugene M. Shoemaker and David Levy, the comet was discovered in March of 1993 and impacted with the planet more than a year later, leaving scars that were, for a time, easier to identify via telescope than the Great Red Spot. However, yet again, once the fervor from that story had abated, the public's interest turned elsewhere. And, for the last hundred-plus years, elsewhere it had remained, explaining the indifference with which Alex's presentation was being met.

"The simple fact is, an asteroid could wipe out a major city tomorrow and we would have no warning," Alex went on, even if only for himself. "This is a scenario we have to start considering. Is the possibility low? Yes. But it is still a possibility. And to dismiss it is to invite disaster."

He opted to change gears.

"I know that there are many people, both in this room and out there in the world, who don't take this seriously," he said. "People who think that the idea of an asteroid striking Earth is fantasy. Something that might spring out of the mind of a Hollywood screenwriter. And that people like me are like Chicken Little, running from door to door warning that the sky is falling. And maybe they're right to a point. But the fact is, an asteroid doesn't even have to hit the ground to cause catastrophe. Back in 2002, an asteroid exploded in midair over the Mediterranean between Libya and Crete. Now, at the time, tensions between Pakistan and India were running particularly high. Both countries were on full nuclear alert. Luckily, the asteroid exploded over the ocean and no harm was done. But what if it had exploded over Mumbai or Islamabad? Who's to say that either country wouldn't have misinterpreted the explosion as a first strike and retaliated accordingly?"

This provoked a reaction, although not the one Alex had intended. The room was filled with the sound of more chairs emptying and more footfalls making their way to the door. He shuffled his papers and looked at his holopad, hoping to find an image or story that could win them over again.

"Excuse me," came a voice from the podium that had been placed in the center aisle. Alex was a little thrown by this. Initially, he had planned on waiting until the presentation was over to take questions. However, given the way the afternoon had been going, he was no longer confident he had the luxury of time. And if this guy was interested enough to ask anything, he certainly wasn't about to admonish him for it.

"Yes sir," said Alex. "And you are . . . ?"

"Senator Mark Rayburn," the man at the podium said. "Alabama."

"The home of Ann Hodges," said Alex brightly, hoping to use the connection to establish a little common ground. "That's a coinciden—"

"Yes," Rayburn said. "I'm a man who believes in cutting to the chase. So why don't you tell these good people, or at least those of us who are left, what it is that you're asking."

"Here's the truth, Senator," said Alex. "This is the only natural disaster that we have a chance at stopping. You can't stop tornadoes or flash floods. You can only seek to minimize the damage that they cause. But with asteroids, we have the means, resources, and technology to prevent them from ever causing us any harm in the first place. We just haven't taken advantage of our options. So what am I asking? I'm asking for your help in funding a system that will allow us to track these things. Specifically, we're hoping to track near-Earth asteroids, which are harder to spot. See, they're naturally dark, and the brightest ones only reflect about twenty percent of the light that hits them, so we need . . ."

Rayburn held up his hand. "And if we track them," he asked, "do we have the means to stop them?"

"Well," Alex said, "that is also something we're working on. We have a number of very promising ideas at the Planetary Defense Coordination Office. In fact, someone there was going to—"

Rayburn clearly didn't want to hear it. He bulldozed over Alex's response to get to his next question.

"I seem to recall a whole big fuss sometime ago about another asteroid that was going to pass us by. Apotheosis or something?"

"Apophis," said Alex. He knew where this was going.

"Uh-huh," Senator Rayburn said. "And what happened there?"

"It missed us," Alex said, "by about nineteen thousand miles."

"Nineteen thousand miles," Rayburn said.

"That's not that far when you think of it in interstellar terms," Alex said. "That's almost ten percent of the distance to the Moon!"

"I see," said Rayburn, as though he hadn't heard Alex's reply. "And since then, how many near misses like that have we had?"

"Well," Alex said, feeling the air slowly running out of his presentation like a punctured air mattress, "none, but—"

Rayburn didn't answer. He just nodded and offered a sarcastic salute on his way to the door. In his wake, the remaining attendees began to gather their things and shuffle out of the conference room. Alex found that his voice was rising, both in volume and pitch.

"That's all the more reason it could happen now," he said. "It's only a matter of time before something enters our atmosphere. Something too big for us to stop. The dinosaurs didn't stand a chance, but we do! We're living on borrowed time!"

When he finished, his words echoed, confirming that he was now addressing an empty room. He blinked like a man just coming to his senses and realized how hysterical he'd probably just sounded. Then he looked down at the small stuffed bear that he had perched on the podium, a good-luck charm from his goddaughter.

"How do you think it went?" he asked his sole remaining audience member.

As he gathered up his papers, he jostled the podium, and the bear tipped over, falling to the floor.

"Yeah," he said. "That about sums it up."

As he was gathering up his papers dejectedly, Alex suddenly heard slow but steady applause echoing through the ballroom. He looked up from the podium at the tall figure approaching him.

"Wonderful presentation, Doctor," a woman said. "You really had 'em hooked."

Although the face had yet to come fully into focus from the glare of the spotlight, Alex didn't need to see it. He'd know Sara Kent's voice if he heard it underwater. He looked at her, shaking his head as he continued cleaning up his presentation.

"Would have helped to have you up here instead of out there," he said.

"Sorry," she said. "I got hung up back at work. By the time I got here, you were already—"

"It will really help what's left of my ego if you don't finish that sentence," Alex said, but his tone had softened. He knew Sara had been busy ever since she'd been named director of NASA's PDCO. The organization's responsibility was the early detection of PHOs—potentially hazardous objects—that might pass by Earth at a distance deemed too close for comfort. Should something fitting that description be spotted, it was up to them to coordinate with FEMA and other government agencies to determine the severity of the threat and come up with solutions.

Sara walked up to the podium. In the ten years since he'd seen her last, she hadn't changed much. She still wore her strawberry-blonde hair in a loose ponytail, and her eyes still had that hint of mischief, like she was perennially about to tell you a joke at a bar.

Once Sara had crossed the distance between them, Alex suddenly found himself going in for a hug. She blocked the attempt with an outstretched hand.

They shook hands and exchanged awkward greetings. Alex had a feeling he'd be replaying the moment again and again in his hotel room.

Sara walked over to the screen behind them and looked up at the slide that still flickered there.

"'Vermin of the Solar System'?" she said, reading the title off the slide.

"Too much?" Alex asked.

"If you're making a low-rent science-fiction movie? No," said Sara. "But if you're looking to rally potential deep pockets to your cause? Maybe just a touch."

"It's a real term," he said. "Astronomers used to think that asteroids were just bits of junk cluttering up the view of more important things."

"I remember," Sara said. "I've got the same Caltech degree you do, if you recall."

"Yeah," said Alex. "But would you have done as well without my help?"

"Excuse you," Sara said with a light shove. In the space of that gesture, Alex felt a real moment of time travel. Walking with her along Colorado Boulevard in Old Town, their futures out in front of them like the lights of a far-off city. *What had happened to those two?* he wondered. But just as quickly as the thought rose, Alex tamped it back down.

They stepped out of the hotel only to find that it had begun to rain. Alex scanned his phone to see when his ride was due to arrive and noticed that the seven minutes he had been promised had now leaped to fifteen. He grimaced. Nothing like being kicked when you're already down. He looked over at Sara.

"What?" she asked.

"No, nothing," Alex fumbled. "I just was wondering . . . you know . . . curious . . . did you ever . . . you know . . . find someone?"

Way to go, Alex, the voice in his head chided. For some reason, he always heard that voice as the Miracle Max character in *The Princess Bride. A million things you could have talked to her about in this moment and you pick at the oldest wound in the book.*

"Never did," Sara said, somewhat awkwardly. "I chose to put my career first. You?"

"Yeah," said Alex. "Didn't take, though."

"With all your charming traits?" said Sara. "I'm shocked."

Her words left an icy trail in their wake. Before the void could be filled with conversation, Sara flagged a cab. When it sloshed up to the curb, Alex lurched forward rather gracelessly to hold the door for her. In doing so, he accidentally almost knocked Sara to the curb. She steadied herself with a rather bemused look, then slipped into the backseat.

"You still coming to the PDCO tomorrow?" she asked. "I'll give you the grand tour."

"Wouldn't miss it."

"See you then," Sara said, and began to close the door. Before she could, Alex reached out and held it open.

"How come you never got married?" he asked, trying to sound casual. "Were you afraid you'd never find someone who treated you the way I did?"

"Not at all," Sara said. "I was afraid that I would."

With that, she slammed the door and the car pulled out into the rain, leaving Alex confused and embarrassed for the second time in one night.

Chapter Nine

The explosion on the *Tamarisk* was almost instantaneous, sending a torrent of fire erupting suddenly from the rear of the ship and working its way slowly and deliberately forward. In the microgravity environment, the blue-and-yellow flames moved almost like liquid. To a dispassionate observer, the effect might have been strangely beautiful. To the crew of the *Tamarisk*, however, it was terrifying. They spoke in breathless shouts, trying to process and relay information amid total chaos.

"Jesus Christ!" yelled Diaz. "What the hell's going on?"

"Dammit," said Tony. "The fuel's ignited!"

"How the hell did that happen?" Caitlin asked.

"There's no time to worry about how," Tony said, already moving aft. "Someone's got to shut the valves down or we're going to lose the whole ship."

"I'll go with you," said Caitlin.

"Stay here," Tony said. "There's nothing you can do. It's a one-person job, and I know the makeup of the engines. Sit tight. If something goes wrong, you're gonna know about it."

He kissed Vee quickly.

"Keep her flying," he told her, and was gone before she could formulate an answer.

Keeping the ship flying was proving to be a tall order as the fire in the engines played havoc with the RCS. Vee and Caitlin worked to try to get the *Tamarisk* under control, but the experience was like breaking a stallion without a bridle.

◆ ◆ ◆

Belowdecks, Tony worked his way through the guts of the *Tamarisk* and cursed the name of Lyman Ross. There was a reason no one used hypergolic fuels anymore, he thought. Designed to spontaneously combust when they came into contact with each other, they were once seen as ideal because no ignition system was required. The two propellants simply flowed through their respective valves and, once they made contact, ignited. The downside was that the chemicals involved tended to be toxic and potentially dangerous. And, in the case of the hypergolics used to fuel the *Tamarisk*, they were the most toxic and dangerous of all. Devil's Venom, as the Soviets had called it in the early days of their space program, was an incredibly powerful fuel comprised of unsymmetrical dimethylhydrazine and nitric acid. However, as powerful as it was, Devil's Venom was also extremely corrosive, to the point that the nitric acid couldn't remain in the oxidizer tank for longer than a few days without eating through the metal.

Tony suspected that was what he was confronting here. He knew the valves on the *Tamarisk* were old and worn, and the ship itself had probably not been assembled in the cleanest shop to begin with. It wouldn't take much for the acid to eat through the pipe. If even a little dripped onto the tube containing the dimethylhydrazine, then a fire would be the inevitable result.

Reaching the engine, Tony saw immediately that the worst had happened. The valve for the nitric acid had been completely corroded. Still, he could try to contain the leak and maybe at the very least buy them time. He accessed the ship's computer and ran a series of commands to shut down the valves and prevent more fuel from mixing. Just as the computer seemed to be responding, Tony was suddenly greeted with a blast of dimethylhydrazine from the corroded pipe. In an instant, he was doused with the caustic liquid.

Pain blossomed all over his body as the chemicals seared through his suit and skin. His eyes burned and he squeezed them shut, trying to keep out the fumes. Deprived of the chance to torment his eyes further, the agents instead entered his mouth, scorching his nose and throat. Almost instantly, he felt as though his lungs were being filled with fluid, a sure sign of pulmonary edema. Tony coughed violently, as if that would somehow expel the deadly materials, and retched up a torrent of blood onto the decks. Even in the throes of agony, he found himself pausing a moment and blinking in shock, experiencing an almost detached amazement at the viscera he had just ejected from his body. He knew that what he was seeing was a sign of something terrible, and that the time he had left in which to be effective could now be measured in minutes, if not seconds.

He tried to work his way forward, but his head swam as though he'd just been sucker punched, tilting him off balance and sending him spinning wildly back down the tunnel. Desperate, he tried to force himself to move, inching his way to the hatch for the escape lander. Hand over hand, gripping the sides of the ship for balance, Tony pushed through the tunnel.

I'm coming, Vee. I'm coming . . .

Around him, the fire grew worse, the smoke and flames aggravating his failing lungs. His hands shaking, he reached for the comm.

In the cockpit, Caitlin and Vee were battling to keep the *Tamarisk* level when they heard Tony on the comm. His voice was strained, as though each word was a struggle.

"Get to the *Alley Oop*," he said. "Now."

"Tony?" Vee asked. "Baby, what's wrong?"

"Nothing, honey," Tony said. "I'm all right. Just go. Now! I'll meet you there."

Before anyone in the cockpit could protest further, something burst somewhere on the ship and it jerked wildly starboard.

"We've got to go!" said Diaz.

They scrambled their way down the hatch and into the *Alley Oop*, bouncing off the walls as they floated nearly uncontrollably in zero gravity. Once inside the lander, they strapped in and locked their helmets into place. Vee and Diaz started the launch cycle while Shaw manned the radar to search for their position in space. Another burst and they were rocked again.

"Tony!" Caitlin yelled into her helmet mic. "We've got to move."

The only response she received to her query was silence wrapped in static. Something was very wrong.

"I'm going for him," she said, and began unbuckling her straps.

Caitlin pinballed her way back up the tunnel. When she reached the top, a terrifying sight greeted her. The *Tamarisk* was now engulfed in flame, making it next to impossible to move anywhere.

"Tony!" she cried into her mic again, hoping he was still alive and able to hear her.

Suddenly, Tony burst out from the wall of fire that led aft and slowly worked his way toward her. His face was covered in burns, his suit slowly being eaten away. He looked up at her, shaking as he tried to speak.

"Looks like God was listening," he said ruefully.

"OK," Caitlin said to him. "It's OK. Just get in the lander and we'll get you patched up. Come on . . ."

"Can't do it," Tony said. "Docking clamp was damaged in the fire. It's got to be released manually."

Caitlin knew what he was trying to tell her. "No," she said. "No, Tony, there's got to be another way. There's got to—"

Another explosion erupted from somewhere on board, and they shifted violently to port. Tony and Caitlin locked eyes.

"Caitlin," he said. *"Go."*

There was no more time. Willing herself to turn away, Caitlin floated back down the hatch, trying her best to hold it together. When she got inside the *Alley Oop*, Vee turned to her.

"Where's Tony?" she asked, the panic growing in her voice. "Where is he?"

"Start the launch cycle," Caitlin said. "We need to be ready to—"

"Where is he?"

"He's gone, OK?" Caitlin said, probably more harshly than she meant to. "He's gone. And we will be too unless we get ready to leave now."

"Babe?"

Tony's voice came over Vee's headset. She answered immediately.

"I'm here!" she said, unable to hold back her tears. "I'm here, honey, but we've got to go, so come on, OK?"

"That's why I'm calling you," he said. His ragged voice grew faint. "I can't make it. You have to go without me."

"No," she said. "No, don't say that! You *are* going to make it, OK? Just a few more feet."

"Babe," Tony said, "you've got to let me go. It's the only way the rest of you stand any chance."

"You can't do this," Vee protested. "I need you. All of this doesn't work without you. It's always been you and me."

"And it always will," he said. "I love you . . ."

Tony hit the manual release from inside the *Tamarisk*, and the *Alley Oop* separated from the burning ship. As it was jettisoned, Vee screamed.

"No!" she yelled, and the sound of her voice tore Caitlin down the center. *"Tony!"*

Vee bent forward, hysterical. Caitlin was left with no choice but to take over pilot duties.

"Where are we headed, Shaw?" she asked.

"I don't know!" Shaw said. "I still don't know where we are!"

Caitlin took a second to gather her thoughts and assess their situation. As she did, it was not long before the inescapable truth hit her like a sixteen-ounce glove to the gut.

"Buckle in," she told everyone. "Prepare for landing."

"Landing?" asked Diaz. "Where the hell do you think we're landing?"

The crew looked out the viewport at the asteroid drawing closer.

"The only place we can."

Chapter Ten

"Caitlin? It's your father . . ."

Her eyes snap open, her disorientation compounded by the realization that she's upside down. She blinks, trying to focus and wipe the fog from her mind when the whine of the rotors forces her back into reality. Air rushes into her lungs, and she clambers out of the fallen helicopter into complete chaos. Gunfire rakes the air from above and around them. The sky above is only a suggestion, concealed by acrid smoke from the ruined copter and discharged weapons as well as particles of sand, dust, and pulverized stone. Some troops, the ones who've survived the crash, are already fanning out into the street, cutting down insurgents and tending to the wounded. Of these, there are several. Whether from impact or from the hail of bullets that descended on them immediately following, much of Caitlin's platoon has been decimated. Men and women alike writhe, bleeding from assorted wounds, some more grave than others. Two things the movies don't tell you about dying in combat. It's never quick and it's never quiet.

She finds Evers huddled up against the wreckage. The same one who, just moments before, ensured everyone on board the helicopter that he was invincible. Even though he is sitting still, Evers is gasping for air, his face a mask of panic. His eyes dart around frantically, searching for help.

"I can't breathe! I can't breathe!" he shrieks. "Please God, help me!"

Caitlin scrambles over to him and takes his face in her hands, locking eyes with him.

"Hey! Hey! You're OK," she shouts. "You're in survival mode! Your body's trying to draw in more oxygen than you can handle! Happens to everyone on their first engagement. Just breathe slow, you'll be OK!"

The private nods, and Caitlin slaps his helmet, moving on. Her head is screaming from the heat and the weight of her gear. Even though she is heavily armored, she feels vulnerable, exposed, mostly because it's damn hard to move. She tries to process the madness around her, to put what's happening into ordered, organized columns, but to no avail. More bullets scream overhead, pinging off the downed helicopter as she works her way through the sand.

The bastards aren't even aiming, *she thinks.* Just laying down suppressing fire to keep us from doing anything other than crawling on our bellies.

As she huddles up behind a mud wall and contemplates her next move, a body lands next to her and she yells out.

"Hey, Taggart!" Ben says. "You made it!"

"For whatever that's worth," she says.

"Fix your eyepro, Boss," Ben says.

Caitlin adjusts her ballistic glasses, which had somehow gone askew in her journey from the helicopter to the wall. Ben gives her a nod.

"Much better," he says. "So what's the plan?"

"I don't know," she says. "It's all gone fubar down here. Are we the only helo down?"

"In this sector, yeah," Ben says. "Looks like it. But who knows what's happening elsewhere?"

"They were waiting for us," she says.

"The Enders?" Ben says. "Hell yeah they were. Are you really surprised?"

"No," she says. "But I'm pissed as hell!"

"Then let's press forward," Ben says. "Maybe we can use that to our advantage."

Caitlin nods and they begin gathering the remains of the platoon, moving forward into the burning hulk of the city.

◆ ◆ ◆

"Are you serious?" Diaz asked Caitlin, eyes full of panic as he looked out at the approaching asteroid.

"I'm completely serious," she told him. "But now is the time for better options. Don't be shy."

Diaz didn't answer, either unable or unwilling to present an alternative. He simply sat back in his seat, rocking back and forth, talking to himself. Caitlin reached over and grabbed him. She placed her hand flat on his chest.

"Hey!" she said. "Hey! Breathe, OK? I need you to breathe."

Slowly, as Diaz regained his composure, Caitlin could feel his chest rising and falling in a steady rhythm against her hand.

"Good," she said. "That's good. Keep it up. Shaw! How are we looking?"

"We've got to slow our rate of descent," he called back. "At our present speed, we're going to slam right into this thing."

Caitlin worked the touch screen controls on the lander, ordering the braking thrusters to fire and slow them down.

"All right," Shaw said. "First things first, we want to aim for the night side of this thing. That should give us eighteen days or so before the Sun comes up and cooks us. Secondly, if we stand any shot of landing this thing, then we've got to match our velocity to the asteroid's, and we've got to keep it slow or we're going to bounce right off."

The descent to the asteroid was measured and precise, with Shaw talking Caitlin down as she gently worked the thrusters to keep the tiny escape craft from bouncing back up into space. Finally, after what felt like hours, the blue contact light flared on the screen, indicating that the sensor probe on the bottom of the lander had touched the surface of the Thresher.

"Contact!" said Shaw.

"Diaz!" Caitlin shouted. "Fire the pitons."

Like the probe and the *Tamarisk*, the *Alley Oop* was also equipped with anchors that could be launched from her landing struts to bite into the rock. Diaz deployed them at once, and the ship came to a juddering halt. It was less of a landing and more of an awkward falling to the ground. Caitlin allowed herself a bitter inward chuckle. The *Alley Oop* wasn't named without a sense of irony, it seemed. It was not the most graceful lander ever built, and Caitlin questioned whether Lyman Ross knew if it was spaceworthy. In fact, if Caitlin were to think things through, she'd most likely conclude that Ross had put the lander on board solely to ensure the *Tamarisk* was up to regulation.

When they hit the surface and the anchoring harpoons fired themselves deep into the rock, all the lights on the ship winked out for a moment and then flickered back on. The team attempted to gather themselves. Diaz was still freaking out.

"Jesus!" he yelled, his eyes wide and frantic. "Jesus Christ, what the hell just happened up there? He's gone! He's gone, man!"

"Pull it together, Diaz!" Caitlin shouted.

He quieted down but continued breathing heavily, trying to collect himself. Caitlin turned to look over at Vee, who had unlatched her helmet and was rubbing her eyes. Her face was stony, although the torrent of emotions swirling underneath was visible. Gently, Caitlin touched her arm. Vee's head swiveled toward her sharply. Instinctively, Caitlin retracted her hand, and Vee looked away.

"Stings like hell, doesn't it?" Caitlin said, trying to bridge the gap between them. "Your eyes? It's because there's very low gravity. The tears can't run down your face, so they just collect in your eyes. Just keep rubbing them. It'll pass."

Vee didn't answer, continuing to look down. Caitlin decided to try a different tactic.

"I know," she said. "OK? *I know*. But right now, we've got big problems in front of us and not a lot of time to deal with them. I need you at your best right now. Or as close as you can come. Can I count on you?"

Tears formed again in Vee's eyes, and she wiped them away angrily, almost defiantly, before they could attempt to lodge themselves there. She turned to face Caitlin again, this time ready to address the elephant in the room.

"You let him go," she said, simply.

"I made a call," Caitlin said. "*He* made a call. The ship was burning. It was him or us. He knew it too. Remember, Vee, he was the one who released the docking clamp. It's not like he was pounding on the hatch to be let in. He sacrificed himself so that we could have a chance at getting out of this alive. And believe me when I tell you that I wish it had been me instead of him."

"Right now, so do I," Vee said.

"I get it," Caitlin told her, regaining her composure. "I've been here before. It's one of the perks of being in charge. You sometimes have to make decisions that get some people killed and other people upset. And you can hate me for it, you can wish me dead, whatever you've got to do to push through this. But I need you. Shaw and Diaz need you. So stow your hate until we get off this rock. Because right now, I'm counting on you. Can I count on you?"

Vee looked as if she would say more, but then turned away, casting her eyes down at the controls. "Yeah," she said. "Yeah, I got this."

Caitlin gave her arm a squeeze. This time, Vee didn't recoil.

"I'm sorry about Tony."

Vee said nothing. Caitlin turned her attention to Diaz and Shaw.

"OK, here's the situation," she said. "First, we've got to assess what we have to work with on the lander. I want us to go through this bucket both inside and out. Fuel, electrical, supplies, everything that works, and everything that doesn't. Does she have enough fuel to get us back to the Moon? And if not, what then?"

"Why are we even discussing this?" said Diaz. "Why don't we just take off right now? Head back home? Hell, let's try and book it to Earth if we can."

"I already said that's my plan, Diaz," Caitlin noted. "I'm hoping that we *can* get back to the Moon. We need to know what we're dealing with in terms of fuel. But Earth? Right now, that's out of the question."

"Why?" Vee asked.

"Because," said Caitlin, "in Lyman Ross's eyes, we've failed. Which means we're on our own. No clearance, no travel pass, no visas. We try to get to Earth, and they'll shoot us down before we can even begin reentry."

"So we're stuck here," Shaw said.

"Just for now," said Caitlin. "Just until we know what we're up against."

Shaw looked at Caitlin, his initial bewilderment giving way to anger. "What we're up against?" he asked. "What we're *up against*? Tony's dead, our ship is destroyed, and in case you haven't taken a peek out the window recently, we happen to be stuck on a goddamn asteroid! I don't think you need to be Stephen Hawking to figure out what we're up against!"

"Are we going to have a problem now?" Caitlin asked him. Shaw turned away, kicking the console. Caitlin let it pass, then turned and faced everyone.

"We knew there were risks when we agreed to take this job," she told them. "But I think we can all agree that things went worse than expected. We can't change what happened. All we can do now is try and find a way to survive. But the only way we're going to do that is if we keep our heads together and *stay cool.* So, anyone who feels like taking a walk outside with me, let's suit up and get moving. Anyone who needs some time to process everything we've been through, this is when you take it. After that, you keep your emotions in check until we're back home, got it?"

"Yeah, Boss," said Diaz. "I'm with you."

Caitlin walked over to him and put out her hand, pulling him up and looking him in the eye.

"We did everything we could up there," she said to him. "You know that."

"But Tony . . ." His voice broke as he looked away. "Tony, he—

"Tony made his choice," said Caitlin. "And it was the right call. He saved us because of it. Now the best thing we can do is try and make sure he didn't die in vain."

Diaz composed himself, staving off the tears, and nodded. Caitlin nodded with him.

"There you go," she said. "Now let's figure out how we're going to get home."

Shaw, Diaz, and Caitlin suited up and prepared to head out onto the surface of the asteroid. Vee opted to stay behind to see what was working internally on the *Alley Oop*. After depressurizing the cabin, Caitlin knelt and pulled open the hatch, preparing to walk outside.

"Man," said Diaz, looking down at the stony cratered surface of the Thresher. "This is not how I thought this day was gonna go."

"Tell that to Tony," said Shaw.

"Easy, you two," said Caitlin. "Let's keep our eye on the ball."

The three miners turned astronauts stepped out of the lander and onto the surface. Almost immediately, they found themselves disoriented in an alien landscape unlike any they'd witnessed before. Time spent on the surface of the Moon had done very little to prepare them for the experience of navigating this new terrain. The topography was jagged and uneven, with ridges and craters dotting the landscape in chaotic, irregular patterns. The ground was covered in a light carpet of ejecta, the effect of centuries of impacts from smaller objects from throughout the cosmos. The light was minimal, as the Sun was presently on the other side of the asteroid awaiting its rising in eighteen days, so everything was cast in a caul of half-light that made them think of a graveyard under a gibbous moon.

As they began to move, they quickly found that walking on the surface of the Thresher was next to impossible. The low gravity made them feel as though every step was going to send them careening into space. To Caitlin, the experience felt more like swimming than walking. A simple push with a fingertip was enough to propel them forward or slow them down. Still, the mini RCS inside their suits helped to combat the effects somewhat, keeping them relatively grounded.

"Watch your thrusters," Shaw warned the group. "Too much force and you could kick up dust and contaminate the RCS."

"Got it," said Caitlin. Diaz, who looked a stone's throw away from vomiting, merely nodded.

Slowly, they learned to walk, using a combination of small hops countered by thruster fire from their suits, an unpleasant and nerve-racking experience. On one occasion, Diaz lost his bearings completely and would have gone tumbling into space were it not for Shaw's quick reflexes.

"Maybe you should check on the lander," said Shaw. "Give yourself something to hold on to."

"Yeah." Diaz nodded, breathing heavily. "Probably a good idea."

Now working more gingerly than ever, Diaz hop-walked around the outside of the *Alley Oop*, holding on to the hull and examining the craft carefully, checking for anything that looked out of place.

"She's a reentry vehicle," he said. "Not just an excursion module. If we decided to make the trip back to Earth, she could get there, except . . ."

"I don't like the sound of that word," Caitlin said.

"Well, you're gonna like this even less," said Diaz. "The heat shield's cracked. It might last long enough to slow our orbital velocity, but after that, we're gonna be charbroiled."

"OK," Caitlin said. "Do we have anything on the ship that can repair it?"

"We might have some non-oxide adhesive in the supply locker," Diaz said. "I can check when we get back inside."

"So the heat shield is cracked," Caitlin said, taking stock. "But can we get close enough to Earth to dock with another ship maybe?"

"Sure, I guess," said Diaz. "But I thought you just said Earth was out of the question. Remember? We're four illegals coming from the Moon. The only ships that are going to come and meet us are either attack skiffs or a prison barge."

"Yeah, I know what I said," said Caitlin. "But I'm rethinking my position. Sitting in a prison barge would still be better than sweating it out on this rock."

"Yeah," said Shaw. "Speaking of that. Don't forget, in eighteen days or so, this asteroid is going to complete its rotation. When it does, there's going to be nothing between us and the Sun, and we're all going to get pan-seared."

"Good point," Caitlin said. "All the more reason to be thinking of an escape plan. With that in mind, we should get back on board and see what our fuel situation is like."

As they turned to go, Caitlin noticed that Shaw was still standing rooted to the surface of the asteroid, a worried look on his face.

"What's the holdup?" she asked.

"There's one more thing," he said. "I've been doing some calculations about our orientation, looking at our position based on the stars, and . . ."

"And?" Caitlin asked, not liking where the line of conversation was headed.

"We're off course," Shaw said. "The fire, the thrust from the *Tamarisk*, the force of the launching of the escape lander, whatever it was, something pushed us off of our original trajectory."

"How bad is it?" asked Caitlin.

Shaw looked into space, and Caitlin's gaze followed his. At once, they both saw Earth rising over the asteroid's horizon. With a horrible sinking sensation, Caitlin suddenly realized what Shaw was trying to tell her.

"It's pretty bad," he said.

Almost as one, Caitlin, Shaw, and Diaz stumbled back onto the *Alley Oop*, unlatching helmets and shedding suits. Vee swiveled around to look at them and give them the rundown of what she'd uncovered during her scan of the ship.

"Fuel situation's not great," she told them. "We depleted most of it getting to the surface. The good news is the low gravity means that we won't need a ton of propellant to make escape velocity. So, chances are good that we'd be able to take off, but getting all the way back to the Moon or Earth might be a challenge. Unfortunately, that's the least of our problems. The ignition system's offline. Not sure if it's electrical or what, but I can't get it working at the moment . . .

"What is it?" she asked, her eyes traveling from one person to the next. Caitlin could tell by the hesitation in her voice that she had read their collective expressions.

"Can you get comms working?" asked Caitlin.

"Yeah, I think so."

"Do it," Caitlin said. "Broadcast a distress signal on ICC channel 24."

"Channel 24?" asked Vee. "That channel's reserved for emergencies."

"Yeah, well, I've got something that will definitely apply."

"What's going on?" Vee asked.

"Let's just say that we might be getting back to Earth a little sooner than Ross or anyone else would have planned," Caitlin told her. "Only problem is, no one's going to be all that happy to see us."

Chapter Eleven

Halfway back to Georgetown, Sara instructed the driver to turn around and take her back to the PDCO offices at NASA headquarters. A lot of her memories of the years she spent with Alex Sutter had sunk way beneath the silt of her mind, and seeing him tonight had stirred them up. She knew her last words to him tonight were harsh. *Probably a little too harsh,* she told herself. After all, she had been just as much to blame for how things ended as he had been. But what did he expect? He had wanted to get married right after graduation and . . . what? Have her play the dutiful housewife while he went on to conquer the world? No thank you. She knew her mother had gone from her childhood home to a dorm room to the house she had lived in ever since. And although her mother would never admit it, Sara occasionally caught glimpses of the longing in her mother's eyes, as though she were scanning some distant horizon for the life that had left her behind. Sara had long ago promised herself that that same longing would never enter her own eyes.

And so Alex had gone off to his career, first at the Jet Propulsion Laboratory and then at FEMA, taking on a position that had brought him back into his old love's orbit. When he had first e-mailed Sara letting her know about the job that involved combating asteroid threats, she knew soon their paths would cross, but she hadn't imagined how it would feel when the moment came. And so she did the thing she always did when she didn't want the vagaries of everyday life encroaching on her psyche. She worked.

It was late when she arrived at the PDCO, and she imagined there would be little to do, but Sara didn't mind. A few hours of mindless distraction would be enough to keep her occupied before she had to see Alex again the next morning.

As she walked through the halls to her office, Sara found herself once again wondering how many people in America even knew the PDCO existed. Even though it was not a common topic of discussion, planetary defense had a history that went all the way back to the 1960s, when a group of twenty-one MIT seniors and graduate students came together to devise a plan to stop an asteroid, 1566 Icarus, from colliding with Earth in June of 1968. According to the data the students received, Icarus would be traveling at a speed of eighteen miles per second and strike the planet with a force equivalent to more than a half-million megatons of TNT. The impact would effectively wash Florida off the map and create two-hundred-foot waves and be felt as far away as Africa.

During the study, the students proposed launching six Saturn V boosters, each carrying a 44,000-pound nuclear warhead with a yield of 100 megatons. The hope was that the first rocket would break Icarus apart and the remaining five would pulverize the fragments, turning one potentially destructive asteroid into a harmless meteor shower.

Of course, 1566 Icarus did not collide with Earth, and the danger was entirely hypothetical. However, it did pass within four million miles of the planet, becoming the first asteroid detected by Earth-based radar. The students themselves published the study in 1968, bringing the threat of an asteroid impact to the public's attention for the first time.

Since then, various groups had come forward to champion the cause of both asteroid detection and deflection. Even Apollo 9 astronaut Rusty Schweickart was an outspoken advocate for planetary defense, helping to found the B612 Foundation in 2002, comprised of scientists, former astronauts, and engineers working toward the goal of maximizing Earth's preparedness for a PHO impact. In 2016, NASA joined the cause by forming the PDCO.

Unfortunately, as the years had gone on, and the hysteria surrounding incoming asteroids had waned, the PDCO's budget had been slashed repeatedly. Then with the Second Cold War and Last Campaign diverting both government funding and public interest away from watching the stars, the organization's funding had been further reduced until the amount of sky they were able to successfully search was minimal, the equivalent of peering at the Grand Canyon through a keyhole. As such, most of the PDCO's days were spent scanning for distant threats, ones that may put future generations in jeopardy. These potentially hazardous asteroids, or PHAs, were what kept Sara busy most days and nights. However, the absence of any really distressing news meant that Sara could expect a night of relative quiet distraction with which to dispel all thoughts of her past life and the roads not taken.

"Sara!" came a voice from behind, approaching fast. She turned to see Ned Peterson streaking her way, his belly bouncing urgently with every footfall. He ran up the stairs to her station and stood there, slightly hunched, as though he was trying to will the wind to reenter his body. Sara watched him piteously a moment and held up a freshly poured cup of coffee.

"Ned," she said, "what am I holding?"

He looked at the cup as though it were a particularly vexing puzzle to be solved. Eventually, Ned came up with the answer, although his tone suggested uncertainty.

"Coffee?"

"Mmmm-hmmm," said Sara with the air of a pleased parent. "And what is the rule about disturbing me while my coffee is still hot? Especially during the night shift."

"I know," he said between desperate huffs of air. "I know, but you're really, really going to want to hear this. We picked up a distress call."

"A distress call?" Sara asked. She set her coffee down on the desk. Now Ned had her attention. "Was it coded?"

"Yes," said Ned, finally composing himself. "But the code wasn't in any of the registries."

"All right," she said. "Let me hear it."

"Channel 24," Ned said.

Sara punched up the channel and listened to the message. As she did, her face went white. She looked back at Ned.

"You said their code wasn't registered anywhere? You sure about that?"

"Yeah, that's right," said Ned. "And I'm sure. I ran it twice."

"What about the asteroid?" Sara asked. "Are you on that?"

"Yeah," Ned said. "I've reached out to Kelly at the Minor Planet Center. They're tracking this thing too."

The fact that the Minor Planet Center was now involved was of definite interest to Sara. Located in Cambridge, Massachusetts, the organization was charged with collecting data on comets, asteroids, and any other object in space deemed to be a "minor planet." They tended to receive more than fifty thousand sighting reports a day. If they were tracking this one, Sara knew it had to be significant.

"All right then, we've done everything we can do for now. Let's answer this woman before someone else does," Sara said. "And let's start waking up the right people."

"Sure, sure," said Ned. "Anyone in particular?"

Sara put on her headphones, preparing to answer the distress call. She looked up at Ned.

"Anyone who'll listen."

◆ ◆ ◆

Caitlin kept sending out the call, waiting for a response.

"Mayday, Mayday, this is Caitlin Taggart of the *Tamarisk*. There has been an incident. Myself and my crew are stranded on asteroid 1222

Thresher. I repeat, there has been an incident on board our ship and we are stranded on asteroid 1222 Thresher . . . which is now on course for Earth. I say again . . ."

Finally, the comm crackled and hissed and a woman's voice filled Caitlin's headset.

"This is Sara Kent, from NASA's Planetary Defense Coordination Office, responding to the distress call. Is this Caitlin Taggart?"

"Yes, this is Caitlin Taggart," she said. "I was the captain of the mining vessel *Tamarisk*, now lost. As I said, we've touched down on asteroid 1222 Thresher and are on a collision course with Earth. Repeat we are on a collision course with Earth."

Silence followed as the message traveled across the void from the asteroid to Earth. The communication delay between Earth and the Moon was 1.3 seconds. On the asteroid, given that they were a little closer, the delay was slightly less, but to Caitlin, it felt like an eternity.

"You don't need to keep repeating that," Sara Kent said at last. "Hearing it the first time was bad enough. OK, Caitlin, can I call you Caitlin?"

"If you've got a way out of this, you can call me whatever you please."

"I'm working on it," Sara said. "But I can tell you this: Whoever you were trying to call, I can promise you that the right people picked up. This is what we've been training for."

Sara was obviously trying to say the words with confidence, but Caitlin could tell when someone was bluffing. Being in the military and a mother, one tended to learn the tells. But if she wanted to bluff for the time being, Caitlin was more than happy to let her. Right now, given her current circumstances, even the pretense of confidence was welcome.

"So what do you need us to do up here?" Caitlin asked.

"Well," said Sara, "what can you tell us about your crew? Are they all OK?"

Caitlin looked at Vee and her eyes immediately shot downward, focusing on the control panel with laser-like intensity.

"We lost one in the fire on the *Tamarisk* before we abandoned ship," Caitlin said. "We're down to four now, but, under the circumstances, we're all holding up as well as can be expected."

"Good," Sara replied. "That's good to hear. Can I ask how in the hell you ended up in this mess?"

"It's kind of a long story," Caitlin told her, "but let me ask you, do you have kids?"

The silence that followed the question somehow seemed longer, even with the delay in communications. Caitlin couldn't say for sure, but something told her that she might have struck a nerve.

"No," Sara said after a moment. "No I don't."

"But you must have someone you care about," Caitlin pressed on. "Someone who cares about you."

"Sure," she said after another pause that felt glacial. "I have."

"And you would do anything for them, right? Anything to protect them, I mean?"

"I suppose I would," Sara said. "I suppose anyone would."

"Then there's your answer."

"Fair enough for now," Sara said. "The rest you can tell me over a beer when we get you home."

"You get us out of this," said Caitlin, "and that beer is on me."

"All right," said Sara. "Now you've done it. Now I have no choice but to help you. We're all going to put our heads together down here and try and figure out what our options are. In the meantime, how are you holding up?"

"Me?" Caitlin asked. "Oh, I'm straddling the line between throwing up and passing out cold, but otherwise, I'm doing just dandy, thanks."

"Just hang tight, Caitlin, we've got you," said Sara. "I'll call back when I've got something more to share, OK?"

"You got it." Caitlin nodded. "I'll be right here."

Sara broke the connection, and Caitlin turned to see the worried faces of her crew.

"What's the story?" asked Diaz.

"The story is that there's a real nice lady down there who works for the government and she wants nothing more than to help us," Caitlin said. "Problem is, right now, I don't think she can."

"So what does that mean?" asked Vee.

"It means that this asteroid is going to hit Earth," she said. She thought of Emily and fought hard to keep her voice level. "And right now, I don't know if anyone can stop it."

Chapter Twelve

The phone on Alex's nightstand buzzed insistently, shaking him out of a deep sleep. For a moment, he thought he was back home in Pasadena, but when he sat up and looked out the window, he saw the Washington Monument glittering in the distance instead of his beloved San Gabriel Mountains. He looked down at his phone and saw that it was Sara calling. Before he could answer, the buzzing stopped.

"Pocket dial," he muttered to himself and flopped back against the pillows. He still had a few hours before their meeting at the PDCO. He closed his eyes and tried to will sleep to come back to him. As he was drifting off again, the phone went off a second time. Now fully awake, Alex sat up, tapped the display, and put the phone to his ear.

"Hello?" he said.

"Alex?" a breathless voice asked from the other end. "Are you awake?"

"Sara?" he asked. "Is that you?"

"Yeah it's me," she said. "Are you up?"

"I am now," he said somewhat irritably. "I was trying to get back to—"

"There's no time for sleep. Hurry up and get down to the PDCO," she said.

"Why?" he asked, sitting up and turning on the bedside lamp. "What's going on?"

"Are you familiar with an asteroid designated 1222 Thresher?"

"Yeah," he said, the fog in his brain beginning to lift. "I think so. It's going to pass between the Moon and Earth at some point, but it's not a threat. In fact, it should miss us by . . ."

Before he could finish, his phone buzzed in his ear, signaling a text. Then it buzzed again and again until he had no choice but to pull it away from his ear and see who was trying to reach him so desperately. He read the texts, all from other NASA and FEMA colleagues, and his stomach did a perfect somersault inside his guts. He put the phone on speaker.

"Sara?" he said. His voice sounded small and timid.

"Yeah, Alex?"

"I'll be right there."

◆ ◆ ◆

Fifteen minutes later, a driver pulled up outside NASA headquarters. Alex quickly gathered up his briefcase and papers and pressed his thumb to the pay plate before getting out of the cab and racing inside. Sara met him at the entrance, waving him in vigorously.

"Hurry up!" she said. "This isn't time for a stroll!"

Nice to know that some things haven't changed, he thought. But he nevertheless obliged, quickening his steps as he made his way toward the building.

"Is this for real?" he asked.

"All of the discovery surveys verify," Sara said. "This is as real as it gets."

There were four teams, all based on Earth and known as discovery surveys whose job it was to watch the sky for asteroids. Catalina Sky Survey and Spacewatch were in Arizona, Pan-STARRS was in Hawaii, and LINEAR watched the heavens from New Mexico. There used to be five discovery surveys, but funding for NEOWISE, the space-based robotic telescope, dried up sometime in the middle of the current century.

"How did no one see it until it was right on top of us?" Alex asked.

"Because it wasn't right on top of us until a day ago," Sara said. "It was going to pass between Earth and the Moon and miss us by several hundred thousand miles. No one was even tracking it."

"Jesus Christ," Alex said. "What shifted its orbit?"

"Turns out someone was trying to mine it," Sara said. "It's a platinum asteroid, apparently. Worth trillions to anyone savvy enough to land mining rights."

Alex whistled at the number, then gave Sara a look.

"I thought asteroid mining was kind of . . . frowned upon."

"Yeah, well, booze was frowned upon in the 1920s," Sara said. "Didn't stop people from trying to make a profit off of the stuff."

"You had to go all the way back to Prohibition to make that point?" said Alex. "I can think of a lot of other dodgy mining operations just since the Moon was coloniz—"

Sara's stare silenced him, and he held up his hands.

"Fine, fine," Alex said. "Booze it is. OK, let's get moving on this. We'll need to start collating the data we've got on this thing and figure out our options. And we should set up a meeting at the White House as quickly as possible. They're going to need to know about this."

"Already done," Sara said.

"So efficient," said Alex. "Let me ask you. How do you think the situation looks?"

"I'll let you decide once I show you all the data," Sara said. "But if I were you, I'd consider relocating."

"To where, exactly?"

"Start by leaving the planet and work your way out from there."

Chapter Thirteen

"This is going to work."

Listening to Diaz, hearing the excitement in his voice and seeing it on his face, Caitlin found herself wishing that she had the same confidence in her plan. Actually, she wished she had any confidence at all at this point. All she had at the moment was a funnel cloud of doubt that kept any rational thought from taking root. She tried to shake herself out of it, reminding herself who she was. During the campaign, she'd always known how to assess a crisis. How to think on her feet. How to react in a millisecond when the plan went from perfect to completely screwed. Right now, though? She was having a hard time getting a handle on the moment. That was part of why she was putting so much into this idea, a symbol of how she tended to deal with extreme situations. Find a way out, even if insane.

"Take us through this again," Vee told Caitlin. "You want to do what, exactly?"

"It's pretty simple," she said. "We strip the *Alley Oop*. We take all the insulation from the descent stage, which, as you know, is made up of aluminum-Mylar foil blankets. Once we've got all the Mylar we can take from the ship, we use it to fashion a solar sail. Then, when we've got it together, we take that little rover out of the hold. Drive the sail out to somewhere on the asteroid where it will be facing the Sun. If all goes well, the sail will slowly start to absorb the Sun's radiation, and the resulting radiation pressure should push us out of the path of Earth.

"Sounds promising," Vee admitted. "What made you think of it?"

"I read about solar sailers on Lake Armstrong," she said. "I was going to take Emily to see them when she came here."

"Hey, you still will, Cutter," said Diaz, smiling broadly. "We're gonna get off this rock! Me? I'm all about this plan. Shaw, what do you think?"

Shaw stared out the viewport, an almost placid expression on his hawkish face. If Caitlin didn't know better, she would have said that he looked bored. "I doubt it will work," he said. "But if it gives us a way to kill some time before we obliterate half the people on Earth? I'm game."

"Your optimism is infectious," said Caitlin.

"Why don't you think it will work, Mr. Wizard?" Diaz asked.

"A perfect sail has to have one hundred percent specular reflection," said Shaw. "That means it's got to be like a mirror. Even ninety percent would work, accounting for wrinkles, curvature, and so on. But assembling it in this environment under these conditions, we're going to be lucky to even get seventy-five percent specular reflection. Then there's the size. A typical sail is about a hundred and twenty yards wide. There's no way can we scrape together that much Mylar from the lander. And lastly, we have to be spot-on as to where we place it. If we're not, we could end up pushing the asteroid in the wrong direction. Maybe even closer to Earth. The margin for screwing this up is just too wide the way I see it."

A potent silence settled in as they all took in Shaw's words. Then Diaz spoke up.

"You know a lot about solar sails, man."

"I was a substitute science teacher back on Earth," he said. "Probably should have stayed one too."

"Well, what do you say you stop sitting here and bitching about it and put that big brain to good use?" said Diaz.

Shaw chuckled and stood up. "What the hell?" he said. "We're all gonna die anyway."

"Great," Caitlin said grimly. "You two get started on the sail. Vee, let's you and I get on the comm. Let them know what we've got planned up here."

"You think they'll go for this plan?"

Caitlin shook her head as she contemplated the truth of their situation.

"Whether they go for it or not, it's all we've got for now."

Chapter Fourteen

Entering his thirtieth hour without sleep, Alex Sutter walked to the Situation Room at the White House like a ghost. Despite the lack of rest, he was still fully prepared to address the president's advisors on the asteroid situation. The president himself, on his way to his retreat in Catalina, was "unreachable." Alex failed to see how that was possible, but he was relieved to hear that, at least for the time being, the commander in chief would not be a part of this discussion. He had spoken with the president once before and found it akin to holding out your hand and shouting "Heel!" at a perpetually barking and foaming dog.

Sara was walking alongside him, and although she had been awake as long as he had—longer in fact—she somehow still managed to look put together and presentable. He had always admired that quality in her, even going back to their days at Caltech. She could stay out as late as everyone else, then walk into an exam the next morning looking like she'd gotten eight hours of unbroken rest, and walk out having aced the damn thing.

Sara looked over at him, and it was in that instant he realized that he had probably been looking at her just long enough to make things awkward.

"What?" she asked, sounding annoyed.

"No, nothing," he said, then tried to think of something to say. "It's just funny, you and I, you know, we were together back at Caltech and then we weren't and now, here we are and we're both . . ."

Sara's expression showed complete disbelief.

"Really?" she said. "Now?"

Before Alex could further contemplate his faux pas, they entered the Situation Room. The president's most trusted team of advisors was gathered around the table. Alex nervously took his place there, shuffling his notes as he did so. Vice President Jason Keating stood up and addressed the room.

"Good morning, everyone," he said. "And thank you for coming here on such short notice. Overnight, the White House was made aware of a situation that has suddenly developed in space, one that may well have grave consequences for our planet. For more information, I turn you over to Dr. Sara Kent of the Planetary Defense Coordination Office and Dr. Alex Sutter of the Federal Emergency Management Agency. Doctors, if you please."

Sara and Alex stood up and walked over to the screen at the far end of the table. Alex punched a few keys on his holopad and an image of the asteroid popped up behind them.

"This is asteroid 1222 Thresher," he said. "It's approximately seven hundred meters in size. It's comprised of mostly rock, clay, and silicate with a large platinum core. We believe it originated somewhere in the belt between Mars and Jupiter and was moved out of its orbit, either by Jupiter's gravity or by another asteroid."

"I thought Jupiter's gravity was supposed to prevent objects like this from getting through," said Dave Seward, Deputy Director of the Office of Science and Technology Policy.

"You're talking about the theory that Jupiter acts as sort of a cosmic vacuum cleaner, I assume?" said Alex, to which Seward nodded. "It's a valid idea, the notion that Jupiter's extreme gravity captures any objects and sucks them in before they can become a real threat. However, that gravitational force can work against us as much as for us. The planet's gravity can toss objects out of our solar system, but it can also toss them back in. A great example is Barringer Crater in Arizona. It's more commonly called Meteor Crater and was formed by a nickel-iron meteorite about fifty meters across that hit Earth sometime during the Pleistocene epoch. The energy released upon impact was equivalent to 2.5 megatons of TNT. The meteorite was quite possibly sent here by Jupiter's gravity. With that in mind, we may be looking at a similar situation with 1222 Thresher. Whatever the circumstances, the fact remains that somehow this asteroid was set on a new course, bringing it close to Earth."

"Close enough to be an issue?" asked White House Science Advisor Bob Lee.

"No, not initially," said Alex. "It would have come very nearby, maybe a few hundred thousand miles, but nothing that we would have had to concern ourselves with. It was on a trajectory to pass by the trailing edge of Earth in its orbit when an . . . incident occurred."

Here, Sara stepped forward and the screen behind her changed to an image of the *Tamarisk.*

"Just twenty-four hours ago, my team and I at the PDCO received a distress call from the surviving crew of this ship," she said. "A lunar tug designated *Tamarisk*. The crew, it seems, were in the middle of an unauthorized mining operation on the asteroid when a fire broke out. Apparently one crew member was lost, and the survivors were able to escape in the lifeboat and make it to the surface of the asteroid."

"Where was the *Tamarisk*'s port of call?" asked Keating.

"She originated from the Ponca City docks, Mr. Vice President," said Sara, somewhat hesitantly. Her eyes glanced over to Alex, and he knew what she was thinking. Unlike the commander in chief, the vice president was smart, calculated, and tended to think several moves ahead when faced with a crisis. Additionally, along with several other members of his party, he was not in favor of many of the policies the president endorsed. But, that said, he was also number two in the chain of command, which meant that he was duty bound to uphold them. Now that he knew the *Tamarisk*'s crew was from the Moon, their chances of getting home might be even more seriously jeopardized.

"So the Moon, then," Keating confirmed.

"That's right," Sara said. "They came from the Moon."

"Excuse me," said Secretary of State Amy Katz, "but, if I'm not mistaken, isn't asteroid mining illegal without ICC authorization?"

"Yes," Sara said. "That is true. And, from what we can tell, the crew of the *Tamarisk* was operating without that authorization."

"Then, on whose authority were they out there?" Katz asked.

"We're still looking into that."

"So we've got a crew of miners conducting an illegal mining and salvage operation in violation of a travel embargo," Secretary of Defense Alan Kittredge said. "And now they've gotten themselves stranded. Have ICC send out a skiff and take them back to the Moon where they can face justice. I'm sorry, Mr. Vice President, but I'm not seeing how this is our problem."

"With all due respect, Mr. Secretary," said Alex, "it's about to become everyone's problem. You see, the incident on board the *Tamarisk* has resulted in the asteroid's trajectory being changed."

"Changed?" asked Secretary Kittredge. "You mean it's now aimed at Earth?"

"Essentially," Sara said. "The catastrophe on board the ship somehow caused the asteroid to change course. We're still looking into what exactly happened. But, as Dr. Sutter noted, it was due to pass by Earth and is now poised for impact instead."

"Try not to think of it as being aimed, per se," said Alex to the room. "It's more just been moved into our path. We are heading toward it as much as it is headed toward us. Eventually, the asteroid and Earth will occupy the same space in orbit around the Sun. Imagine you're crossing the street. When you do, you're occupying the same space that cars, trucks, motorcycles, and what have you also occupy. You're just not doing it at the same time. Now, imagine you step off the curb and something happens a few miles back. An overly long traffic light, someone running late for an appointment . . . a thousand little things to change the pattern of traffic, and suddenly a car happens to also be right where you put your feet at that same instant. And when that happens . . ."

"Are we talking about the end of the world here?" asked Katz.

"Not exactly," said Sara. "But the damage will be extensive, and the death toll will be catastrophic."

"How catastrophic are we talking?" Katz asked. "Let's not sugar-coat it."

"If the asteroid impacts Earth, it will do so with the force of about two hundred thousand megatons. About four times the strength of the Tsar Bomba explosion in 1961. The most powerful man-made explosion in history. If it strikes water, any coastal cities in its path will be obliterated by tsunamis more than a quarter mile high. If it strikes land, we're talking earthquakes, fires, people being immolated where they stand . . ."

"And that's just the initial impact," Alex said. "Afterward, we'd be looking at acid rain for months, a global drop in temperature by about forty-six degrees Fahrenheit, no summer, worldwide devastation of the ozone layer, allowing harmful UV rays to penetrate the atmosphere . . ."

He looked around the room and saw the stricken faces of everyone present staring back. He realized that he may have gone a bit too far. Alex adjusted his glasses and cleared his throat.

"Terrible," he said, his voice reduced in volume. "Let's just leave it at really, really terrible."

"Do we know where it will hit?" Keating asked.

"It's hard to say for sure at this stage," said Alex. "But, based on what we know of the asteroid's current trajectory, it looks like it might hit somewhere off the Pacific coastline."

"My God," said Katz. "We have to start evacuating that region."

"That needs to be done carefully and precisely," warned Kittredge. "If you have the president go on TV and announce that an asteroid is coming to wipe out California and everyone needs to clear out, you're going to have a mass panic on your hands."

"I agree," said Keating. "Let's try and solve the problem first before we alert the public."

"I think Secretary Kittredge is right," Alex said. "I can work with FEMA to coordinate an evacuation plan that makes sense given the short time frame we have to work with."

At the mention of the words "short time frame," the room fell silent. All eyes, including Sara's, fell on Alex, who was suddenly keenly aware of having said too much.

"How long do we have?" Keating asked.

Sara and Alex were quiet, exchanging looks. He knew he didn't want to be the one to break the news, and he suspected she felt the same. Finally, Sara took a deep breath.

"Twenty-seven days," she said.

A rumble of voices erupted as everyone reacted. Some were louder than others. Keating rapped the table, calling the room back to order.

"OK," Secretary of Defense Kittredge said, speaking up. "I assume we have a plan to knock this thing out of the sky? Nukes or something?"

"There's a chance we could use a nuclear weapon to divert the asteroid or to break it up before it enters our atmosphere," said Sutter. "And while that might lessen the impact, we'd still be looking at a devastating situation."

"But it's an option?"

"Yes," said Alex. "But there are other factors to consider."

"Enlighten us."

"We could nudge the asteroid off course and skip it out of our atmosphere," Alex went on. "Like a stone over a pond. But we could also simply pulverize it and then run the risk of turning one large falling object into several. Or we could knock it off course but send it somewhere else. In essence, the pieces could wind up missing North America but strike other countries that weren't originally in its path. Putting aside the devastation, the international implications of deliberately redirecting an asteroid into the heart of another country are, well, considerable."

"What countries could be affected?" asked Vice President Keating.

"Are you seriously considering this?" asked Sara.

"Right now, Dr. Kent, I am considering everything and anything," he said. "Believe me, it's not an attractive option, but I need to know so that when the president asks me, I have an answer for him. So, again, what countries could be affected?"

"Well," said Alex, "we've run some preliminary scans, and based on the Thresher's current trajectory, if we were able to redirect the asteroid and it didn't skip out of the atmosphere, the most likely point of impact would be somewhere in Siberia."

"That's a sparsely populated region," said Kittredge, almost to himself.

"There's also the question of the crew," said Sara, as though by changing the subject she could steer the room away from this line of thinking.

"I'm sorry?" asked Kittredge.

"The surviving members of the *Tamarisk* crew," said Sara. "They're still up there."

"How many people are we talking about?"

"Four," said Sara.

"Four?" Kittredge asked in disbelief. "We are looking at potential loss of life in the millions, and you're going to quibble with me about four people? Four people who assumed the risk of undertaking an illegal mining operation, and might I add, are in violation of an embargo put in place by our president!"

"One of them is Caitlin Taggart," said Sara. "She was a hero in the Last Campaign. Fought at the battle of Samarra."

"I don't care if it's Jim Morrison and Janis Joplin and they're back to spread flower power to the entire free world. Four people against millions, Dr. Kent. Do the math."

"All right, Alan," said Vice President Keating. "You've made your position clear. Dr. Sutter, do you have other ideas outside of using nukes?"

"Trust me, Mr. Vice President. We are working the problem."

"Well, I'm afraid you and your team have got to work it harder," he said. "You're running out of time."

Once the meeting adjourned, Sara and Alex ducked out of the Situation Room and began walking down the halls of the White House to Alex's car. Alex took note of the portraits of former presidents on the walls, great men and women who'd found themselves at one time or another faced with a decision that would affect the lives of millions of Americans, not to mention people around the world. But had any of them faced anything like this? The potential annihilation of countless human lives by a force from beyond the planet?

He stopped in front of the famous portrait of Kennedy, arms folded, looking down. He looked at Sara and pointed at the picture.

"Do you know this was based off of Ted Kennedy's posture at JFK's funeral?"

"What?" Sara said, almost as though she wasn't sure why she was being asked.

"Yeah," Alex said. "Jackie had the painting commissioned after the assassination, and the artist, Aaron Shikler, he didn't want to do the same old portrait that had been done before. He found this picture of Ted at the funeral and, just like that, came up with probably the most famous presidential portrait in the White House."

"OK," said Sara. "Thanks for the history lesson. Now comes the part where you tell me that you have a plan, any plan, that doesn't involve launching nuclear missiles into the upper atmosphere."

"Come on, Sara," Alex said, starting to walk again. "We've run simulations on everything from knocking the asteroid off course with a laser ablation to sending up a ship and attaching booster rockets to blowing the asteroid back with a blast of steam."

"Right, I know," Sara said. "We run the same simulations at the PDCO every week. And of those simulations, shall we talk about how many of them were successful?"

Alex looked at her, pushing his glasses up the bridge of his nose.

"None," he said flatly. "None to date."

"Exactly."

She began walking again. Alex hurried to catch up to her.

"But you know that we're close," said Alex. "Really close."

"You know what else is close?" Sara asked. "That goddamn asteroid. And if we don't come up with a workable solution, our president is going to blow it out of the sky and turn a big problem into a million smaller problems."

"Forgive me for saying so," said Alex, "but I don't think the nukes are what's got you so upset."

"Then please share with me what you think has got me so upset in your infinite wisdom."

"You're worried about the crew," he said. "Specifically, this Taggart woman."

"She's got a daughter, Alex," said Sara.

"I know. But she violated a travel embargo," he countered. "She was mining an asteroid illegally. She's broken countless ICC *and* federal regulations. Even if we brought that rock to a soft landing on the Mall, they'd clap her in irons the second she stepped off of it."

"At least she'd be alive," said Sara. "I think her daughter would prefer that."

"Sara, I understand your compassion," Alex said. "I even admire it. But what the secretary of defense said is true, ass though he may be. We're talking about four people weighed against millions. Right now, those millions are our priority."

They left the White House and walked over the Ellipse, where they had parked earlier in the afternoon. Sara started to get back into the car. Alex touched her arm gently.

"Look," he said, "if I can figure out a way to save them *and* the crew, I'll do it."

Sara smiled at him. "That's good enough for me."

She started to get into the car and then turned and looked back at Alex.

"It was a cool story," she said.

"What?"

"The painting," Sara said. "It was an interesting story."

"Oh, yeah, well, I'm full of interesting stories," he said.

He closed the door behind her and walked around to the driver's side. As he did, he sighed.

"Now all I need is an idea."

Chapter Fifteen

PDCO headquarters had become asteroid central. Nearly all other work had stopped and every available mind was focused on staving off the impending devastation from space. One of the conference rooms, or, as the scientists were calling it, CIC for command information center, had been turned into the nerve center of the operation and was abuzz with activity. People brushed past each other, moving in and out of the door carrying printouts, photographs, and old binders filled with yellowing reports. Anything that could shed any light on asteroids. How they moved, what their properties were, and what, if anything, could be done to stop them.

The room itself looked like a cross between a science lab and a frat house, walls dotted with SMART Boards covered in equations, algorithms, and thumbnail sketches of asteroids entering Earth's atmosphere. The table was littered with a mosaic of coffee cups, soda cans, takeout containers, and textbooks. Somewhere in the background, music played on a constant loop in an effort to keep the team awake and engaged. It was coming up on two days since the discovery that the Thresher had moved into Earth's path, and people were starting to get punchy.

Into this chaotic scene came Alex and Sara, fresh from their meeting at the White House. Sara clapped her hands, bringing everyone to attention.

"All right, everyone," she said. "Let's all get on the same page!"

"How'd it go at 1600?" asked Ned.

"Not great," she said. "Everyone here has been given clearance to receive any information related to this crisis, so I'll fill you in. Let me remind you of your professionalism and the expectation that you will keep these briefings completely confidential. First, people, let me introduce, for those who haven't already met him, Alex Sutter from FEMA. He's been working with us for some time now on asteroid defense, and he's agreed to stay here until the crisis has passed."

Alex waved somewhat awkwardly to the room.

"Excellent," said Sara. "Now that we all know each other, let's get caught up. Any new info here?"

"We've been looking into what happened up there to set the asteroid on a course with Earth," said Ned. "The fire on the *Tamarisk* wouldn't be enough to redirect an entire asteroid. So we've tried to piece it all together."

"What have you come up with?"

"Well," said Patricia Delgado, a theoretical physicist on loan from MIT, "from what we can tell, when the *Tamarisk* exploded, the shock wave broke off a piece of the asteroid, which went off in one direction, while the remaining section was pushed closer to the Moon."

"The Moon's gravity then captured the asteroid and swung it onto its present course," said Ned.

"Right in our path," said Sara. "Good work, guys. As you know, Alex and I were at the White House today to bring everyone up to speed on what's happening."

"What do they want to do?" asked Daniel Kim, a young scientist who had joined the PDCO from the Jet Propulsion Lab.

"The president wants to use nukes," said Sara.

"Can he even do that?" asked Ned. "I thought there was a law or something that prevented using nuclear weapons in space."

"There is," said Alex. "The Outer Space Treaty. But most of the nations involved have agreed that, under certain circumstances, the ban could be lifted. The potential eradication of millions, if not billions, of human lives from a space-born PHO apparently applies."

"Are they even sure it would work?" another young astrophysicist asked from the back of the room.

"They seem to believe that, with a large enough warhead, a nuclear blast will break the asteroid up into smaller, more manageable fragments," said Alex. "I for one happen to think that they're dead wrong. But that doesn't mean a nuclear option isn't a viable one."

"Explain," said Sara.

"If the bomb were detonated near the asteroid, the surface would be irradiated by the X-rays and neutrons released by the detonation," Alex explained. "Those X-rays and neutrons would, in turn, create so much heat on the surface that portions of the Thresher would be vaporized. As the vaporized material is blown from the asteroid, it could create a change in momentum. Theoretically."

"That makes sense," said Patricia. "But do we even have a nuke big enough to cause that kind of detonation?"

"We've got it," Alex said. "Shortly after he took office, the president ordered the construction of the largest nuclear missile ever built. Sixty-eight megatons. The warhead sits on an old SLS booster left over from the shuttle program. The missile's called the Thunderclap. He's got it stored in a silo somewhere outside Topeka."

"Moving on," said Sara. "We know the missile is an option, but we also know the risks. It would have to detonate near the asteroid at just the right angle to be effective. Any miscalculation and it's raining rocks all over the world."

"That's exactly right," Alex said. "The Thunderclap nuke is a last resort. Which means we've got to come up with a whole lot of other resorts before we get there."

"So what have we got to work with here?" asked Sara. "What have you bright young minds been cooking up?"

"Our options are slim," Ned began. "We've run through everything again and again. We thought maybe we could use a ship as a gravity tractor, employing its gravitational field to alter the asteroid's path."

"I don't think that'll work," said Sara. "Not in the time we have. A gravity tractor only works after years of station-keeping with an asteroid. A spaceship has minimal gravity. Anything we could launch in the time frame we've got to work with would be too small to make any difference."

"That's what we found," Ned agreed. "We were also thinking of an enhanced gravity tractor."

"What about a kinetic impactor?" asked Patricia. "We launch something right at the asteroid. A craft of some kind. It hits the Thresher with enough force and, boom, knocks the asteroid out of the way. It's been done before."

"Yeah," Alex agreed. "With a comet. It's an intriguing idea, but where are we going to find a ship that can get the job done in time? This is a big bastard we're talking about and for something to hit it hard enough to knock it back, that something would have to comprise a decent portion of the asteroid's mass. But let's keep that one in our back pocket. Let's check with NASA. Maybe they've got something that can get the job done."

"On it," said Patricia, gathering up her notes and leaving the room.

"Is a laser ablation out of the question?" asked Ned.

"It wouldn't be if we had a strong enough laser," said Sara.

"We have no directed-energy weapons available?" Ned persisted. "Nothing from the military?"

"Most of the more powerful DEWs were decommissioned and dismantled after the Second Cold War and the Last Campaign," she said. "The government felt the resources and materials would be better directed elsewhere. There are some laser weapons in use on naval vessels, but they're used to shoot down missiles. They're not powerful enough to handle something of this size."

Clicking his pen over and over again, Daniel stared at the ceiling. His face wore the expression of a man to whom an idea was slowly but surely coming.

"What about the Yarkovsky effect?" he said, still studying the ceiling tiles.

"Go on," said Alex.

"The idea that sunlight can heat the asteroid and change its trajectory," said Daniel. "So what if we painted the asteroid's surface white? The side facing the Sun, right? That way you alter the amount of radiation it absorbs. When it rotates, the irradiated side would start emitting infrared photons, generating a small amount of thrust, and whoosh, we're saved."

Sara and Alex were silent a moment. "And how do you propose we paint the asteroid?" she asked.

"I don't know," he said. "I haven't thought that far ahead yet."

"OK," said Alex. "Let us know when you get there. But I like the way you think. Think weird, people. It's what we need."

"Also," Sara said, "we're all going to be burning the midnight oil on this one, so I want everyone to start working in shifts. Sleep is critical. When it comes to asteroid deflection, every measurement counts, and we can't risk disaster because someone was pulling an all-nighter. All good?"

Everyone nodded in agreement and then went back to scanning their notes, holopads, tablets, and phones. Sara looked over at Alex.

"I don't want to side with the president on this or just about anything else," she said, "but our choices are frighteningly scarce."

"I don't want to side with him either," he said, "but show me a better option."

Just then, the door burst open and a nervous-looking technician ran in.

"Dr. Kent?" he said. "Comm channel's buzzing. It's Caitlin Taggart. She says they have a plan."

Chapter Sixteen

While Diaz and Shaw were outside assessing what they would need for the solar sail, Vee and Caitlin began a thorough checkup of all the *Alley Oop*'s flight systems to see how easily they'd be able to get her flying. Of course, even if they were able to get off the surface, they still had to consider the cracked heat shield. They did have materials on board to repair the damage, but how effective those materials would be was anyone's guess.

"How are you holding up?" Caitlin asked Vee as she ran through the preflight checklist.

"Fine as wine," she answered. Then she looked up at Caitlin. "I didn't mean what I said earlier, you know. When I said that I wished it had been you instead of him? I didn't mean that."

"Yes you did," Caitlin said. "And you'd be nuts if you didn't. He was your husband, Vee. And, for whatever it's worth, I wish that I could trade places with him for you, believe me."

Vee was quiet a minute, then began tinkering with the control panel again. "But if that's your way of saying you forgive me," Caitlin said, "then I can live with that."

"Forgive has nothing to do with it," Vee replied, shaking her head. She wiped her eyes quickly. "What happened happened. And even if things had gone differently and Tony was still here, so what? It'd be five of us stuck on this asteroid waiting to die instead of four."

"Don't think like that," said Caitlin. "We're gonna get off this thing."

"What makes you so sure?"

"Because you're a stone-cold badass and I'm the goddamn Mama Bear," she said. "What chance does some four-billion-year-old rock have against the two of us?"

Vee shook her head and went back to work.

"You're crazy," she muttered. "That's all there is to it."

"Sometimes I wish that I was," said Caitlin. "It would make every day so much easier. Now, what about this ignition problem?"

"The good news is that the ignition isn't the problem," said Vee. "The bad news is that it's something else."

"Something such as . . . ?"

"I'm not sure yet, but I've been running diagnostics, and I think this bucket is a hell of a lot older than we thought. It's still got an EDS setup."

Caitlin whistled. That was surprising. In the early days of spaceflight, the vehicles that were used to propel the astronauts to the stars carried explosive device systems designed to perform a wide range of tasks, from separating stages to deploying parachutes. The Saturn rockets that ferried men to the Moon carried more than two hundred of them, while the Curiosity rover that landed on Mars in 2012 employed seventy-six different pyrotechnic devices, each one designed to fire at a specific moment during the landing. However, over the last fifty years or so, pyrotechnics had been phased out on most spacecraft in favor of pneumatic separation systems that allowed for quicker reusability.

"Jesus," said Caitlin. "Where the hell did Ross find this thing?"

"Black market, probably," said Vee. "I'm guessing this thing is Russian, or maybe Chinese. It might have been an old lunar lander that's been retrofitted."

Caitlin called up the *Alley Oop*'s schematics on the screen and began running tests of her own. She had always had an interest in gear from the time she was a kid, fixing cars in the driveway with her dad. Even as an adult, tinkering with something took her mind off worry and distress. She looked intently at the display, swiping through screens of system checks until she zeroed in on a potential problem.

"I've got something," she said. "Looks like the computer's reporting a failure in the guillotine system."

"And that's bad?"

Caitlin nodded. The explosive guillotine was a particularly key piece of tech, which, when fired, would sever the umbilical cables connecting the *Alley Oop*'s ascent and descent stages. If the charges didn't ignite and propel the blade down with enough force to cut the umbilical, they'd be stuck on the asteroid for a long time.

Before Caitlin and Vee could consider their circumstances further, the comm lit up with an incoming message. Sara was back on the mic.

"Looks like your girl's finally picked up," said Vee.

Caitlin switched on the comm. "It's about time," she said. "Where were you? On a hot date?"

"Oh, nothing special," said Sara. "People here are telling me you've got a plan."

"That's right." Caitlin broke down what she had come up with. Sara took it all in.

"I like that you're thinking proactively up there," she said, "but I'm going to be blunt. I don't think it's going to work."

"I appreciate the direct approach," said Caitlin. "Care to tell me why?"

"The amount of Mylar you've got on that lander compared to the size of the asteroid just isn't enough to make a difference," Sara said. "It would be like putting a handkerchief on an elephant."

"We've got a science teacher here who kind of told us the same thing," said Caitlin. "But we've got to try something."

"I understand," said Sara, and then she told Caitlin to hold on. After a moment, another voice came on the line.

"Hi, Capt—Mrs. . . ."

"Caitlin's fine," she said. "Who's this?"

"Dr. Alex Sutter, Federal Emergency Management Agency. Dr. Ken—Sara's just told me about your plan, and I have to agree with her assessment. It's risk versus reward. And, from where I'm sitting, it doesn't balance out."

"That's fair, Dr. Sutter," said Caitlin. "But my father always thought it was bad form to shoot down someone else's idea without presenting a better one. So . . . I'm all ears."

Alex fell silent in response to Caitlin's challenge. Then he sighed in resignation.

"OK," he said. "The people on your crew who will actually be working on the sail itself are going to need to be very careful out there. There's no magnetic field on an asteroid, as you know. So they're at the mercy of the Sun. If there's suddenly a solar flare or a coronal mass ejection, the consequences could be very grave."

"Thanks for the heads-up, Dr. Sutter," said Caitlin. "We've been talking over the risks up here and have an idea of what we're up against. But I'll be sure to remind them again to watch their backs."

"Great, that's great," Alex said. "How far out do you think you'll need to go to place the sail where it will be effective?"

"Shaw thinks we'll have our best shot placing it somewhere on the asteroid's terminator," said Caitlin. "As it rotates, the sail will begin to catch the Sun's light and hopefully make a difference. Should take us about an hour to get out there and another hour back."

"Sounds like a plan," said Alex. "Um, I'm going to run some numbers on this and see what we can do for you back here. In the meantime, I'll, uh, hand you back to Sara now. You, you watch your back too."

"Will do," Caitlin said. A moment later Sara came back on the mic.

"You there?" she asked.

"Well, you may have been on a date," said Caitlin, "but it doesn't sound like it was very hot."

"Ha ha," said Sara drily. "The man you're insulting just might be responsible for saving your life, you know."

"OK, OK," said Caitlin. "Just trying to keep it light."

A silence passed between them as though they were each trying to think of what to say next.

"Look," the two women said at once before laughing.

"You first," Caitlin said.

"No, you go ahead."

"OK," said Caitlin. "If this doesn't work . . . even if it does, we both know that getting off of this thing is kind of a long shot. God knows I'm going to give it everything I've got, but I also have to accept that this might not go my way."

"You don't know that."

"Trust me, Sara," said Caitlin. "A few years in combat and you learn to read the field. But I knew the risks. I knew there was a chance this could happen. Well, maybe not this, but I knew I was flirting with disaster. But I also knew why I was taking that risk. And why it was worth it."

"Your daughter," Sara said.

"Exactly," Caitlin said. "Which is what I wanted to bring up. I want you to get her. I'll give you all the information. I want you to get her and bring her to DC."

"Caitlin," Sara said, "I don't know if I can keep her from going into the system. Under the circumstances—"

"I know," said Caitlin. "I know. But maybe, if she's there . . . if she's with you, then I can at least talk to her. Tell her what happened. And why I did it."

"Caitlin . . ."

"Please," she said, and she heard her own voice break. *Dammit,* she chided herself. She had been trying to keep it together.

"All right," Sara promised. "You've got my word that I'll do what I can."

Caitlin took a second to compose herself. "Thank you," she said. "Really. And up here, I can only promise that we'll do the same."

◆ ◆ ◆

The four surviving crew members headed out to the surface of the Thresher and started meticulously taking off the *Alley Oop*'s multilayer insulation blankets piece by piece, salvaging as much Mylar as they possibly could to use with the solar sail. Working in near-zero gravity was a bear. The bulk of the suits and their onboard RCS helped to keep the team relatively grounded, but the process was a constant battle. No matter how secure they actually were, they felt as though one strong sneeze would send them tumbling into deep space.

"You do realize," said Shaw as he worked, "that if we strip this thing of all its MLI, and then we do end up having to take off, there's nothing to keep the instrumentation cool? The Sun could fry the ship's innards before we can even think about doing something about it."

"Have a look at where we are and what we're up against," Caitlin told him. "You think I'm worried about what the Sun's going to do to our instruments if we happen to make it off this rock?"

"Just giving you a heads-up, Boss," he said.

"Noted," said Caitlin. "And don't get me wrong; I appreciate it. Now, here's my question: Once we get this sail fashioned, how are we going to actually use it?"

"Well," said Diaz, "I've given this some thought . . ."

"And what have you come up with?"

"In a perfect world," he said, "we'd be able to take the Noser and drive the sail out to the horizon to a point on the asteroid that gets the most sunlight. Then we'd bolt it down somehow, head back to the *Alley Oop*, and let Mr. Golden Sun do his work."

"You're saying we can't do that here?" Caitlin asked.

Diaz looked doubtful. "It's possible, but I've got concerns," he said. "The core of this thing is platinum, sure, but the surface is so granular, I can't be a hundred percent sure you'll be able to hold it down."

"We were able to grip it with the ARM on the *Tamarisk*," said Vee.

"The strength of that thing versus anything we might have back on the ship is a night-and-day difference. Down here on the surface, there's no guarantee that anything we use to anchor the sail will hold."

"So it's like trying to pitch a tent on the beach," Caitlin said.

"I wouldn't know," said Diaz. "I've never been to the beach."

"Right. Sorry." Caitlin sighed. "I forgot. So what are you proposing?"

"Once we get the sail fashioned," he said, "someone's going to have be the one to bolt it into the rock. Then they're going to have to stay out there to make sure that, once the thing is down, it stays down."

"Sounds like a dangerous job," Vee said. "Maybe even a suicide mission."

"Maybe," Caitlin replied. "But the consequences of not doing anything are going to be much worse."

Chapter Seventeen

With the Mylar gathered, the crew began assembling the sail. As the resident science expert, Shaw took the lead, checking and rechecking everyone's work as though he were back in the classroom.

The sail was a three-axis design that almost looked like a giant kite reinforced by carbon nanotubes they had harvested from the ship's instrument panel. Assembling the sail was laborious and difficult, but they worked diligently. As they did, Shaw watched and shook his head.

"I have to say, I'm impressed," he said. "I still have my doubts that it'll work, but seeing the thing put together has made me more optimistic."

"Someone please note the time," Diaz said. "Shaw said something positive!"

"That said," Shaw continued, "I'm still not convinced that, even if we get this thing to work, there's any guarantee the Sun will push the asteroid in the right direction."

"And there he is again . . . ," said Diaz, punching Shaw in the arm affectionately.

They went back to work and Diaz looked at the sail.

"You know, Boss," he said to Caitlin, "you were talking about people using these things to race on Lake Armstrong? I saw them once when I was a kid. Sun riders, they called them. Small little boats with these big reflective sails. They could move too. Faster than you'd think. They were all different colors. Red, blue, gold. They even had this crazy shiny green color. I'd never seen anything like it before. Later on I found out it was called 'drake's neck,' because the color looked like a male duck's head. What did I know? I'd never seen a duck before. But the boats, man. They looked like little pencils just shooting across the water. Everyone was betting on the races, of course, but I was too young. So my grandmother let me bet her. I chose the blue one and she chose the red one, and we bet on every race. At the end of the day, my guy had won more races. So, I'm thinking it's just a bet for fun, you know. And then, all of a sudden, my grandmother hands me something. It's hard and rough and it kind of feels cool in my hands, kind of like a rock that's been in the shade, you know. I'd never seen anything like it before."

"What was it?" asked Vee.

In answer to Vee's question, Diaz reached into one of the pockets in his suit and extracted something small and round. He held it up so that it was illuminated in the lights of the ship's cabin.

"An acorn," he said, grinning. "She must have brought it to the Moon when she left Earth. I have no idea how she got it through quarantine."

Caitlin looked at the small, ovoid object in Diaz's hand. Instinctively, almost unconsciously, she reached out her own hand.

"Can I . . . ?" she asked.

Without a word, Diaz turned his wrist and placed the acorn into Caitlin's palm. When the seed touched her skin, she felt something electric. It was the first natural object from Earth she'd touched since leaving its surface so long ago. She turned the small nut over in her hand, feeling the leathery shell under her fingertips and wondering about the suns that had warmed it, the snows that had covered it.

"Nice, right?" said Diaz. "I've kept it with me from that day since. It's always brought me luck, and I think it's going to today as well."

"Lake Armstrong, huh?" Caitlin said. "I've known you for a year, and somehow I didn't know you grew up in the city. Shame on me."

"How very un–Mama Bear of you," said Diaz. "Oh yeah, I was real high society back in the day."

"Must have been nice," said Vee.

"It was," Diaz said, then looked down at his work. "For a while."

"Something changed?" asked Caitlin.

"Something always does," said Diaz. "I was living with my grandmother in the city, and then when she died, I got shipped out here to live with my uncle Santiago."

"Doesn't sound like you enjoyed that much," said Vee.

"What gave me away?"

"I had an uncle Santiago in my life," said Vee. "Only I called him Dad."

"You're right," said Diaz. "He was a thief and a fool. He and his cronies had me and some of the other kids running all around the Hive, stealing whatever they could. Wasn't too long before he got caught, us along with him."

"What happened then?" Shaw asked, his face uncharacteristically inquisitive.

"Uncle Santiago was a lost cause," said Diaz. "They shipped him off to Roosa Penitentiary on the far side. But me and the other runners were given a choice. Go to juvie or work off our sentences. So I took a job in the motor pool at Guanghang. Not too many years later, here I am riding a rig with you fine people."

"And now here you are," said Shaw, "about to die on an asteroid in the middle of space with these fine people. Ain't life grand?"

"Maybe I am going to die," Diaz mused, "but I'd still rather be with you people."

"Why?" asked Vee.

"Because with all of you, I finally found what I was looking for," said Diaz. "Family."

"You ready for this, Diaz?" Caitlin asked. After endless and tedious hours building the sail, the two of them were finally on board the Noser, the ungainly lunar truck from the cargo hold of the *Alley Oop*, ponderously making their way across the surface of the asteroid. The ride was surprisingly smooth but incredibly slow. Due to the microgravity, they could only travel at about one mile per hour or risk losing contact with the surface. The good news was, should they flip over, the rover's onboard solar panels, placed all around the vehicle, would power tiny motors that would flip the vehicle back onto its wheels.

As the Noser carried the sail, Caitlin wondered if, instead of Diaz, she should be asking herself how ready she was.

"Oh yeah," said Diaz, looking around at the alien landscape. "This is my moment!"

Diaz had spent the last hour stubbornly insisting that he go out on the asteroid alone, but Caitlin had very gently made it clear to him that there was no way in hell that she was going to sit back in the *Alley Oop* while one of her crew risked themselves for the rest of them. In the campaign, she had always tried to lead by example and would never ask anyone under her command to do something she wasn't willing to do herself. Besides, she reasoned, this was her idea, and if it was going to blow up in anyone's face, it was going to be hers.

All three of the crew, and Diaz in particular, took care to remind Caitlin that this wasn't the military and that no one was under anyone's command, at which point she simply informed them exactly what they could do with their logic and said that she was going anyway.

It was a compulsion, she knew, the need to take control of a situation, even if it meant putting herself in harm's way. For Caitlin, control was a comfort. She had been in too many situations in life where she had been unable to have power over circumstance, and she was determined to no longer let that happen. And so, here they were now, trudging their way across the asteroid, en route to either salvation or doom.

"Well you should know that our friends on Earth are listening in," Caitlin told Diaz. "So if you screw up, we're not the only ones who'll know about it."

"Great," he responded. "Good to know. Because I wasn't really feeling any pressure about all this. So that helps a lot."

After a laborious drive, the rover came up over the asteroid's horizon, and the duo saw the sunlight flaring above the landscape of stone and ice. The rays filtered through the particulates and ice crystals floating around them, creating a kaleidoscope of colors and refracted light. For a moment, Caitlin could almost forget where she was and what she was up against and simply took in the sight.

"OK, you two," Shaw said, his voice popping in their ears. "You're just about there. A few more steps and you should be in a good spot. Remember, you're not going to have much time. There's no protection from the Sun, so at worst, you'll be incinerated where you stand. At best, your organs will get microwaved and sometime in the next five years you'll sprout tumors the size of star fruits."

"That's beautiful, Shaw," said Diaz. "Really, thank you for that. You're a poet."

"All right," Caitlin said, bringing the rover a few more feet. "Are we good?"

"Yes," Shaw said. "Looks like you've got a perfect spot there. Tie 'er down."

They unfolded the sail, and Diaz unlatched the pistol-grip rock drill from his belt.

"Good thing we thought to bring this baby with us," he said.

"Prepare and prevent, don't repair and repent," said Caitlin.

"What's that?"

"Just something my dad used to say. Kind of sounded silly at the time, but it obviously stuck with me. Anyway, let's fire up the drill, shall we? Maximum torque, sixty revolutions per minute."

Diaz nodded and began drilling into the rock and securing the solar sail to the asteroid. Caitlin held up her hands as he did.

"Watch it now," she said. "You're going to start kicking up rocks. And in this gravity, or lack thereof, they could potentially tear through our suits."

"I'm being careful, Boss," Diaz said, not taking his eyes off his work. "Besides, these suits are self-healing. You know that."

"I know," said Caitlin. "But those are for small nicks or tears. I don't know about you, but I'm not prepared to test their limits."

They worked carefully and methodically, Diaz cutting into the asteroid with a surgeon's precision and Caitlin securing the sail. It was hard work, and the asteroid fought them at every step, the RCS on their suits getting a workout. Eventually, they were able to get the sail completely unfurled and totally bolted down.

"All right!" Diaz said, pumping his fist as well as he could in the low gravity. "Team *Space Invader* represent!"

Caitlin gave him an exhausted smile as she took a moment to admire their work.

"Freddy Diaz," she told him, "we may have just saved the people of Earth."

Diaz beamed at her and all the cockiness that usually masked his true feelings was gone. In that instant, Caitlin could see something in him that she thought he rarely showed to anyone: the desire to make someone proud. To have someone recognize his accomplishments and validate him, even just for a second.

"Now let's call Earth and see if all this was worth it," said Caitlin, switching on the comm. "You reading us?"

"Loud and clear," Alex Sutter's voice came over the comm. Caitlin and Diaz could hear the excitement in his tone.

"How are we looking down there, Boss?" Diaz asked. *"Bien?"*

"Uh, well, I might not go so far as *bien*," Alex said, "but would you be OK with *así*? Solar sail pushes are relatively tiny, so it's going to take some time before we have any numbers to crow about. But you've definitely given it your best shot possible for now."

Caitlin looked over at Diaz and gave him an approving nod.

"You did good," she said to him. "Real good."

And just then, it all went horribly wrong. An alarm suddenly went off inside Caitlin's suit, and she frantically searched for the source, scanning her heads-up display for any sign of depressurization. Then, after a few seconds of searching, she realized that the alarm wasn't for her suit, but Diaz's. Because they were designed to work in such dangerous, high-pressure circumstances, the suits were linked so that every team member was aware if someone else had a problem. "Boss?" Diaz said suddenly. Caitlin could see the fear slowly spreading on his face. "Something's wrong."

Caitlin quickly looked at her HUD, which was flashing on the inside of her helmet's faceplate. She swiped through until she could locate the problem with Diaz's suit. After a second, she saw what was happening.

Oh no.

"Dammit!" she said. "Diaz, the RCS on your suit is failing."

"What?" Diaz asked. "What's failing? What's happening?"

Caitlin heard the terror in Diaz's voice and she felt for him, but there was no time to discuss the situation. With no RCS jets to hold him in place, Diaz would float off the asteroid before it even dawned on him what was happening. Quickly she toggled the jets on her own suit, stopping and starting them so that she could hop quickly over the surface and get to Diaz before something terrible happened. She could see him panicking as she leaped toward him.

"I can't hold on, Cutter!" Diaz was screaming. "I'm starting to drift!"

"Just hold on!" Caitlin called out. "I'm coming to get you!"

On Diaz's suit, the jets began to sputter and die like an old combustion engine that had given out. Horrified, Caitlin could see his feet beginning to hover above the asteroid. She was losing him.

"Cutter!" Diaz called out. *"Caitlin!"*

Screw it.

Caitlin disengaged the RCS jets and pushed off hard, floating in space with her arms outstretched. The terror in Diaz's eyes was plainly visible as Caitlin drew closer.

"Hang on!" she yelled.

They crashed together and Caitlin engaged her own RCS, forcing them both back down to the surface, locked in an embrace. They looked at each other a moment, both breathing heavily.

"Where do you think you're going?" Caitlin asked, finally allowing herself to smile.

"Can we get out of here before something worse happens?" asked Diaz.

Before Caitlin could even think of formulating an answer, they were both blasted apart by something that rocketed up from underneath them. Diaz was suddenly and forcibly ripped from Caitlin's arms. She reached for him, but his fingers just missed her own, and he was sent into space, tumbling end over end as he left the asteroid's surface. She could see the look on his face as he was suddenly carried away, a look she knew would be the stuff of her nightmares.

Instinct took over, and she fired her jets and was pushed back to the surface. Safe on the ground, all she could do was watch. As she lay there, she saw something enter her field of vision, turning gently over and over before floating upward and away. A shard of ice went through Caitlin's heart as she realized what it was. A tiny acorn.

"Diaz!" she screamed.

But he was already gone.

Chapter Eighteen

"Caitlin?"

Back in the PDCO office, Sara continued trying to hail the *Alley Oop*, hoping to hear something back from the team, something that would assuage her growing fear. She and Alex had been listening as the event unfolded, sitting helplessly as they listened to the panicked cries of Caitlin and Diaz. Sara had been trying to reach Caitlin ever since, but all she had been getting in reply was static. Then finally, Caitlin's voice, thin and reedy, came over the airwaves and confirmed the worst.

"He's gone."

The line went dead, and Sara was left to process the news on her own. She hurled down her headset and put her face in her hands. Then, as quickly as the rage and frustration came, it was gone, replaced by steely resolve.

It can't end like this.

She looked over at Alex, who was busy scanning the numbers on the asteroid's trajectory, trying to discern whether Diaz's efforts had made any difference. He looked back at her, and his face wore an expression that matched her own. He was upset and saddened as well, but he also knew that there was much more that needed to be done, that the story couldn't end here for any of them.

"What the hell happened up there?" Sara asked.

"I don't know," Alex said.

"Gas pocket," said Ned, coming into the room and walking over to them. "Water ice on the surface of the asteroid sublimated as it drew in the Sun's heat. It created a gas jet. Without anything to hold them down, there was nothing to keep them on the ground. It all comes down to basic physics."

"Jesus Christ," Patricia said, tossing a pencil onto the table and leaning back, her hand over her eyes. "What was water ice doing on the surface of an asteroid? Aren't they usually found on comets?"

"We've been seeing it more and more," said Sara. "The sheets aren't usually thick, less than a micron in most cases. But they're out there."

"But we didn't lose them both, right?" said Alex. "Diaz and Taggart?"

"No, we've still got Taggart," Ned said. "But Diaz . . ."

Before he could proceed, Alex looked up from the screen, wearing a lopsided, vaguely optimistic expression that Sara assumed was his attempt at being encouraging.

"Good news?" she asked.

"A little of both," Alex said. "Which do you want first?"

"Give me the bad news," Sara said. "It's that kind of day."

"There was more than one gas pocket," he said. "The sail has been damaged. How badly I'm not sure, but it's definitely going to affect its ability to push the asteroid out of the way."

Sara closed her eyes and sighed, placing her head in her arms.

"The good news?" she asked, head down.

"It's too early to tell for sure," he said, "but it looks like the sail may have made a slight difference. I don't think we're out of danger yet, but it might have helped, even just a little bit."

"Great," said Sara, feeling the helplessness swell up inside her. "So we all might die on Saturday instead of Tuesday?"

"Come on, Sara," said Alex. "I'm grasping at straws here."

Sara composed herself. "I know," she said. "I know, I just . . . I don't like feeling so out of control like this."

"If feeling out of control upsets you," said Alex, "you picked the wrong line of work. Half of what happens up there is out of our control."

Sara gave him a look warning him not to test her, and he backed off with his arms upraised.

"OK, OK," he said. "Why don't we take a walk? Just a few minutes to clear your head. They're going to be regrouping up there, so there's not much more we can do down here at the moment. Come on. The fresh air will be good for you."

Sara looked intently at the computer monitor that showed the asteroid's slow but relentless approach, then, after a deep breath, turned and stood up, preparing to walk outside with Alex. Before they exited the room, she pointed at him with a stern yet playful expression.

"Just don't try to hold my hand, OK?"

"My own hands will remain squarely in my pockets," he promised. "On my honor."

It was late when they stepped outside, and the traffic along East Street Southwest was light, with only a handful of cars gliding past. Their tires shushed as they made contact with the rain-washed streets. The air was a cool and welcoming contrast to the choked and stifling closeness of the PDCO offices, and Alex and Sara breathed it in gratefully.

"Feels good, doesn't it?" Alex asked, seeing the expression on Sara's face.

"I don't know if good is the right word at a moment like this," Sara said. "But will you settle for better than I was before?"

"I'll take it." Alex reached for the inside pocket of his coat before closing his eyes and shaking his head.

"Jeez," he said. "Twenty-two years since I've quit and I'm still reaching for a smoke when I get stressed."

"I remember," Sara said. "Not one of your more charming traits."

"Lucky I had so many more to balance it out."

"Hey, whatever helps you sleep at night," she said.

"I don't sleep at night," he said. "Why do you think I became an astronomer?"

"Touché."

Alex looked up at the night sky. The rain had stopped, and the clouds were clearing away, allowing a thin sliver of stars to peek through.

"'Who knows whether, when a comet shall approach this globe to destroy it, as it often has been and will be destroyed, men will not tear rocks from their foundations by means of steam, and hurl mountains, as the giants are said to have done, against the flaming mass?'"

He turned his gaze away from the sky and looked over at Sara.

"'And then we shall have traditions of Titans again, and of wars with Heaven.'"

"You've got me at a disadvantage here," Sara said, looking slightly puzzled.

Alex grinned slightly. "Lord Byron said that," he said. "In 1822. He knew this day was coming and believed that, when it did, the world would have the means to fight back. And yet here we are, with the end of days right on top of us and we're blindly stumbling our way through the dark."

He kicked at a pebble on the sidewalk and watched it skitter away before it came to rest in a puddle in the street.

"Hey," Sara said, "we're still fighting. All of us are. Down here, up there. That's all we can do. Fight like hell until we can't fight anymore."

"Still the fount of wisdom, I see."

"The question is," she asked, "are you going to listen this time?"

"Maybe," he said. "Maybe . . ."

Alex glanced at Sara and again felt that strange sense of traveling through time. He saw her through different eyes and wondered how he could have ever let her go in the first place. In the space of that glance,

Alex reflected on the various choices he'd made throughout his life, wondering how many had been the right ones.

"You're doing it again," said Sara.

"What?"

"Looking at me like a weirdo peeping through a window. If you want to say something, say it."

"OK," Alex said. "I wanted to say that what happened between us was—"

Sara's upraised hand stopped him cold.

"Let me rephrase," she said. "Say anything but that."

"Come on, Sara," Alex said. "We should talk about it sometime."

"Why? We've gone fifteen years without talking about it. So why now?"

"Because . . . who knows what's going to happen in the next few days. And if I'm going to die, I don't want to do it carrying regret around."

Sara gave him a long and contemplative look, and then laughed.

"You're lame," she said, although there was no malice in her voice. Alex took that as progress.

"Nice," he said. "Nice. I'm opening up to you, and this is what I get. I'm going to go back inside now and find a big desk to hide under."

"All right," said Sara. "I'll be right behind you. I'm going to take another minute out here."

Alex turned to leave but looked over at her one last time before he did.

"You OK?" he asked.

"Maybe," Sara said. "Do you have any more Lord Byron quotes?"

"Uhhhh," Alex said. "I don't think so. How about Kansas? Dust in the wind, you know?"

He started to sing, and Sara's laughter drowned him out.

"Please," she said. "I've changed my mind. Let's go back before someone calls the police."

Alex gave her a thumbs-up, and together they walked inside. As he headed up the stairs, his phone buzzed in his pocket. When he looked at the display, his face lit up.

"What is it?" Sara asked.

"Just got a message from Patricia," he said. "Remember we wanted her to look into using a kinetic impactor, something to knock the asteroid out of the way?"

"Yeah . . ."

Alex grinned broadly. "We've got one."

Chapter Nineteen

The Chinese called it the T'ien Lung, after the mythical dragon charged with keeping the gods from falling out of the sky. It was originally built by Starfire, a private spaceflight and exploration company, sometime during the last century. In the early days of lunar travel, Starfire had done brisk business as a delivery service, ferrying people and parcels to and from the Moon. Looking to branch out into other areas, they saw an opportunity in the area of asteroid deflection and built the craft that they dubbed the Rocinante, Don Quixote's horse. Unfortunately, sometime during the war, Starfire went bankrupt and their assets were acquired by another private company, Tai Shan Enterprises out of Beijing. However, aside from changing the name of the impactor, they had done little else with it, and for the last twenty-five years the vessel had sat unused in a hangar on the Moon. After Patricia reached out to NASA, someone searched the archives and found Starfire's original plans and proposal. From there, the team at the PDCO were able to trace the craft to Tai Shan. After negotiations between NASA, the China National Space Administration, and Tai Shan Enterprises, the Chinese had agreed to launch the T'ien Lung from the Moon to intercept the asteroid. The last hurdle to clear was to get the president on board via a last-minute video conference to his Catalina Island vacation home. On the call were Sara, Alex, the president, and Xu Zhao, the president of

Tai Shan Enterprises. All of them looked tired, except for the president, who was his usual blotchy shade of exasperated.

"Take me through this one more time," said the president, "like I'm a six-year-old."

"What we're looking to do, Mr. President," said Alex, rubbing his temples as though he could jump-start his already overstressed brain, "is hit the asteroid nose first."

"So, knock it out of the way?" he asked. "Like a billiard ball?"

"Not exactly," Sara said. "What we're hoping that it will do is slow the asteroid's velocity down so that it arrives at Earth three and one-third seconds later. Earth moves at thirty kilometers per second in its orbit, so if the T'ien Lung is successful and slows the asteroid down by that much, then in theory, Earth should simply, in a manner of speaking, scoot out of the way."

This explanation was greeted with silence. The president stared at them from the video screen blankly. Alex whispered out the side of his mouth to Sara.

"I think you lost him."

Sara nodded and looked back at the screen.

"Like a billiard ball," she said. "Just like a billiard ball."

The president nodded in return, smiling widely as though pleased with himself that he had been able to follow the scientific line of thinking.

"Good," he said. "That's real good. But now let me ask you something."

Everyone tensed in anticipation.

"If all we need is a big damn spaceship," he said, "why not just evacuate the Global Space Station and hurl that thing at the asteroid?"

"Well, there are a number of problems with that solution, Mr. President," said Alex. "For starters, the time it would take to evacuate the station would be incredibly costly. Every minute we spend on something else is another minute the asteroid gets closer. Additionally, the GSS wasn't designed for this type of mission, whereas the T'ien

Lung was. Yes, it might make a slight difference, but not as significant as the Chinese ship would make. Additionally, even if we considered this option, by the time we could launch the GSS, its proximity to the asteroid means that it would never be able to generate the velocity needed to make a significant impact. And since energy increases as the square of the velocity—"

"All right, all right," the president said. "Don't talk my damn ear off. I was just throwing it out there. And what about the Chinese? You people are willing to provide us with the vehicle?"

"Yes, Mr. President," said Xu Zhao. "On one condition."

"Jesus Christmas, is this really the time to be discussing conditions?" asked the president.

"It is a simple one," Xu said, "and I believe you will be amenable to it."

"Lay it on me," the president said, leaning back in his chair.

"We want mining rights to the asteroid."

"Are you serious?" said Alex.

"Very serious, Dr. Sutter," Xu said. "We believe that, although the T'ien Lung will deflect the asteroid from its present course, we can recapture it and safely bring it into lunar orbit, which I believe was the miners' original intention, was it not?"

The room fell silent in the wake of Xu's question. The fact that the asteroid had been set on a collision course with Earth due to a man-made accident caused by a failed mining attempt had not yet been made public knowledge. This made for a somewhat delicate situation when it came to formulating a response. Xu, looking as though he could feel the discomfort radiating from the other side of the screen, simply smiled.

"We too have our means of uncovering secrets," he said. "So, do you agree?"

"To your own point, sir," said Sara. "Attempting to mine the Thresher asteroid was what caused this disaster to begin with. Do you really want to court disaster by trying to mine it again?"

"You will forgive me for saying so, Dr. Kent," Xu said, "but I believe we are better equipped to handle the delicacies of asteroid mining than this particular group of rogues."

"They weren't rogues," said Sara, leaping to their defense. "They were . . ."

"Yes, we are well aware of the circumstances surrounding their predicament," said Xu. "And furthermore, we are aware that all of the miners involved were employees of the Guanghang Mining Company, a Chinese organization. Chinese employees, Earth citizens, lunar refugees. This is a very complicated matter. A simple agreement can uncomplicate it greatly."

"And what are we supposed to do if your people screw things up and send the damn thing falling back on our heads?" asked the president.

"With all due respect, Mr. President," said Xu, "I am not going to fence with you on this any longer. Those are our terms, both of Tai Shan Enterprises and the Chinese government. Do you accept?"

"What choice do I have?" the president grumbled. "You people have got me and mine by the short and curlies here."

"A vulgar analogy," said Xu, "but also an apt one."

"All right," the president said. "You've got my consent. Now, what do you need?"

"We need information," Xu said. "The T'ien Lung has been dormant for some time, and many of the schematics on how to operate it have been lost. Your national space agency has some of the data we need in order to intercept the asteroid successfully."

"You're talking about how much thrust and weight is required to make the impactor effective, correct?" Alex asked.

"That's right," said Xu.

"No problem," Alex said. "We can transmit that to you immediately."

"Excellent," Xu said. "I will contact our people at the launch facility and tell them to have the rocket ready to take off within a matter of hours."

"Thank you, Mr. Xu," said Sara.

"It is my pleasure, Dr. Kent," he said. "Hopefully, this will work to all our mutual benefits."

"Sure," said Alex. "We avoid destruction, you get filthy rich. I can live with that."

Xu gave another thin smile. "So can I," he said, and cut the transmission. Without another word, save for a dissatisfied grunt, the president did the same.

"Well, that went as well as can be expected," said Alex. "Now we've got to get this plan in motion."

"Absolutely," Sara agreed. "Let's get in touch with the team on the asteroid. With any luck, we can get them off that thing before the impactor hits."

◆ ◆ ◆

"What's it called?" asked Caitlin.

"A kinetic impactor," said Sara. "Basically, a huge battering ram that will crash into the asteroid and kick it square in the teeth and away from Earth."

"And us along with it," Caitlin mused. "Not an appealing option."

"That's why I recommend you take off as soon as you can," said Sara.

"All well and good," said Caitlin, "except we've still got a cracked heat shield and an engine that won't turn over."

"Dammit," said Sara.

"My thoughts exactly," Caitlin replied. "Any other ideas?"

"Look, there's still a chance you can get off of the asteroid even after it's been deflected," Sara said. "Based on our calculations down here, your ship should be far enough away from the impact point and will protect you from flying debris. So, when the time comes, all you've got to do is just sit tight and hold on to something."

"That's terrible advice," said Caitlin.

"I'm sorry," Sara said. "That's all I've got to give right now."

"That seems to be the norm these days," Caitlin said. "But thanks for trying. I'll round up the crew and let them know what to expect."

"Great," said Sara. "And while you're at it, can you let me know what to expect as well? Because right now, I have no clue."

Chapter Twenty

After hours of preparation, the T'ien Lung stood on the pad at the Yutu Launch Center, ready for its date with the Thresher. A squat, Mylar-encased craft with a single engine and eight tanks of fuel, the T'ien Lung was all about function over form, carrying no moving parts, solar panels, or anything that could slow its velocity. Atop the craft was an octagonal battering ram made of pure copper. The entire craft was designed for one purpose—to gather as much speed as physically possible and deliver a powerful-enough blow to any near-Earth object to send it permanently out of the way.

"T'ien Lung launch in T minus ten seconds," announced the flight director from Yutu Mission Control.

Back on Earth at the PDCO, Sara, Alex, and their team all watched the video feed from the Moon.

"If this doesn't work . . . ," Alex said.

"It's going to work," said Sara. "It has to, or we're all royally screwed."

"Three . . . two . . . *one* . . ."

Silently, the T'ien Lung lifted off from the Moon's surface, prepared to embark on the most important mission it would likely ever undertake.

◆ ◆ ◆

On the surface of the asteroid, Shaw had opted to venture outside to see if he could spot the impactor heading toward them. He had assured Caitlin that he would go back inside the lander before the ship made contact, feeling a little like a kid promising his mother he wouldn't play on the train tracks.

"What do you see out there?" Caitlin asked.

"Nothing yet," answered Shaw, scanning the stars. The heads-up display in their suits also had the ability to switch to telescopic vision, allowing them to see far distances without having to resort to binoculars. Responding to electrical impulses sent from the gloves' fingertips, the display could zoom in and out with an opening or closing of Shaw's fingers. He looked around, trying to get his bearings. A long time had passed since he'd had to rely on celestial navigation to orient himself, but he was glad he'd paid attention as a kid, both in science class and to his grandfather, who would quiz him mercilessly during their annual camping trips to Cedar River in the Adirondacks.

Finally, after several minutes, he zeroed in on an object moving in the star field above him. It was a small pinpoint of light, like a satellite viewed from Earth.

"I've got it!" said Shaw. "Coming in at about twenty degrees north."

"We're tracking it too," said Sara into Shaw's headset. "I'd get back to the lander before impact."

"OK," said Shaw. "Just a little longer."

Sara, Alex, and the team watched intently as the T'ien Lung raced toward the Thresher, powered by its single engine. In Washington, Catalina, and China, the scene was a similar one. No one spoke or moved. All eyes were fixed on the screen, waiting to see what would happen when the rocket made contact with the asteroid.

"Impact in thirty seconds," the flight director announced from the Moon.

"Roger that," said Vincent Whittemore, his NASA counterpart, who was also monitoring the rocket's trajectory from Houston.

◆ ◆ ◆

"Shaw, get out of there!" said Caitlin. "When that thing hits, it's going to bounce you right off the surface!"

"I don't know, Boss," he said. "Something's wrong."

"Impact in twenty seconds," the Chinese flight director warned through Shaw's headset.

"Roger twenty seconds," echoed Whittemore.

"Shaw!" said Sara. "Caitlin's right. Move now before it's too late."

"I'm not so sure," Shaw said.

"Impact in fifteen seconds."

"Copy that, fifteen seconds . . ."

"Shaw!" said Caitlin. "Now!"

"Ten seconds . . . nine . . ."

"He's not going to make it," said Sara.

"Eight . . . seven . . ."

"Come on, Shaw," said Caitlin.

"Six . . . five . . . four . . ."

"Three . . . two . . . one . . ."

On the surface of the Thresher, Shaw stood placidly and watched as the T'ien Lung sailed overhead, missing the asteroid conservatively by hundreds of miles.

Chapter Twenty-One

"Can somebody tell me what just happened?" asked Sara. "Seriously! What *the hell* just happened?"

"I don't know," said Alex. "But I'm going to find out right now."

As he left the room, Sara radioed Shaw.

"You OK up there?" she asked him.

"Yeah, Dr. Kent," he said. "I'm doing all right. Heading back to the lander now. Wish I could say we were a little better off than we were before, but I guess you already know that by now."

"Yeah, I'm afraid I do," she said. "Mind telling me what you saw that no one else managed to pick up on?"

"The rocket was off course," Shaw said. "Coming in at a completely wrong angle. I couldn't tell at first, but the closer the impactor got, I could see from the surface that it was going to miss us. I don't know who was doing the calculations up there, but someone goofed big time."

"Looks that way," Sara said, feeling sick to her stomach. She could only imagine what the president was saying right about now. "Listen, we're going to try and put the pieces together down here, and we'll get back to you when we've got something more to report, OK?"

"Yep," said Shaw. "We're going to regroup ourselves up here."

"Talk to you all in a bit, then," said Sara, and cut the line. As she did, Alex walked into the room. He looked absolutely green.

"What?" Sara asked.

"I don't even want to tell you," he said. "Seriously, it's that bad."

"I'm going to find out sooner or later," she said. "It may as well be from you."

"Come on," he said. "Let's take a walk."

Sara followed him as they left the CIC area and went back into her office. Alex closed the door as she took a seat behind her desk.

"As you know," he said, "we sent the Chinese the data for how much thrust the T'ien Lung needed in order to reach the Thresher and knock it off course, right?"

"Yes," Sara said. She said the word slowly, trying to draw it out almost as a means of delaying Alex's response.

"We sent them a number for how many pounds of thrust," Alex explained. "They entered the same number . . . in newtons."

Sara closed her eyes. She felt her neck muscles loosen, and her head fell forward into her hands almost involuntarily. While the US still measured booster thrust in pounds, China was on the metric system and measured everything in kilograms and newtons. The ratio of a pound-force of thrust to a newton was over a factor of four, meaning the amount of thrust they had programmed into the rocket's navigation system was catastrophically off base.

"Jesus Christ," she muttered. "How the hell does something like that even happen? Please tell me! What do they have, kids doing the calculations over there?"

"It's not unheard of," Alex said. "The screwup, I mean, not kids doing the calculations. It happened once before, back in the late twentieth century. The Mars Climate Orbiter disintegrated in the Martian atmosphere because of a mix-up of English and metric units."

"The Mars Climate Orbiter was a Martian weather satellite," Sara said. "This was a rocket whose goal was to save Earth from destruction. Kind of apples and oranges, don't you think?"

"I guess when you put it that way . . ."

"Look, we've got a major mess to clean up," said Sara. "Not only in terms of figuring out what we're going to do about the asteroid, but also politically. The president, the Chinese government, Tai Shan Enterprises, they're all going to want answers."

"I agree," Alex said. "Why don't I go to the White House? I've been yelled at by the president before, so I can deal with it. You and the team can stay here and see if we can come up with a Hail Mary play that will get us out of this."

"All right," said Sara. "Let's get to work."

As Alex turned to leave, his phone began buzzing in his pocket. He pulled it out and read the screen.

"I've got to get to the White House," he said, looking pale.

"I know," said Sara. "That's what you just—"

"No," he said. "I mean *right now*."

"What is it?" Sara asked.

He walked over to her. "I think you should head back inside and try and reach the team on the asteroid," he said. "They're going to need to hear some friendly voices right now."

He turned his phone to Sara so she could read the message he'd just received. On the phone, a text from a FEMA colleague was glowing insistently.

The news is out.

As Alex headed to the White House to deal with the fallout from the breaking story, Sara hurried back from her office to the CIC. She walked through the halls in a sort of dreamlike fog, unable to fully process that the story they'd been sitting on for days was now public knowledge. For a time, she had felt as though they were in a kind of protective cocoon and all they had to focus on was Caitlin, her team, and what was happening on the asteroid. Now, however, they had to contend with input and opinions from an angry and confused world.

Throughout the PDCO offices, every channel was now turned to the news, where announcers and anchors were chattering away in stentorian tones about the approaching end of humanity. Asteroid 1222 Thresher was spotted by an amateur astronomer in the Ruby Valley near Bozeman, Montana. He'd had his telescope pointed at the right part of the sky at the right time, wielding enough intelligence to know exactly what he was looking at, and more importantly, what it meant for Earth. A few well-placed e-mails later and the story was splashed all over every news outlet on the planet. Details were still sketchy, and Sara doubted they knew all the particulars, specifically that there were currently four miners (*three*, she corrected herself, feeling an icy pinch in her stomach as she did) riding atop the asteroid.

She entered the CIC to a burst of voices asking different variations of the same question. She held up her hands to quiet them all.

"I don't know any more than any of you do," she said. "That's the plain truth. Right now, I'm going to try and raise the team up there. We need to fill them in on what's going on. After that . . . I don't know what I'm going to do. But for now, *nothing changes*. OK? We keep working the problem and trying to knock this thing out of our way."

Colleagues muttered assent and went back to work as Sara got on the mic to try to raise Caitlin.

Chapter Twenty-Two

"Did you see me, Mommy?"

"Of course I saw you," Caitlin says.

They are walking home from school, Emily's hand folded neatly with her mother's. The Sun has almost set, casting the world in a hazy golden hue. The trees that haven't surrendered their leaves are a riot of orange and red, while the ones that have stretch their bare arms to the dusky blue sky, as though they are pleading for the return of spring. Around their feet, dead leaves spin, caught in the grip of the fall wind. But the wind isn't cold. It's brisk, invigorating. The world may be preparing for its long winter sleep, but for now, it still looks, feels, and smells vibrantly alive.

"Did you think I was good?"

"Are you kidding?" says Caitlin. "You were terrific!"

"But I was just a tree," says Emily. Then her eyes tilt downward. "Patty Grayson got to be a Pilgrim, and she's a whole month younger than me!"

Catlin lets go of Emily's hand and draws her arm around her daughter's shoulders, squeezing her in close and kissing the top of her head.

"Let me tell you something, baby girl," she says. "This is true for school plays and for life itself. It doesn't matter if you're a Pilgrim or a tree. It only matters what you do with what you're given. If you're a Pilgrim, great. But if you're a tree, then you just be the best tree you can."

Emily appears pleased at this notion, confident that she has done her best and made her mother proud. She draws in closer, and the two hurry home against the November chill.

◆ ◆ ◆

"Caitlin?"

Sara's voice, distant and wreathed in static, shook Caitlin out of the near-trance she wavered in and of following the double disasters of losing Diaz and the failure of the T'ien Lung. She had never been one to lose hope, but in the wake of recent events, Caitlin found hope slowly beginning to ebb. The only thing that was keeping her going at all was the thought of Emily. Every time she remembered Diaz's terrified face receding into the void, she replaced that image with one of Emily to try to keep going. Vee and Shaw had headed back out to the asteroid's surface, trying to see if they could salvage anything from the sail. Caitlin wanted to go out and help them, but found that the energy had left her body.

She couldn't figure out why the loss of Diaz was hitting her so hard. She'd lost people under her command before, but nothing had hurt quite like this, at least not for some time. The suddenness, the stupidity of it, the feeling that they shouldn't have even been here in the first place, those were all familiar emotions to any combat veteran. But somehow losing Diaz cut even deeper. Almost from the moment she'd met him, she'd recognized Freddy Diaz as a kid who was in search of a role model, always looking for someone to guide him, to steer him out of trouble and back onto the right path. And for the past year, Caitlin found that she was happy to take on the role. She had seen the potential in him, the talent and intelligence he brought to the table. So, in a way, she felt like losing Diaz was akin to losing a child. And somehow that loss made her feel even farther away from Emily.

Standing up and exhaling, Caitlin decided that, rather than sitting there feeling sorry for both herself and Diaz, she would instead do what she always did when she needed to distract her mind: tinker. She had to get the pyro circuit on the guillotine working again or they'd be permanent residents on the Thresher.

Removing one of the control panels that covered the umbilical severance system, Caitlin examined its inner workings and made a distressing discovery. Even if they'd made a perfect landing under completely stress-free circumstances, they'd probably be facing the same situation. The system was impossibly old, its wires stripped and corroded. If they attempted to take off, chances were there wouldn't be enough power to fire the charges and activate the guillotine.

Caitlin knew that in order to get the system to work, she would have to try to transfer power from other systems in order to ramp up the voltage on the guillotine. Unfortunately, she didn't know enough about these old landers to know for certain which system she was drawing from. She sighed. A long afternoon was on the horizon.

"Caitlin?" Sara's voice came suddenly again. "Are you there?"

Despite not wanting to talk to anyone, Caitlin knew she had to find the strength to answer. Her hands shaking, she swiped the display from Mute over to Talk.

"Yeah," Caitlin said, although the words came out in a choke. "Yeah, I'm here."

"How are you feeling?" asked Sara.

"Feeling like I just watched one of my crew die in front of me," said Caitlin. "And that there wasn't a damn thing I could do to stop it."

"I hear that," Sara said. "Believe me; I do. If it makes you feel any better, early readings are showing that the sail might have worked. Your course has been adjusted slightly."

"So we're out of danger?" asked Caitlin.

"Oh no," said Sara. "You're still driving headlong into danger. But there's a chance that you might not kill as many people as you would have before."

"You're right. I do feel better. I'm so glad you called."

"Well, now that I've successfully wrecked your day," Sara said, "why not go for broke and wreck your whole week?"

"Do it up," said Caitlin, not caring what Sara had to tell her.

"The word's out about what's coming to Earth."

That did get Caitlin's attention. She sat upright in her chair.

"What?"

"Yeah," Sara said. "Some skywatcher in Montana picked you up and lit the signal fires. The press is all over it. But, look, don't worry. It was only a matter of time. Something that big and coming in that fast wasn't going to stay hidden for long. It's actually kind of a miracle they didn't find out sooner."

"Do they know about us?" asked Caitlin.

"Not yet," Sara said. "But, the truth is, it might not be too much longer before someone puts two and two together. Once they figure out that the asteroid was being mined, there are going to be some online detectives who might be able deduce who you all are and where you came from."

"Emily," said Caitlin. "If they find out about me, they could—"

"Emily's already on her way to DC," Sara said. "She and your friend Ben are going to stay with my sister in Ashburn for now. She'll be safe for the time being."

Caitlin breathed a heavy sigh of relief, but she also knew that relief was only temporary. Sara was right. Soon, someone somewhere would figure out how 1222 Thresher ended up playing the world's worst game of chicken with the people of Earth. And once they had that piece of the puzzle, anyone who knew how to ferret out information would have no trouble turning over the right stones to uncover the *Tamarisk*.

"You OK?" Sara asked.

"Is that a rhetorical question?" asked Caitlin.

"Kind of," Sara said. "But I can feel the weight on your shoulders from down here. You feel like unburdening yourself?"

Caitlin let forth a bitter chortle that broke off midway through.

"I wouldn't even know where to start."

"Well," Sara said, "why don't you start with how you ended up there in the first place?"

"How did I end up here?" she asked. "Bad choices. A string of them, in fact. A lovely daisy chain that starts on Earth and stretches all the way to the Moon."

"Bad choices, huh?" Sara asked. "If I could turn my bad choices into cash, I wouldn't be stuck sitting here talking to you."

That produced a real laugh this time, and Caitlin started to feel better. Or at least a little less doomed.

"I just thought it would be different, you know?" she said to Sara. "My life, my job, everything. It feels like since I came back from the campaign, nothing has made any sense. Then Emily came along, and I saw a glimpse of what life could be like. Of what *I* could be like. And I don't mean to say that I didn't have an identity or anything before I became a mother, but suddenly, for the first time since the war, I had a mission, if that makes sense. I was going to give her the best parts of myself. All the things I could have been, all the things I'd wanted to be but wasn't, I was going to pass those on to her. I was going to fill her up with everything that I'd been denied. Everything I'd denied myself. She deserved that. She deserved so much and what she got . . . it just wasn't right. I'd promised myself that this wouldn't happen to her. That she'd never be left alone the way I was when my dad . . ."

She couldn't finish the thought. Trying to speak hurt, like forcing something sharp and spiny from her throat.

"Hey," Sara said, "what happened to you wasn't your fault. You ended up on the Moon because of circumstances you could never have foreseen! You were caught up in something completely beyond your control."

"That's true, I guess," Caitlin said. "And now we all are."

"Yeah," Sara said. "We're all caught up in this. Which means we're all in it together. You've got the best minds in the world down here trying to figure this out. And I know you fou—three are doing the same thing up there. Now, I don't know you all that well, Caitlin, but everything I do know tells me you're a fighter. And every fighter gets knocked down. The question is, how long are you going to stay that way?"

Against the odds, Caitlin found herself smiling. She liked this woman more and more and found herself hoping that they would have a chance to meet so that she could tell her so in person.

"I'll take your silence for consent," Sara said.

"Yeah, yeah," Caitlin responded. "Are you going to start charging by the hour now?"

"I could definitely use the money."

"Tell me about it," Caitlin said.

"Hey," Sara went on, "if you don't mind my asking, what happened to your father?"

"Caitlin? It's your father . . ."

Something dark crossed over Caitlin's heart and she fumbled to answer, only succeeding in making stilted hemming and hawing noises. In the wake of all that had just happened, she wasn't prepared to talk about her dad.

"Sorry," Sara said, backing down immediately. "I didn't mean to pry. Just, the way you talked about him, it didn't sound like . . ."

"No," Caitlin said to her. "No, it's OK. I mean, I may as well tell you now, right? I don't know if we'll ever get to talk about it over glasses of rosé on my couch."

"Never say never," Sara said.

"He died when I was fifteen," Caitlin said suddenly, not wanting to dance around the subject anymore.

"Oh, Caitlin," said Sara, now realizing the full extent of the wound she had been picking at. "I'm sorry. I didn't—"

"It's all right, really," said Caitlin, brushing off Sara's pity with the words. "It's fine. It was just one of those things. We'd been on Earth for about nine years by that point, and I guess his heart couldn't take it. He'd been living on the Moon since it was first colonized, so his body just wasn't ready for the strain of Terran gravity. I came home from school one day, and my mother told me. She'd found him in his study. She said he looked like he was asleep . . ."

"That's awful," Sara said. "I'm sorry I brought it up."

"I was going to go to California that summer," Caitlin continued. She suddenly realized that it was the first time she'd talked about her father's passing to anyone, including her ex-husband, since it had happened. She felt oddly liberated. "I had signed up for a four-week biology camp along the Napa River Ecological Reserve."

"Biology camp," Sara said. "So you were one of the cool kids?"

"Oh, you have no idea," Caitlin said. "But it didn't pan out that way. After he died, I stayed behind to help my mother, then dropped out of school to work at my father's mill. And when that went under three years later, I was off to the army."

"Did you ever get back to Napa?"

While talking about her father, the question felt somewhat random and unexpected. Caitlin paused.

"Sorry," said Sara again. "I'm sure that's kind of out of the blue, but it's important. Sometimes life gets in the way, you know? The things we plan for ourselves never materialize. The little things fall by the wayside, and we promise ourselves that there'll always be time to come back around to them. Then we wake up and it's twenty years later."

"No," Caitlin told her. "I never did get back there. After the war, I came back home, married Eric, and set in motion the events that led to you and I having this conversation right now. I regret it, though, you know? Never getting down there. Even for a wine tasting or something. Like you said, I guess I always thought I'd have more time."

Sara paused for a moment.

"You know what I think?" she said.

"What's that?"

"I think that everything that's happened to you is the reason you're going to make it out of there alive. I think that life has hit you so hard and so many times that you're just waiting for your chance to hit back."

"We'll see," Caitlin said simply. There was more that she wanted to say, but the words were lost. "So what about you?" she said instead. "What's your tale of woe?"

"That's going to have to wait," Sara said. "I've got to get back to this whole saving Earth thing. Meanwhile, any ideas you have about how to get yourselves out of this mess, I'm all ears."

"We'll keep thinking," Caitlin promised her. "And I'm going to hold you to that story."

"Oh yeah, girl," said Sara. "But you've got to bring the rosé."

"It's a deal," Caitlin said. "Straight from Napa Valley."

"Now you're talking," Sara responded. "Catch you later."

A click and the line went dead, leaving Caitlin alone with her ghosts.

Chapter Twenty-Three

The scene at the White House was nothing short of total chaos. Although news of the asteroid's approach was only a few hours old, it had traveled quickly through the circuitry of social media, galvanizing everyone in the world into panic or action. As a result, when Alex returned to 1600 Pennsylvania Avenue, he found the presidential residence surrounded by protestors. Some were angry with the government. Some were angry at society. Others were just perpetually in search of something to be angry about, and this new catastrophe gave them the perfect opportunity. People danced, formed human chains, and cried up at the sky while shaking their fists. On a makeshift dais, a band performed a rousing, punk-infused cover of "Eve of Destruction." A handmade banner hung behind them, proclaiming the event to be the "First (and Last) Annual 'Rock' Concert." Amid the bedlam, some enterprising souls sold merchandise, ranging from homemade, cheap-looking T-shirts to equally off-brand mugs and bumper stickers. The items were doing a brisk business.

All along the avenue, signs were everywhere, bouncing up and down angrily inside clenched fists. Most were covered in colorfully worded invectives directed at the president, many repurposed from previous protests. However, to his complete and total shock, Alex saw that some of these signs were actually *pro*asteroid. "Rocks Have Rights,

Too," said one, while another one blared "They Were Here First." He shook his head.

"Maybe we deserve to get wiped out," he muttered to himself.

After what felt like an interminable wait, the White House gates opened and he was waved inside. Parking his car, he raced into the building, where he was met by Chief of Staff Dawn Meyers. She looked ashen and worried, as though she had gone a long stretch between rests. He imagined that, if he could see his own face, it probably wouldn't look all that different.

"Thank you for coming over so quickly, Dr. Sutter," Dawn said as they began walking briskly down the hallways of the White House. "In light of everything that's happened with China and with the news getting out all over the world, the crisis has become much more complicated."

"No problem at all," Alex said. "Are we headed to the Situation Room?"

"No," Dawn said, "we're going right to the Oval Office."

Alex felt his sudden pallor. "The Oval Office? I thought the president was still in California on vacation."

"He cut it short," said Dawn. "As much as he loves golf, he loves his approval ratings more. A crisis like this couldn't go ignored, especially after the impactor plan failed so spectacularly. So he's back, and he wants answers. And, as you know, when he wants answers . . ."

"I know," said Alex with a weary sigh. "You'd better be prepared to give them to him."

They walked down the narrow Oval Office corridor, past offices where various staffers were busily receiving and relaying information from around the world. Screens everywhere were lit up with images of the asteroid and the faces of various press secretaries and communications officers from around the globe as the president's staff strategized and planned for the coming disaster.

A few more steps and Alex found himself being led through the oddly angled door and into the Oval Office, where the president was seated behind the Resolute desk and bellowing into the video display on it. His face was practically purple, his suit rumpled and oversized, his tie impossibly large. As the president shouted, phlegm rattled in his throat, making his various demands sound like a gargle. At first, Alex couldn't quite make out what he was shouting about to the person on the other end of the video conference. Only that he was angry. That wasn't a surprise. As Alex drew closer, however, the conversation became clearer.

"Look, I'm not saying that the thing is going to drop right in that damn wasteland you got up there in that country of yours, Yaroslav, only that it *could*."

"Mr. President," said the person on the other end of the video conference, whom Alex immediately identified as Yaroslav Visiliev, the president of Russia, "please understand that if American scientists redirect the asteroid so that it enters Russian airspace and puts our people in jeopardy, my government will have no choice but to interpret this as an act of war."

"An act of . . ." The president just about spluttered. "Did your mother drop you on your head, son? This ain't an act of war. Hell, it's an act of God!"

"Nevertheless, if you intercede and Russia bears the brunt of your actions, then we will have no choice but to retaliate. The peace that our two nations have worked so hard to achieve over the last sixty years will be undone, perhaps irrevocably."

"Well, you undo whatever you have to, my friend. Right now, I'm just trying to figure out how to save *my* people."

Alex bristled at the use of the term "my people." With what was approaching, the idea of "yours" and "mine" seemed outmoded at best. He wished the president felt the same way, although it was no surprise that he did not. To him, the world was a big playpen, and the only goal was to amass the most toys and devise the best ways to keep them out of everyone else's hands.

"Then I believe that our goals are the same," Visiliev answered in clipped, measured tones. "Our best scientists are trying to come up with a solution as we speak."

"Well, hell yeah they are," said the president. "What in the blue-blooded Christ do you think we're doing over here?"

As the president yammered on, Alex looked around the Oval Office, thinking of the other men and women who'd served the nation. He remembered reading that William Taft had created the Oval Office in 1909, modeling it after the White House's Blue Room. The Blue Room had been created as a formal meeting place for dignitaries and prominent people from around the world, a tradition held over from English court. With all the guests in a circle, everyone was at an equal distance from the president, the perfect representation of democracy. Alex's eyes now fell upon the ruddy-faced, boorish man seated in front of him and wondered what Taft and the other occupants of this office would make of its current resident.

Taking stock of the president fuming behind his desk like the world's biggest two-year-old, Alex still couldn't figure out exactly how he'd been elected. A loudmouthed rabble-rouser from Alabama, he had risen from car dealer to congressman in a short amount of time and ridden the wave of public paranoia and fear all the way into the most powerful office in the world. During the time of his campaign, tensions between Earth and the Moon were growing, and the tide of opinion against Moonborn travelers to humanity's home planet was taking a turn for the worse. Still, for all his shortcomings (and they were many), he was a great orator, and he'd used that skill to his advantage time and again. In speeches from small towns to massive convention halls, the president had played on the country's anxieties masterfully, gently stoking the fire until it grew into a conflagration. One that, as far as Alex saw, was now threatening to engulf the world.

Also in the room were Secretary of Defense Kittredge, Secretary of State Katz, and White House Press Secretary Karen Peralta. They were talking among themselves over the din of the president's tirade. Alex considered approaching them, but given his last encounter with Kittredge in the Situation Room, he opted to hang back.

Finally, the president pressed the screen on his desk with a meaty thumb and ended the call, turning around in his chair. His eyes seemed to look past the people in the room to a point somewhere off in the middle distance. His gaze was glassy and his eyes flicked back and forth nervously, the look of a man slowly becoming unhinged.

"Mr. President—" Dawn began.

"Who's this?" the president barked, seemingly to no one in particular.

"Alex Sutter, Mr. President," he said, extending his hand. The president eyed the hand as though being presented with something offensive, but then shook it briefly. "We've met before. We—"

"Oh, you're the asteroid doctor, huh?" the president said. "Well, you sure got us into a real mess, didn't you?"

Alex was puzzled. "Um, I'm sorry, Mr. President, I don't see how I got us in—"

"You don't see, huh?" the president said. "Seems to me that's exactly your damn problem. But I see a little different, and what I see is a goddamn Chinese rocket that just zipped past your asteroid without leaving so much as a scratch on the surface."

Alex opened his mouth to offer some sort of an explanation, but the president's glare tamped the words back down his throat.

"Like I said," the president continued, "a real mess. So what are you going to do to get us out?"

Alex, deciding that the initial line of questioning was no longer worth pursuing and would in fact invite further controversy, took a seat in front of the president's desk and opened his notes.

"Well, Mr. President," he said. "We've run through a number of scenarios and—"

"Have you got something or not?" the president asked, his voice sharp and bellicose.

"We have a lot of promising ideas," said Alex. His words came out in a defeated rush, like the sound of a deflating balloon.

"Promising ideas?" the president shot back, his eyes going wide. "We're about to be annihilated in a matter of days, and you're talking to me about promising ideas? And, if you will, please define 'promising' for me? You mean like that Chinese rocket that just shit the damn duvet? The one I went to bat for and got into bed with the Chinese government over asteroid mining rights? Promising like that?"

The president sat back and folded his hands over his prominent belly. He rocked back and forth in his chair, seeming to be lost in thought, then sat forward and looked directly at Alex, waiting for an answer.

"What happened with the Chinese impactor was a grave error," he said. "I'm not going to sit here and attempt to argue that. But we're trying—"

"You know I've got a nuke big enough to punch a hole right through Jupiter, right?" the president said.

"Um, yes, Mr. President, I am aware of that fact."

"And you know that my secretary of defense tells me that it most likely will be effective in knocking this thing right the hell back into space? A theory that you yourself corroborated right here in this very building not so very long ago, if I'm not mistaken?"

"Again, sir, that is correct, but—"

"Then what am I talking to you for?" he said. "I've got the damn codes, I've got the tools, and I've got the backing of just about everybody in my cabinet. And, I have a feeling that, when I address the nation later tonight, I'm going to have the backing of the entire goddamn country. And, probably the whole damn planet too. So, as far as this old boy is concerned, sold American and case closed. We're gonna nuke the sucker. Kittredge, make it happen. Now, if you'll excuse me, I'm busier than a moth in a mitten here—"

"Excuse *me*, Mr. President," said Alex.

The president blinked a moment, unused to being challenged. The other people in the room instinctively shrank back as well, looking like dogs that had unknowingly defied their master.

"I'm sorry to be so blunt, sir," Alex went on, "but it's not as simple as that. What about the people on the asteroid?"

"The people?" the president asked, then turned his narrow eyes to the others in the room. "What the hell is he talking about?"

Dawn's eyes closed as if asking, *why did you have to bring that up when we were so close?* Karen stood up and approached the president's desk.

"Dr. Sutter has a point, Mr. President," she said. "There are three miners up there. They were working on the asteroid when it changed course."

"Aw hell," he said, tossing his fountain pen onto the desk. "You could have mentioned that to me up front."

"It's in the report on your desk, sir," Karen began. "It's . . ."

A flurry of papers appeared as the folder was thrown in Karen's direction. The president's final word on what he thought of her report.

"Jesus H. Barking Mad Christ," he said. "What the hell do I pay you for?"

He leaned back again, spinning around in his chair a few times. This seemed to relax him, and when the final revolution concluded, his expression was calmer.

"So what do we have to do here?" he asked. "A damn rescue mission of some kind?"

"There's not enough time," said Alex. "To mount a mission of that size in the time frame we have just wouldn't be . . ."

Another squall of papers as the president expressed his absolute disdain for Alex's reply. Again the chair revolved and again the president returned placated. This time, however, he wore the look of a man who'd just been struck by a thought.

"Where the hell are these miners from?"

Four sets of eyes all flicked back and forth at each other. No one wanted to answer the president's query. Finally, Alex opted to take the bullet.

"The Moon, sir."

More hurled papers, accompanied this time by profane yet colorful turns of phrase delivered in a molasses-smooth drawl.

"The Moon?" he said. "Well, holy shit in the henhouse, you four don't know whether to scratch your ass or check your watch. Now, if these dumb sons of bitches broke an embargo and got themselves in a mess that could endanger the lives of everyone on Earth, that's their goddamn problem. I say we nuke the thing and file those three under 'acceptable losses.'"

"Ordinarily, I would agree with you, Mr. President," Karen said. "But there are some political factors to consider."

Everyone braced themselves for another paper shower, but it didn't come. The president was now strangely poker-faced.

"Such as?" he asked, a single eyebrow slowly rising.

"Sympathy for Moonborns is growing," Karen said. "It's been a year since the bombing, and there are a lot of people who've been so negatively impacted by the travel ban that it's softened their stance on the situation. Now that the world knows about the asteroid, it's only a matter of time before word gets out about the people trapped on the asteroid. And when that happens, there will be people here on the ground who will advocate for them vocally."

"So what do you propose I do?" the president said. "Sit back and play pocket pool while this thing turns California into a water park just because some people are protesting over three illegals? Hell, they've been protesting me since the day I took office."

"I'm not saying that you shouldn't do anything," said Karen. "But we can't just ignore them completely."

"You could mention it in your address to the nation," Dawn suggested. "Make it seem like they were heroes. That they were trying to stop the asteroid from hitting Earth and they failed. Their sacrifice won't be forgotten and so on."

The president nodded, his blotchy face splitting into a grin. "I like that," he said. "That makes both them *and* me look good! Dawn, that's why I pay you the big bucks. OK, it's settled, then; we nuke the bastard. Kittredge?"

The secretary of defense stood up. "Yes, Mr. President?"

"How long after I give the OK can you have that bird in the air?"

"Sir, it will take a few days to fuel the missile," Kittredge said.

"It's not that simple," Alex cut in. "It's also a question of waiting until the asteroid is in the proper position in space. We don't want the Thunderclap to actually hit the asteroid dead-on. The detonation has to be close enough to shift its track, but not so close that the nuke strikes the asteroid directly."

"And why not?" asked Kittredge.

"We want to deflect the asteroid, not destroy it," said Alex. "A direct hit could break up the asteroid, turning it from one falling object into many, with no way to deflect or control the debris. By detonating the nuke in just the right spot, the force of the blast should push the asteroid away. With that in mind, we have to wait for it to be in range."

"All right," he said. "How long will that be?"

"About forty-eight hours, we think," said Alex.

The president looked over at Kittredge. "Can you have that bird ready in forty-eight hours?"

"We'll double our efforts," said Kittredge. "Do whatever we have to in order to get her there."

The president's eyes went back to Alex. "All that sound good to you, Einstein?"

Alex nodded. "Yes," he said. "Yes, it does. But, Mr. President, I implore you to consider other options. The nuclear solution could make an already bad situation worse. As I've noted, the timing has to be perfect. And, if you'll forgive me, the T'ien Lung incident doesn't inspire confidence."

"You say you want us to consider other options?" said the president, and then leaned back in his chair again. "What have you got? Thrill me."

Alex fell silent.

"I didn't think so," the president said. "Now you head on back to the bughouse, and if you and your crew come up with something that blows my skirt up, we can talk. But otherwise, I'm addressing the nation and letting them know that, in two days' time, this thing goes boom. All good?"

Everyone said that it was, though their lackluster tone suggested that they thought otherwise, then thanked the president and filed out of the room. Dawn looked at Alex as they walked back down the hall.

"In the grand scheme of things, that could have gone a lot worse," she said.

"I would really hate to consider how," said Alex.

"At least he made up his mind," she replied. "I've seen him stare off into space for ten minutes while supposedly considering a proposal, then suddenly snap back to reality and go off on a tangent about some random person who's supposedly wronged him. This time, at least we've got a course of action."

"Yeah," Alex said. "But is it the right one?"

"Well, it's like the president said," Dawn told him, "you've got forty-eight hours to convince him otherwise."

Chapter Twenty-Four

Vee and Shaw returned from their last EVA with bad news. Next to nothing was left of the sail where Diaz and Caitlin had put it down. This revelation was particularly demoralizing to Caitlin. Not that she had put much hope in the sail to begin with, but to see that it was completely destroyed somehow made the situation feel more hopeless. As hard as she tried, she couldn't shake the feeling that Diaz had died for nothing. And worse yet, that he should never have been out there in the first place.

"OK," she finally said, guilt threatening to overwhelm her. "We need to start focusing our attention on getting off of this thing. Right now, our only goal is going to be to get the *Alley Oop* up and running, then we're going to take off from the asteroid and get on a course to Earth."

"What about ICC?" asked Vee.

"We'll take our chances," Caitlin said. "Better than sitting around here waiting to die. So here's what's going to happen. We need some rack time. Combat naps only. Enough to recharge and get focused. Then, Shaw, start plotting a course to Earth. Vee, you and I are going to go back outside and run some final diagnostics."

"What do you have in mind?" she asked.

"We've got a heat shield to try and repair."

◆ ◆ ◆

An hour later, Vee and Caitlin were back on the asteroid, trying to work their way underneath the *Alley Oop* and fill the cracks in the heat shield with non-oxide adhesive that they had managed to find in the ship's hold. NOA was standard issue on most reentry vehicles. For years it was called NOAX, with the *X* standing for "experimental," but anyone who had crewed on a ship that traveled in and out of the atmosphere knew the agent by its common name: hot sauce.

The theory behind NOA was fairly simple. The stuff went on like a paste, and when it was heated during reentry, the polymers fused into ceramic and, hopefully, acted as a makeshift shield from the extreme temperatures. In the case of the *Alley Oop*, it wasn't that simple, however, because hot sauce usually tended to degrade after about thirty days or so without use. And, judging by the look of the container they had found, this batch was more than a little past the sell-by date. Still, they reasoned it was the only port in a storm.

As they worked, Caitlin knew it was time to reconnect with Vee.

"So," she said, "are you going to tell me your name or not?"

Vee shook her head in amused disbelief. "Why are you asking me now?"

"Why not now?" Caitlin said. "In a few days' time, we're either going to slam headlong into Earth, be blown into the stars by the world's biggest nuke, or burn up somewhere over Pacoima. Seems like the perfect time to me."

"I don't like to talk about my name," she said.

"Why not?"

Vee started to formulate an answer, her face distant. To Caitlin, she looked as though she wanted to reveal her thoughts but something was holding her back.

Eventually, the light returned to Vee's eyes, and she looked over at Caitlin.

"It just reminds me of a different time, that's all," she said. "One I'm not too eager to relive."

"That's fair," said Caitlin. "I'll tell you what. I'll tell you a secret if you tell me your name."

"Are you kidding?" Vee said. "I already know all your secrets!"

"All right," Caitlin said, gently squeezing more NOA into the heat shield. "Your loss. It was a good one too."

"I'll try and live with the disappointment," Vee said.

Just then, Shaw radioed the two of them.

"Yeah," said Caitlin, "go ahead."

"We're getting a call from PDCO," he said. "Someone wants to talk to you."

"OK," said Caitlin. "Send the feed to our helmets."

"Trust me, Boss," Shaw said. "You'll want to be sitting down for this."

Vee and Caitlin worked their way back into the lander to answer Sara's call. Once inside, their fingers touched the screen to activate communication with Earth.

"Sara?" Caitlin asked. "You there?"

"Yeah, Caitlin," said Sara. "Me, Alex, we're all here. The whole team."

"Wow," she said. "Must be big news."

"It is," Sara replied. "There's someone important who wanted to wish you well up there."

"Hi, Mom!"

Whoa.

The tears started at once. And, just like Vee's, they hurt like hell.

"Hi, baby!" she managed at last. "What are you doing there?"

"Dr. Kent let me come," Emily said. "She thought you'd like to talk to me."

"Well, Dr. Kent is a very smart woman," Caitlin told her. "And she knows me pretty well."

"She's nice," Emily said. "And her sister's nice too. Me and Ben are staying at her house."

"Oh yeah?" asked Caitlin. "Have you been having fun?"

"Yeah," said Emily. "They let me stay up and watch movies."

"Nothing too scary?"

"Mooo-om," Emily said, "I'm not a baby."

"I know, I know," Caitlin said, "but you're *my* baby!"

"Oh please," said Emily, but the tone in her voice hinted at her happiness.

"I'm also reading the book you gave me," Emily went on. "There's a part in it that made me think of you and where you are right now."

Caitlin chuckled. "Is this the part about believing as many as six impossible things before breakfast?"

"No," said Emily. "But I like that part too. No, it was where Alice asks the cat which way she should go."

"'That depends a good deal on where you want to get to,'" said Caitlin, quoting the book back to Emily. She knew just about every word by heart. Her father had read it to her over and over again, sometimes starting over the second he'd finished the last page.

"'I don't much care where,'" Emily said. "'So long as I get *somewhere*.'"

"'Oh, you're sure to do that,'" Caitlin said, now unable to hold back her tears, no matter how much they stung. "'If you only walk long enough.'"

"When are you coming home, Mom?"

"I'm working on that, baby," said Caitlin. "Mom's working real hard. And all those people down there with you, they're working real hard too."

"OK," said Emily. "Just remember one thing . . . be the best tree you can."

"I'd never forget that," said Caitlin. "And I'll be home real soon. But you know, even if you can't see me, I'm still right there with you."

"I know that, Mom," said Emily. "And even though you're not there anymore, I still love you to the Moon and back. What about you? Do you still love me from the Moon and back?"

"Oh, baby girl," Caitlin said, "I'm so much closer than that now."

They said goodbye with a promise to talk again very soon, and then Sara came back on the line.

"Hey," she said, "you holding up OK?"

"I'm guessing you didn't bring my daughter to talk to me just to brighten my day," said Caitlin, still trying to collect herself.

"OK, then," said Sara. "Tell me why you think I did."

"To soften the blow," said Caitlin. "You've got some bad news for me, and you thought being able to talk to Emily might make it easier to hear."

"That wasn't why I had you talk to Emily. She's been asking from the minute she touched down at Dulles. But you're right," Sara said. "I've got some bad news. And there's no way to sugarcoat it, so I'm not even going to try. The president is going to use the nuke. When Thresher is close enough, he'll launch the rocket and detonate near the asteroid, and whatever happens, happens."

"What about us?"

"He's got a nice little story to tell the country about you," Sara said, not bothering to hide the bitterness in her voice. "You're all going to be heroes who tried to save the world and, having failed in that attempt, nobly agreed to sacrifice your lives so that the world may go on."

Caitlin looked around at the others on board the *Alley Oop*, and tried to make sense of this new revelation. Basically, the people of Earth had just told them in one voice that there was no help coming. Worse yet, in a relatively short amount of time, they were either going to be blown to cosmic dust or punched into some far corner of the galaxy by the big fist of a planet that wanted nothing to do with them. The news was a lot to take in. To Caitlin, it was shocking and upsetting, but also, strangely, she felt ashamed. Almost dirty, as though her status as an "illegal" had made her in some way untouchable or unworthy of a second thought. Although she had no way of knowing, she imagined that Shaw and Vee were feeling something similar.

Finally, Caitlin said the first thing that came to mind.

"Well that sucks."

"Nicely put," said Sara. "If we had more time, more resources, then maybe there would be a chance. But we just don't. I'm sorry, Caitlin. I'm so sorry."

"Why are you sorry?" Caitlin asked her. "You didn't do this."

"I know," said Sara. "And I want you to know that we're not out of ideas down here. We're going to keep working on this until we come up with a solution. I just can't help feeling like I failed you."

"You didn't fail us," said Caitlin. "You've given us an opportunity."

"How do you figure that?"

Despite the circumstances, Caitlin had a feeling of optimism.

"Because now I know it's up to us to save ourselves."

Chapter Twenty-Five

Sara disconnected from Caitlin and put her head in her hands. She felt like she had not only let the three miners down but herself as well. She had told Caitlin that she was working on the problem, but what did that mean? Every solution they had come up with was shot down because of time and money.

Alex came up and sat down next to her, laying a comforting hand on her shoulder.

"No one can say that we aren't doing everything we can," Alex said.

Sara looked at him through eyes growing blurry with tears.

"Do you really believe that?"

"Would it matter if I did?" said Alex. "The odds were against us from the beginning. This thing was coming at us too fast from too close. We barely stood a chance."

Sara gave a rueful laugh. "Tell that to that little girl."

"I know," Alex said. "But I'll tell you something. I read about Caitlin Taggart. The things she did over there in the campaign. And if I were going to put my money on anyone who could find a way out of this, it's her. In fact, she kind of reminds me of you."

Now Sara's laughter was more genuine. "Nice try, Sutter."

"I'm serious!" he said. "Look, remember back in college, you were struggling in your first year, and that professor told you you'd never make it as an astronomy major. And what happened? You doubled down on all your courses and graduated with honors. You've never known how to quit, and something tells me she doesn't either."

Sara and Alex looked at each other for a moment and something passed between them. The moment wasn't unpleasant, and, shockingly, Sara found herself wanting to stay in it a little longer.

"We've got something!" Patricia Delgado said, running into the room and raising her arms in triumph.

Sara looked up, both irritated at the interruption and relieved. Plus, the idea that her team may have come up with a solution produced another emotion: elation.

"What is it?" she asked.

Ned dropped a stack of printed pages on the table.

"Firelight," he said.

Sara flipped through the pages, looking them over.

"OK," she asked. "What's Firelight?"

"It was an old Russian orbital defense platform," Patricia said. "Built sometime in the middle of the century during the Second Cold War. By the time of the Last Campaign and the formation of the New Coalition, it was deemed to be no longer necessary and never brought online. But, nevertheless . . . it's still up there."

Sara also looked over the pages showing old schematics and blueprints of the design and layout of the Firelight platform. Most of the lettering was Cyrillic, making it hard for Sara to decipher how it was supposed to work. Still, she thought, there was something familiar to her about the design.

"All this time we didn't think that a laser ablation was a possibility because we didn't have a powerful enough laser," said Ned. "Now we do."

Alex looked thoughtfully at the image of the weapons platform in his hand.

"It's been up there for decades," he said. "Its orbit hasn't decayed?"

"Doesn't seem like it was ever fully decommissioned," said Patricia. "Maybe the Russians were keeping one hand on the switch. Just to be on the safe side."

"If it hasn't been decommissioned," Sara said, "then there's a chance the Russians could get it up and running again."

"Yeah," said Alex. "But would they?"

"Hell yes, they would," said Sara. "Remember, the president's nuclear diversion plan could end up planting the asteroid somewhere in Siberia. Plus, I think the Russian president would activate Firelight just for the chance to stick it to our own commander in chief."

"All right then," said Alex. "Let's first reach out to the Russian science team in Moscow. They'll be able to tell us whether they think this is a viable option. Maybe they've already thought of this themselves and are working on it as we speak."

"Sounds like a plan," said Sara. "And then?"

"Then I think it's time we set up a conference call between the White House and the Kremlin."

As Sara, Alex, and their team were busy putting their new plan into action, the world was busy coming apart at the seams. If the revelation of the asteroid's approach to Earth had caused panic, once the president addressed the nation informing of his intention to use nuclear weaponry against it, the entire mindset of the planet shifted into full-blown madness. During his speech, he had elected at the last minute to leave out any mention of Caitlin Taggart and her crew. And, given the way the public reacted to his speech as it was, he felt relieved that he'd stayed mum. The streets were swarming with people, all hysterical for one reason or another. Hysterical that the world was quite possibly about to end, hysterical that they were only just finding this out. Citizens wanted answers, whether it be from God, the government, or someone in between. If Terrans had knowledge that three lunar residents were also caught up in the crisis, political tensions could have boiled over into an even less manageable mess.

On TV and online, the president was both hailed as a man who took decisive action in a time of crisis and derided as a buffoon whose shortsightedness and bigotry had led the nation directly to this point. Religious zealots came out in droves, calling the asteroid a punishment for the world's wickedness, the cleansing fire God had promised in the Bible.

"But the day of the Lord will come as a thief in the night," shouted a preacher on a street corner in New York as homeless vagrants and suit-clad office workers stood side-by-side in attention. "In which the heavens shall pass away with a great noise, and the elements shall melt with fervent heat, the earth also and the works that are therein shall be burned up."

Crime rose in incremental waves as the realization dawned on people that, in a relatively short amount of time, the consequences of their actions, if there were any, would be meaningless. Within a day of the president's address, the looting began. Store windows were smashed across the country, with inventory both large and small plucked, snatched, and hauled off shelves and outdoors. Cars were overturned and lit aflame. Those who didn't want to loot or celebrate or bemoan the approaching end of the world simply hunkered down and stayed indoors, too afraid of what awaited them outside or in the skies above.

In the White House, the president was, as expected, apoplectic. Although he was in a red-faced, blotchy rage most of the time, his staffers now noticed something different. In his eyes, there was a hint of fear. There was the palpable sense that he had been treating the presidency like the world's greatest game and now someone had just sat him down and told him that it was all real. He threw a tablet down onto the desk, pointing at the headline on CNN.

NUCLEAR BOOR: President's Missile Plan Spells Doom for Entire Planet!

The article went on to list all the reasons why, at this late stage, a nuclear missile fired at the asteroid would do more harm than good and then presented a detailed analysis of precisely why the president was too stupid to know any of this.

"Goddammit!" he screamed. "Who the hell reads this crap?"

"Fifteen million people daily, Mr. President," said Karen, "according to our latest numbers."

"We need to formulate a response," the president said. "Draft a message for social media. It should say . . ."

"What we need to do is keep our eye on the ball," said Dawn. "Now, with everything that is happening, and with what might be coming in the next several days, I think it's time we considered Operation Ark."

The president's face drained of color. He, like all his predecessors, had been briefed on Operation Ark, but, just like all his predecessors, he had never believed that he would ever consider using it.

"Are you serious, Dawn?" he asked.

"I have never been more serious, sir," she replied. "We should have been talking about this from day one, from the minute Sutter and Kent gave their presentation in the Situation Room. It's time to start notifying the ticket holders and initiating the lottery."

The president, in a rather uncharacteristic move, slumped into his seat. To those present, it looked as though the weight of what Dawn was proposing was too much to carry. How right they were. Operation Ark was a plan for both the continuation of government and, if the worst should happen, the preservation of life on our planet. It was first enacted during the frenzied, paranoid days of the First Cold War, and the plans were laid out in secret. A massive underground city, all connected by a subterranean network of tunnels large enough to drive a fleet of tractor trailers through it had been built with funding from some of the largest corporations and defense contractors in the world.

Beginning somewhere underneath the Allegheny Mountains and extending all the way to Mount Shasta in California, Ark City was the stuff of urban legends and conspiracy theories. People had claimed aliens were living down there, using the tunnels as a base of operations from which to abduct unsuspecting humans. Others claimed that the city would be where the secret power brokers and puppet masters known as the Illuminati would flee once their plan to exterminate the population had been put into effect. This last theory was somewhat closer to the truth. Although there were no nefarious banking families pulling the strings, Ark City was to be populated primarily by the elite of humanity who either had the public profile or economic means to gain entry. But a significant portion of the general population would also be allowed in except for those over sixty-five, and truthfully, even that was pushing it. (There were those in government who believed that no one over fifty should make the cut.) If the president put the plan into effect, one million random Americans would receive a text message with a phone number and a verification code. Calling that number and entering the code would grant that person and their family—provided that family was no larger than four people—access to Ark City should the worst happen. Once the city was at capacity, the doors would be sealed until such time as the surface was habitable again. It was an extreme plan, one no president wanted to consider, least of all this one, who was only just grappling with the awesome responsibilities of his job.

"We're not there yet, Dawn," he said dismissively. "Now about the CNN situation—"

"Mr. President, please—"

"I said we're not there yet, Dawn, goddammit!" he shouted.

"Well, when *will* we be there? Do you mind my asking?" she asked, slamming her fist down on the desk. "Jesus Christ, Mr. President! The country is falling apart around you. And in a few days' time we could be facing a global crisis on our hands the likes of which no administration has ever seen before. And what do you care about? Your public image. My God! You're worried about what they're saying about you in the press? Trust me, they're saying a whole lot worse about you in their homes. Since Truman first dropped the bomb on Hiroshima, every president who has ever sat in this office has wondered how he or she would face the end of the world. Would they stand tall, or tuck tail and run? What would they do when the final hour came? Well, Mr. President, that final hour is here. How will you face it? Burying your head in the news, or turning to look the problem in the eye?"

The president stared Dawn down as everyone froze in place. The tension in the room felt like the electricity in the air just before a summer thunderstorm. But before he could properly explode, the door to the Oval Office burst open and his assistant came in.

"Mr. President?" he said, suddenly becoming aware that he was interrupting something. He cast his eyes around the room nervously before plunging ahead. "I'm . . . sorry to interrupt, but you should turn on the TV. Channel 415."

"Oh Christ," muttered the president. He threw up his hands and leaned back against the desk as Dawn clicked the remote, turning on the screen at the far end of the office. On the TV, a reporter was silently speaking.

"Turn off the mute, dammit!" barked the president.

Dawn punched the proper button on the remote, and the reporter's voice filled the room.

". . . repeat what we have just been told. It seems that a group of miners are stranded on the Thresher asteroid currently making its way toward Earth. It would appear that they had been contracted to mine the asteroid by Lyman Ross, the son of Texas senator Hamer Ross . . ."

"Dawn . . . Karen," said the president slowly, "we need to make some phone calls."

"Yes, Mr. President," said Dawn. "Who would you like us to call?"

"Everyone."

◆ ◆ ◆

Once the news revealed that there were three people stranded on the asteroid and that the president had most likely known about them before ordering a nuclear strike, everything exploded. Human rights groups were up in arms. Supporters of Moonborn families began making speeches wherever their voices could be heard, from protest marches in front of embassies around the world to speeches before Congress on national television. Nightside began making threats anew, promising that, before the asteroid wreaked havoc upon Earth, they would prepare the world for its arrival with a fire that would engulf the planet.

On the other side of the debate were those who sided with the president and felt he was a national hero for making the decision to use the missile, and that by choosing to nuke the asteroid—and, by extension, the people who were on it illegally—he was sending a brave message of zero tolerance to anyone who dared violate the embargo.

"The president is a man of great conscience," said Dallas Hudder, the spokesman for the People of a Free Earth, an anti-Moon society that had rumored ties to the presidency. "And his decision to inflict a righteous punishment upon the three criminals whose wanton ignorance and disregard for the laws of our country and planet have jeopardized our way of life stands as evidence of his greatness."

The day after that interview aired, the fires began.

Nothing was safe from the wrath of the public. Churches, temples, mosques, and homes around the country went up in flames overnight. At first it seemed as though there was a pattern to the burnings, that people who were perceived as being either in support of or, worse, in collusion with the president were the first targeted. But after a while, the carnage became hopelessly random. No one seemed to care what they burned down, only that it *did* burn down. In a very real way, the fires became the physical manifestation of the nation's hatred, hot, constant.

Standing on the Truman Balcony at the White House, the president looked out over his smoldering country. Fires raged in the dark, and sirens screamed into the night. Overhead, churning through the orange-and-black sky, helicopters thumped, their searchlights scanning the blackened landscape. The president looked at the turmoil, absently swirling the scotch in his glass, and slipped a hand into the pocket of his robe. He sighed, unable to figure out how it had come to this. He had been elected the leader of the most powerful nation on Earth and had promised to turn it into a paradise. He knew that the public and the press had branded him as a bully and a rabble-rouser—and he regularly acted the part—but he *had* wanted to make the country a better place. And yet, on his watch, it had become a war zone. He looked down at the lawn, unable to gaze upon the conflagration on the horizon any longer.

"Are you coming to bed?"

The president turned to see his wife standing in the doorway. Age, excess, and the ravages of his time in office had altered his appearance to a near unrecognizable state, but she was just as feisty and spry as ever. Her hair was no longer the chestnut brown it had been when she was still a student at Alabama, back when it would reflect the Sun's rays and make her look as though she was crowned in gold. But its silver color conveyed a different elegance. Wise and confident. She never colored it or tried to hide it, whereas he had fought the onset of the years tooth and claw. Coloring his skin, dyeing his hair, combing whatever strands he had left into an assortment of shapes to give the illusion of thickness. Standing here now, with the ruined city behind him and his elegant wife seeing right through him, the president suddenly felt small, like a child who'd been caught playing a foolish prank.

"Martha," he said, and the word came out sounding like a prayer, the desperate calling out of a man on his knees. "Oh, Martha. Did I cause all of this to happen?"

"You want the answer that will help you sleep or the answer you need to hear?" said Martha. The delicate twang in her voice was completely devoid of pretense.

"I want the truth," said the president. "The kind of truth that can only come from you."

"Well, then, I'll tell it to you straight," Martha said. "Looks to me like you screwed the pooch and you didn't even have the courtesy to give him a Milk-Bone afterward."

The president's eyes widened slightly. Martha walked over to him, reaching for the bottle of scotch. She poured herself two fingers and downed them quick, as though to give her strength, then poured two more and sat down, gesturing for him to join her. They sat together a moment, and she looked him in the eye.

"What the hell did you think was going to happen?" Martha said. "You filled their heads with fear and hatred. Told them that the boogeyman was waiting in every closet. You turned this country into a pressure cooker with your anger and your rhetoric. It was only a matter of time before the damn thing blew. Chances are this would have happened even if that damn rock hadn't tumbled out of the sky."

"You warned me about all of this," he said. "I see that now. And I never listened."

"No, you sure as hell didn't," Martha said. "I've been telling you from the first moment they discovered the asteroid that you had to handle this situation with kid gloves. But there's no stopping you when you get the way you get."

The president was indignant. "And just how do I get?"

"Like a damn dog in a hubcap factory," Martha said, taking a sip of scotch. "Just barking your head off at every little thing you see, and nothing short of turning a hose on you will calm you down any. I warned you day in and day out, but you were so convinced that you were right that you wouldn't hear it. You just kept telling me that you were going to stay the course and walked away. So let me ask you, Mr. President. Are we still on course?"

The president was quiet a moment, thinking over all the roads he'd taken to get here. All the things he had said and done. As he recounted them all, shame began to radiate inside him, a coal being stoked. He wanted to offer his wife an explanation.

"I just wanted to be strong for them," he said. "I wanted to be a leader who would get things done. For years, I sat back and watched all those other politicians say the same things, make the same promises, and get nothing done. I wanted to cut through all of that. To be the kind of president who met the people on their level."

"Maybe 'on their level' isn't where the president needs to be," said Martha. "Maybe he should give the people an example of what they should be striving for. Not a reflection of where they are."

The president had no answer for this. He could only look at the flickering orange skyline and wonder what he could have done differently and what he could still do with the time he had left.

"I wanted to be strong . . . ," he said quietly.

Martha took his hand and squeezed it. "There are other ways of being strong," she told him. "You don't just have to be right."

The president stood and walked to the railing again. He thought about Sundays in their hometown, of church services and picnics with potato salad. Of simpler times when the world seemed to make sense. In those days, all he could think about was how to get out. How much better he considered himself to be than everyone around him. Now all he wanted to do was to go back and never leave.

"'Immediately after the tribulation of those days the Sun will be darkened, and the moon will not give its light,'" he said.

Martha walked up behind him and slid her arms around his waist from behind, resting her chin on his shoulder.

"'And the stars will fall from heaven, and the powers of the heavens will be shaken,'" she said.

"Matthew chapter 24, verse 29," the president said.

"You always remembered your verses." She nodded.

"If you'd been raised by my mama, you would too," he said, chuckling slightly. He then thought a moment. "That verse talks about the end of days. When the son of man will return to judge us all. Could it be that day has come?"

"Maybe so," Martha said. "I guess the question is, if that's the case, how do you want to meet him?"

She kissed his cheek lightly and turned to go back inside, leaving him a moment to consider what she'd said.

"They'll hate me," he said and was angry at how small the words sounded when they came out.

"News flash, Commander in Chief," said Martha, "they hate you already. But all's not lost. I'm still here."

"Are you sure about that?"

"Hell yes," she said. "You think I'm going to go back to Fairhope a disgraced, divorced ex–First Lady? Good Lord, my mother will self-destruct right on the pier."

The president chuckled, and it sounded as though it was coming from a stranger.

"C'mon," Martha said. "Come to bed with me. I don't think the whole city'll burn down in one night."

"I'll be right there," he told her.

As she turned to go, the president called after her.

"Martha?"

"Yes?" she asked, turning in the doorway.

"What reason did you ever have to marry me?"

"I married you because I saw something in you," she said. "Who knows? Maybe I'll see it again sometime."

And with that, she was gone. The president watched her leave and wondered, If all the American people had been as unflinchingly honest as the former Martha Tomlin of Fairhope, Alabama, would he ever have even bothered running for office? Then he looked at what remained in his scotch glass and hurled the contents out onto the lawn, feeling resolve wash over him.

He knew what he had to do.

Chapter Twenty-Six

The next morning, the president asked his assistant to clear his calendar and call a press conference. When she arrived at the White House, Karen was shocked to hear the news and, given the usual outcome when the president shifted gears, a little concerned.

"What are you doing?" she asked when he finally strolled into the Oval Office. "We haven't even had time to prepare a speech."

"Don't worry, Karen," the president said. He held up a stack of handwritten pages. "I've got it covered. Going to do this one from the heart."

He turned to walk out the door, then turned back to her.

"And, for whatever it's worth," he said, "I'm, uh . . . I'm sorry for the way I've treated you this last year. You're a damn good press secretary. You always know what to say . . . and what not to say. I wish I'd taken the time to absorb some of that quality."

Karen stood for a moment as he turned to leave. She was trying to figure out what to say, and then blurted something out that the president could only assume was the first thing that popped into her head.

"Senator Whitmore once called you a pontificating bag of gas," she said, almost shouting the sentence out. "At the White House Correspondents' Dinner. And I didn't disagree with him. I just sipped my drink and nodded."

The president stopped in the doorway, then looked back at Karen.

"Like I said, you always know what not to say."

He walked out the door, whistling "Farther Along," as he did.

After a long walk down the corridor past the Cabinet Room, the president turned right and entered the James S. Brady Press Briefing Room. The press corps stood to greet him as cameras whined and flashes popped. Quietly, he walked up to the podium and spoke.

"Good morning," he said. "I appreciate your all meeting me here at such short notice, and I promise that I will keep my remarks brief."

The president paused, like a pitcher winding up on the hill. Almost in unison, the corps leaned in, waiting to hear what he was going to say. He shuffled the papers on the podium and looked up, folding the papers and tucking them back into his jacket pocket.

"Let's do this the old-fashioned way, shall we?" he said. "While I was jotting all this down, I was thinking of other people who'd held this office, and my mind turned to Lyndon B. Johnson. He inherited one hell of a mess from Jack Kennedy, and the public roasted him for it pretty much every chance they got. And he once said, 'A president's hardest task is not to do what is right, but to *know* what is right.' That stuck with me. Now, I used to think that I did both pretty well. How about you?"

A nervous titter came from the room, but they were warming up. This wasn't the president they were used to. He held up his hand to quiet the reporters down.

"On second thought, don't answer that," he said. "I hear enough mean things about me on the TV. I don't need to hear it in my own house. But Johnson's words . . . they've been resonating with me as of late. Because, really, how can you know what's right in times such as these? How can you know what to believe, when your beliefs can get you killed? How can you know who to be when everyone is telling you who you are is an offense? And . . . how can you put your faith in your fellow man when he's willing to burn down everything you hold dear?"

The room was strangely quiet in the wake of the president's words. Even the cameras had fallen silent.

"You know," he went on in a convivial tone, as though he were speaking at a Lions Club dinner back home instead of addressing the most influential group of journalists in the free world, "there are people outside this very house holding up signs that say this asteroid is a sign from God. And who knows? Maybe it is. Then again, depending on what you believe, maybe it's not. Maybe it's just dumb luck, or the universe simply correcting itself. Restoring the balance somehow. Or maybe it's one of a million random acts that have happened over the course of history to shape the cosmic events that have led us here. But, let me ask you, whatever you believe, *can* it be a sign? From God or the universe or whomever you choose? Can it be a reminder that, despite our perceived mastery of all that we survey, the truth is that we are at the mercy of forces that we can't combat or even comprehend? And if that is the case, then shouldn't it be a reminder that we need to be turning toward each other instead of pushing each other away? That we should be extending our hands in friendship rather than curling our fists in anger?"

Here he paused and looked down at the podium, seemingly centering himself. He was keenly aware that he had spent the better part of his political career acting in stark opposition to the words he had just uttered. And he would be a fool to try to pretend otherwise.

"Of course," he said, "I'm not one to talk. I helped ignite the very fires that are burning across our once-great nation. I fanned them with my hatred and called it strength. I fanned them with fear and called it courage. I fanned them with ignorance and called it enlightenment. And where did it lead me? Rome is literally burning, and this good old boy is reaching for his fiddle. Well, no more. It ends today. There are going to be some big changes, and they start now. Effective immediately, I am putting in motion plans to rescind the travel ban to and from the Moon."

A clamor erupted. He held up his hands and raised his voice slightly.

"All Earth-generated travel visas will once again be valid," he continued. "And all travel to and from the Moon, whether it be commercial or private, will again be legal once this crisis has passed. I have also opened a dialogue with the lunar ambassador, and with a little luck and maybe a few mea culpas, I hope we can put this whole ugly situation to rest once and for all."

He paused a moment to let his announcement take hold. He was sure that his cabinet was having a collective panic attack and that many of his constituents were tearing his signs off their lawns at that very minute. But the speech wasn't over yet. He held up his hand again to quiet the press corps down.

"There's more," he said. "And it won't be easy to hear. As you know, we are working very hard to figure out how we can stop this asteroid from striking our planet. But we also have to face the reality that we might not be able to. We must plan for the survival of our species. Therefore, effective immediately, I will be implementing a program that has been in place for more than a century, Operation Ark."

The president went on to explain the particulars of the Ark City plan to the press, many of whom looked shocked and mystified that such a place could have existed under their feet for their entire lives, as well as the lives of their ancestors, without them ever knowing about it. Perhaps even more shocked were the members of the intelligence community who had not been briefed on the president's announcement and were now going to have to scramble to figure out a plausible explanation as to why the plan had been kept secret for generations.

"I want everyone across the country to know that I did not come to this decision lightly," the president said, "which I know may come as a shock to most of you. But I have seen where rash thinking leads, and the time has come for cooler heads to dictate the courses of action we all must take. So, with that in mind, let me proceed. I started this off with a quote from LBJ, and I'm going to wrap it up with a little wisdom from the Chinese. There's an old proverb that says that, of all the stratagems, the best one is knowing when to quit. Now, I've never quit at anything in my life, and I don't believe that's what I'm doing now. But this country needs to be led, not told what to do. As such, when this crisis has passed, I will be resigning as your president and appointing Vice President Keating as my successor."

Now the tumult in the room was impossible to keep quiet. Every reporter present stood and began shouting. Initially, he had planned not to take any questions but changed his mind. He was interested in hearing their assessment of everything he'd just laid at their feet. Rubbing his hands together in anticipation, the president pointed to Jenny Lewis, a young reporter from CNN.

"I'm going to be bold here," he said, "and see what CNN has to say about me."

"Mr. President," Jenny said, "you've announced that you would resign after the crisis has passed. Why after? Why not step down now?"

The president laughed, a genuine and uncharacteristically self-deprecating sound.

"For those of you who might not have read between the lines on that one," he said, "Ms. Lewis basically asked me why don't I just leave and try not to let the door hit my ass on the way out?"

Now the pressroom was laughing too, and everyone appeared to be in shock.

"Well," the president continued, "I'll tell you why. Because for all my shortcomings, I am a man who believes in finishing the job and taking responsibility for his own mess. Now, as you have heard, there are three miners trapped on that asteroid. So I am not going to walk out of the Oval Office until we bring them home."

Chapter Twenty-Seven

An hour after the president's press conference, he met with Alex and Sara in the Situation Room to go over the new laser ablation proposal. They had both been dreading the meeting, especially given Alex's play-by-play description of his last visit to the Oval Office. However, the two found themselves talking to a very different president.

"Which of the three spirits do you think we have to thank for this?" Alex whispered to Sara as they watched the president cordially greet everyone upon walking into the room, a far cry from the grunts and churlish stares that kicked off most meetings.

"My guess is the wife had something to do with it," said Sara.

"That's usually the case." Alex nodded.

"Good morning," said the president, addressing Alex and Sara. "I understand you have some news for me. Some kind of breakthrough?"

"We hope so, sir," said Alex. "In researching potential solutions to the Thresher crisis, our team stumbled across an abandoned Russian program, Firelight, which may provide a solution. Joining us via videoconference is Valentin Kuznetsov and Dominka Lebedev of the Russian Space Research Institute in Moscow. Also with us is President Yaroslav Visiliev. Doctors, Mr. President."

The two Russian scientists returned the greeting enthusiastically, but President Visiliev, still no doubt stinging from his last encounter with the American president, merely offered a taciturn nod. Alex went on.

"Now, to give you some background, Firelight was an orbital platform designed for defense during the Second Cold War. It was completed but never activated. However, it is still fully functional, and we believe it represents our best chance for deflecting the Thresher asteroid without any residual damage to the people of Earth."

"All right, folks, you've got my attention," said the president. "How's the damn thing work?"

"For the technical details, Mr. President," said Sara, "we would like to turn you over to Drs. Kuznetsov and Lebedev. Doctors, if you please?"

"Yes, of course," said Lebedev in clear, heavily accented English. "As you no doubt know by now, there are many different proposed methods for deflecting an asteroid and preventing it from hitting our planet. These range from kinetic impactors to gravity tractors to nuclear missiles. However, a laser ablation is the most promising option currently available to us. The laser strike will not result in fragmentation of the asteroid, and the laser itself is powered by plutonium, ensuring a pulse powerful enough to effectively redirect the Thresher. Additionally, a laser ablation can be conducted with a relatively short preparation time as opposed to the hours, days, or even years needed for other deflection methods."

"For the uninitiated in the room," asked Vice President Keating, "can you explain to us how this process works in layman's terms?"

"Yes, Mr. Vice President," said Kuznetsov. "In essence, the light from the laser irradiates the surface of the asteroid. The heat then causes the surface to sublimate, essentially turning it from a solid into a gas. Once this happens, the ablated material ejects from the surface and provides a controlled thrust, pushing the asteroid out of the way of Earth. A simple interpretation of Newton's equation of equal and opposite reactions."

"Sounds promising," Keating replied. "But I want to go back to the president's original question. How does it work?"

"Firelight was designed to target multiple areas at once," said Dr. Lebedev. "Upon activation, the platform will release a series of small, plutonium-powered robotic craft, which we call 'lightning bugs.' Each of the bugs is equipped with a fifteen-hundred-watt laser. The plutonium stores the laser's energy and then releases it in a short but incredibly powerful energy pulse. We will send the bugs to the Thresher, where they will effectively swarm around the asteroid in a strategic array. Once they are in position, they will fire their lasers in a concentrated pattern. If all goes well, their combined heat and energy should successfully ablate the asteroid's surface, diverting it to the point where it will skip off Earth's atmosphere like a stone."

"It should be noted," Alex interjected, "that the design of the Firelight platform is based on a project proposed sometime in the last century by the Planetary Society called Laser Bees. Their primary objective, as it happens, was the deflection of asteroids."

"How long before it can be activated?" the president asked.

"It will take a few hours to get the system working, sir," said Kuznetsov. "But within a day we should be able to launch the lightning bugs. Based on the asteroid's current position, they should reach it within forty-eight hours after launch."

"That's cutting it close," the president said. "If we go with this plan, and it doesn't work, can we still launch the nuke?"

Sara stepped forward and hit a switch. One of the massive screens changed to a computer-generated image of Earth with the Thresher asteroid approaching. Between the two was a perforated line running along the planet's curvature.

"The PDCO has come up with this imaginary line of demarcation," Sara said. "Once the asteroid reaches this line, the only option will be to fire the nuke or risk the planet."

"All right then," said the president. "So we have until this son of a bitch reaches this imaginary line in space to try out the Russian laser. After that . . ."

"After that, we have no choice but to hit it with the Thunderclap," said Sara. She then looked down at her papers, as if trying to steady herself. "No matter who's still on it."

"Speaking of which," said the president, "what are we doing about getting the miners back to Earth?"

"We had hoped to launch a rescue shuttle to them," said Alex, "but the asteroid is four times farther away than the Moon. We're not sure if they'll reach them in time before the lightning bugs are deployed. They may have to rely on their lander to escape the asteroid. We're coordinating with the crew on that front as well. Luckily the craft wasn't damaged when it landed on the asteroid, so it should be able to take off before we even deploy the bugs."

"Well then," the president said, "sounds like we've got our ducks in a row. Or at least as much of a row as we can put them in for now. I just have one question."

Everyone in the room paused as they waited to see whom the question would be addressed to.

"If you Russians knew about this laser platform thing," the president said, "why are you even bringing it to us? Why not just blow the damn thing up yourselves and take all the credit?"

The Russians all considered the president's question a moment, and then finally President Visiliev spoke up.

"The Firelight system is complex," he said. "And, in recent years, with the reconstruction after the Second Cold War, we are . . . short on qualified technicians."

"So you all have the technology, but you need our help to make it work?"

"Yes, Mr. President," said President Visiliev, "it would appear so."

The president gave a brief chuckle. "I bet that burns you up, doesn't it?"

The Russian president responded to this remark with a chuckle of his own.

"More than you know, Mr. President."

Chapter Twenty-Eight

The city is falling down around them. Smoke belches from the wreckage of burned-out buildings. Sewers, blown open from the constant pounding of artillery shells, have vomited their contents onto the street, resulting in a river of waste sluicing around the platoon's legs as they run. At this pace, there will be nothing left for them to even fight for. Caitlin and Ben have managed to regroup with a few other soldiers, some from their helo, others who fast-roped in from the other helos that didn't crash.

Once they are off the main street, the team battles their way through side streets and alleyways, dodging Ender fire that seems to erupt from balconies and doorways. Muzzle flashes appear at random like sunlight glinting off mirrors. Gun barrels can be seen poking out everywhere, from windows to cracks in the walls. Finally, the platoon punches through to the courtyard of a large, bullet-riddled building. Gunfire rattles in the distance, coupled with the cries of Enders rallying others to join them. Caitlin shouts to Ben over the roar of the bullets.

"This is it!" she shouts. "This is Hamza's compound!"

They both look up in amazement and a small amount of trepidation. The imposing structure looks as though it has been constructed by haphazardly joining other buildings together, with no sense of architecture or logic. Stairways rise along impossibly high walls, some leading to small entranceways, others leading nowhere. Elsewhere the walls are covered in a latticework of scaffolding, small platforms, and makeshift bridges that string the buildings together like yarn. An M. C. Escher painting as reinterpreted by a psychotic artist.

"This is going to be a real bitch," Ben says.

Before Caitlin can respond, they hear the screams rising above the chaos. They look to the center of the courtyard and see a pair of soldiers huddled behind the bodies of dead enemy combatants. They are pinned down by gunfire from above. Caitlin looks over at Ben and reacts in an instant.

"Suppressing fire!"

Ben nods and rakes the balcony above them with bullets, holding back the attackers as Caitlin runs into the courtyard. She grabs one soldier and drags him back to their position, then repeats the movement as she rescues the second, a young blonde who looks like she might have been cheering for her high school just a month ago. They hump it back to their position, and the girl presses herself against the wall and looks at Caitlin with wide, panic-stricken eyes.

"Are you in charge?" she screams.

Caitlin gives her a nod. "What's your name?" she asks.

"Roarke, Private First Class," the soldier says.

"What's your unit, PFC Roarke?"

"Fourth Infantry," she says. "This is my first deployment. We were supposed to land at Ramadi on the other side of the Tigris to handle exfil when we got shot down."

"Sounds like you got the same raw deal we did, Private," said Caitlin. "You stay on my six and I'll get you out of here, you got it?"

"Yes ma'am," Roarke says.

"What about you?" Caitlin asks the other soldier she rescued. "What's your story?"

"Davidowitz," the man shouts. "Second Lieutenant. We fast-roped in and then shit got stupid. Mortar fire began hitting us from the second we touched down. Everyone scattered. I took Roarke and tried to work my way to the target."

"Good work, soldier," says Caitlin. "You found it."

"What's the plan, Captain?" Davidowitz asks.

"It looks like we're all that's left," Caitlin says. "At least as far as I can tell. That means it's up to us to try and take out Hamza."

"I'll follow your lead, Captain," Davidowitz says.

"Roger that," says Caitlin. "Roarke?"

Roarke moves close to Caitlin's side like a small child huddling next to her mother.

"You stay with me, got it?" says Caitlin. "Don't shoot unless you have to. Muzzle awareness, OK? You know what that means?"

Roarke shakes her head, and her face looks as embarrassed as it does scared. Caitlin nods at her.

"It's OK," she says. She points at the barrel of Roarke's gun. "You see this? Don't point it at anything you don't intend on destroying."

Roarke nods and swallows, trying to get her nerves under control.

"All right," says Caitlin. "Let's move!"

The four race out into the courtyard, laying down suppressing fire and dodging enemy bullets. Roarke does not fire; she merely stays at Caitlin's side, as though her presence alone is a shield that will keep her from harm.

They work their way up one of the staircases, pressing themselves against the walls as the courtyard drops farther and farther below them. Caitlin has never been afraid of heights, but after a few steps, even she suppresses the urge to look down. Inside the compound, the situation isn't much better. There is no order to the layout, and getting one's bearings is an impossible task. The hallways twist and turn in no order, unfolding endlessly into darkness. The soldiers attempt to navigate the labyrinth of passageways, trying to work their way around the blind spots and avoid the gunfire that seems to be coming from all directions, lighting up the darkened halls like strobes. When they reach the top floor, they find a door at the end of a long hall, slightly ajar. Caitlin's eyes flick over to Ben.

"Do it," she says, and Ben nods, tossing an Mk 141 into the room.

There is a jarring bang and a brilliant blaze of light. The four soldiers flatten themselves against the wall and press forward. They enter the room and find Hamza Mahmood, an AK-47 in his hands. He is dazed from the effects of the grenade but is still brandishing the weapon and shouting incoherently. Caitlin, Ben, Roarke, and Davidowitz all point their guns at Mahmood, each one ordering him to put down his gun and surrender. The room becomes a torrent of cross talk and shouted curses.

Suddenly, two other Enders rush out from a back room, all armed and shouting. Caitlin and her unit react in an instant, firing almost as one. There is a brief eruption of gunfire, and the three Enders, Mahmood included, drop unceremoniously to the floor.

"Clear!" shouts Caitlin, and her words are echoed by Ben and Davidowitz.

Caitlin doesn't take a moment longer to think about what they've done or to consider the three bodies in front of them. Now is the time to act.

"OK, I want hard drives, flash drives, data packets, anything that has information and isn't nailed down."

"On it!" says Ben.

As Ben rushes off to get to work, Caitlin scans the room and her eyes fall upon a terrible sight.

◆ ◆ ◆

"All right," said Caitlin, "I think the plan is simple. We fire the ascent stage from the *Alley Oop*, and we get the hell off this rock before the president rams this nuke up our asses. Vee, how's our fuel situation?"

"Not bad," Vee said. "Given the low gravity here, it won't take much for us to reach escape velocity. The problem is going to be whether or not that heat shield is going to hold. Not to mention that, without the Mylar insulation, it could get a little hot in here."

"At this point, that's a risk I'm willing to take," Caitlin said. "The other question is ICC. Once we enter Earth's influence, we're going to be intercepted and detained. Is everyone prepared for that?"

"Both of those words sound much more inviting than 'pulverized,'" said Shaw.

"I have to agree with the science guy on that one," said Vee.

"Then it's settled," said Caitlin. "Let's prep the ship for takeoff."

Just then, the comm lit up with an incoming transmission from Sara.

"Hello up there," she said, sounding surprisingly upbeat given the circumstances. "We've got some good news from the people of Earth."

"Go ahead," said Caitlin. "We could all use some good news."

For the next twenty minutes, Caitlin, Vee, and Shaw listened as Sara outlined the president's sudden change of heart, the Firelight program, and the collaboration with the Russians. When it was over, the crew sat back and tried to take it all in.

"So what do you need from us?" Caitlin asked.

"Just try and get your asses off that rock as soon as possible," said Sara. "Once the bugs are in place, they're going to knock the Thresher back into space, and if you're not off it, you're going to go along for the ride."

"You don't have to tell me twice," said Caitlin. "We're going to prep the *Alley Oop* for takeoff and contact you when we're ready."

"We'll be waiting," said Sara, and ended the connection.

"Their plan won't work," said Shaw. "And it's our fault."

"Why do you always have to bring everybody down?" asked Vee.

"I'm just being realistic," Shaw said. "Trust me, once they run the numbers down there, they're going to come back with the same thing. The Russians and the PDCO are overpromising. And they're about to underdeliver in a big way. The bugs' lasers aren't powerful enough. When they ablate the asteroid, the material will come off too slowly to provide enough thrust."

"And the asteroid will still hit Earth," said Caitlin.

"So that's it?" asked Vee. "We just give up?"

"On the contrary," said Shaw. "This is the part where we go to work."

"I'm listening," Caitlin said.

"OK," said Shaw. "As I noted, the asteroid is on a current trajectory that will not be sufficiently affected by a laser ablation. Not without additional thrust, at least."

"I'm following you," said Caitlin. "How do you propose we generate this thrust?"

"You remember what happened to Diaz?"

The two women nodded somberly. Caitlin was certain she would never forget.

"I know it's not pleasant, but it's given me an idea," Shaw continued. "We know that this asteroid has water ice, yes? And we also know that, when exposed to a heat source, that water ice tends to sublimate and form pockets of gas. So . . ."

Caitlin's eyes brightened. "So with enough water ice gathered together, when the lightning bugs hit the asteroid . . ."

"It will create a geyser of steam that should give us the extra thrust we need to push the asteroid out of the way," said Shaw.

"OK," said Caitlin, "that sounds completely bonkers."

"And it might be," agreed Shaw. "Ice is very reflective, so there's always the chance that these lasers will just skitter harmlessly off the surface. However, there's every reason to think that it *isn't* 'bonkers,' as you so perfectly put it. Think of it like a kernel of popcorn, OK? You heat it enough, what happens? Bang! It explodes outward, right? This is the same basic principle. And if it works, it could put us and everybody else out of danger."

"If you want my two cents," said Vee, "that is just about the most ridiculous plan I've ever heard. But . . . I don't have a damn thing better to do today, and it's a lot more preferable to sitting around waiting to die. How do you propose we gather the water ice?"

"We're miners," said Caitlin, her smile widening. "We dig."

◆ ◆ ◆

Back at the offices of the PDCO, Sara received another communication from Caitlin, who gave her the full download of Shaw's plan. Sara listened to everything Caitlin outlined and then delivered her honest opinion.

"That's completely insane," Sara said.

"You're not wrong," Caitlin said. "We've pretty much come to the same conclusion up here. But it's the only chance we've got."

"Maybe so," Sara agreed, "but you're running on borrowed time. One way or another, those lightning bugs are going to orbit the Thresher in the next few hours and hit it with everything they've got. And, if that doesn't work, the president's going to have no choice but to fire the nuke."

"What am I doing sitting here talking to you, then? Sounds like I've got work to do."

"My point exactly," Sara replied. "Sounds like you guys have a plan, so I suggest you put it in motion now."

"On it," said Caitlin.

"Over and out," said Sara.

"You just need to say 'out,'" Caitlin said.

"What?"

"'Over' implies there's more to be said. 'Out' means the conversation's ended."

"Oh," said Sara. "Thanks for the tip. Now, get moving!"

"Out," Caitlin said. Sara stood up and went over to Alex, who was reviewing the Firelight schematics with the rest of the team.

"Are you ready for this?" said Sara.

"At this point, I'm ready for anything," Alex replied. "What's up?"

"I just got off the line with Caitlin," she said. "They're going to use the rover and scoop up as much water ice as they can into one of the asteroid's craters. Once the lightning bugs fire their lasers, the ice will turn to steam—"

"And turn that crater into a massive thruster?" said Alex. He shook his head, tapping a pencil on the desk as he considered what Sara had just told him. "It's implausible, but not entirely impossible. We've been going over the trajectory of the asteroid ourselves, and if this little plan of theirs works, it might give us the extra boost we need to guarantee that it misses Earth."

"Hang on a second," Ned interjected. "This plan sounds ludicrous at best. At worst it's completely suicidal. As it is, all of our plans to deflect something that big are usually measured in years. And you're talking about pulling something like this off in a matter of days? A week at most? All our scenarios say that it takes years to deflect an asteroid."

"The numbers are shaky, I'll admit," said Alex. "But none of the scenarios you're talking about factor a group of miners blasting tons of material off the damn thing. So yes, I'd like to be working within a better time frame. But think about it, Ned. In a strange way, it makes sense. It's really all about conservation of momentum. If you move enough mass at a high enough velocity, something's got to give."

"I get that," Ned said, "but I have to say I'm still not buying this plan."

"Imagine you're standing on ice skates," said Alex. "If you hold up a desktop fan, you'll move, right? Maybe only incrementally, but you will move. Now imagine you have a box fan."

"You really feel that confident about this plan?" Sara asked.

"Archimedes said that he could move Earth if only he had a place to stand," Alex replied, somewhat enigmatically. "We have to move a lot less, and Firelight is as sturdy a footing as we're going to find for ourselves."

"And what happens if they fail?" Ned asked. "If the asteroid reaches the demarcation mark before the lightning bugs can accomplish their goal?"

"Then the three of them die heroes," said Alex. "All we can hope is that they die alone."

Chapter Twenty-Nine

For the next several hours, the team on the asteroid worked diligently, using the Noser's backhoe and scoop to break up as much water ice as possible and gather the remnants into one of the larger craters.

The team had to be careful of how fast they worked in the asteroid's microgravity. If they pushed the ice too hard, it would continue to keep moving right over the crater. So they had to keep the momentum just slow enough that when the ice hit the crater's edge, it simply floated down and inside. And they were mindful of Shaw's concerns regarding the ice's reflectivity, trying to ensure there was enough dust and rock mixed in to diminish the effect. The extra material also increased the mass inside the crater, which would theoretically result in a greater push when the time came. Shaw had proposed lining the crater with pure ice, in the hopes that the reflectivity would boost the laser's power, but the consensus was that they didn't have enough time or resources to separate the good ice from the dirty ice. They'd simply have to cross their fingers and hope for the best.

After they had come close to filling the first crater, they stepped back and admired the results of their efforts. Caitlin, Shaw, and Vee looked over the edge of the crater at the lagoon of rock, sediment, and dirty ice they had created. It glowed silver and gray in the light of the stars, like moonlight falling on a frozen lake. Caitlin gave Shaw a complimentary nod.

"Not bad for a day's work," she said.

Shaw's face wore a worried expression, and he shook his head in reply. "It's not good either," he said. "At least, not good enough. I've been running through this plan over and over in my head as we've been working."

"It's never a good outcome when you run things over in your head," Caitlin said.

"Here's the thing," Shaw said. "The way this asteroid is going, we've got to move it about a hundred kilometers for it to miss Earth, right? That means, at our current rate of speed, we should hit the planet in approximately ten days."

Shaw turned his wrist and began punching numbers into the touch pad on his sleeve. "All of this means that we've got to divert it by a velocity of about 11.6 centimeters per second," he said.

"That doesn't sound so bad," said Vee.

"Not when you look at it just in terms of the number itself," said Shaw. "But the big picture is far more troubling. This asteroid has a mass of twelve million metric tons, OK? The volume of water ice in this crater, combined with all that we've been able to fill it with, is thousands of times less. When the bugs hit it with the lasers, it's going to shift the asteroid, but not by nearly enough."

"Which means . . . ?" asked Vee.

"Which means in order to reach 11.6 centimeters per second," said Shaw, "we've got to fill seven craters of equal size or greater. So, basically, we've got to do this six more times."

Caitlin looked at the crater, thinking of everything they'd just completed and would now have to do all over again. She cursed under her breath.

"Let's get Sara on the line," she said. "They're not going to like this."

"Are you serious?" said Sara.

"This isn't really the best time for jokes," Caitlin replied. "Shaw's been crunching the numbers all day, and according to his calculations, this is what we're looking at. But I think we've got a plan."

"This I've got to hear," Sara replied.

"We've already got one crater filled," Caitlin said. "We're going to work in shifts, two miners out, one back at the *Alley Oop* for rest and replenishment of oxygen and supplies. Every crater we fill, you hit with the bugs. One, maybe two craterfuls a day. So, instead of diverting the whole thing at once, we slowly nudge it out of the way over time."

"OK, that's a decent plan, even if I still think it's nuts," said Sara. "But the more time you take up there, the closer to Earth this thing is getting. And when that happens, sooner or later the president is going to be forced to use the Thunderclap."

"Copy that," said Caitlin. "I wish there was a better way, God knows, but I don't see it from here. Not right now at least. This is all we've got to work with here."

"All right then," said Sara. "Do what you have to do. I'm going to let the team know that they're going to be working overtime for the next few days. In the meantime, you'd better get to digging."

"Way ahead of you, partner," said Caitlin. "Shaw and Vee are out there now. We're going to rotate out in an hour."

"Got it," said Sara. "You know, with the time frame we're looking at, and the amount of work you have to do, there's a good chance you're going to be out there when the lightning bugs start firing."

Caitlin paused briefly, her stomach flipping over as she tried to assess this rather troubling piece of information.

"Just tell whoever it is manning the trigger that they'd better not miss," she said.

Chapter Thirty

The news that the asteroid ablation mission would take days instead of hours was not well received by the world. The further revelation that the asteroid's present trajectory would place it somewhere in the middle of the Mojave Desert, thereby leveling both Las Vegas and Los Angeles as well as their surrounding environs, was met with even less enthusiasm. This was further compounded by the implementation of Operation Ark. As some people received their text messages while close friends and family members did not, the bad blood continued to boil. Some elected to give up their space in Ark City in favor of a friend or relative. Others chose to stay behind and face whatever came their way. Weddings sprang up overnight as the chosen hoped to be able to bring their new husband or wife in tow. Within twelve hours of the initial messages going out, the streets and highways were choked with traffic as the selected people made their way to Ark City entrances around the country, all of which were being guarded and patrolled by armed troops.

For those left behind, it was as bad as if the asteroid had already struck. The rioting that had been consuming many of the major cities grew worse. Although the president had enforced a strict mandatory curfew in the wake of the fires that had broken out around the country, he had not yet fully authorized the deployment of military personnel into American neighborhoods. That changed when homemade bombs began going off in Detroit, destroying buildings and killing innocent civilians. The day after, the president invoked the Insurrection Act, and tanks began rolling down the avenues of every city and suburb in America. While the initial response to the incursion was even more hostility, the sheer force of the enterprise was enough to quiet down the rioters. Within a few days, the fires died down, the bombs stopped detonating, and everyone looked up from the wreckage to nervously watch the skies.

At the offices of the PDCO, everyone worked tirelessly to adjust the Firelight plan to accommodate the changes outlined by Caitlin and her team on the asteroid. On the American side, Ned and Patricia would alternate in shifts operating the lightning bugs, assisted over in Moscow by Drs. Kuznetsov and Lebedev.

Finally, after long, tedious hours of preparation, they were ready.

"I've gotten word from Caitlin that they've got two craters already filled," said Sara to the team gathered around the control room. "So that's enough to get us going. They're back in the lander now and will head out in a few hours to begin on the third. But in the meantime, it's up to us."

"That's a lot of responsibility," said Ned.

"Tell me about it," said Patricia, who, having gotten her degree in robotics, had been selected as the first to fly the lightning bugs.

On one of the massive screens in front of them, the Russian scientists were live via videoconference.

"Good morning," Alex said to them. "Or, afternoon, in your case."

"We are pleased to be working with you," said Dr. Kuznetsov in clipped, cordial tones. "Now, if you are ready, we are bringing the Firelight platform online now. Are you reading us?"

"We've got her," said Ned. "We have control of the platform and the drones."

"OK," said Patricia. "Detaching bugs now."

Although it had been in orbit around Earth for generations, in preparation for this crucial mission, the Firelight platform had been relocated to a lunar orbit along Lagrange point L2. This point was one of five discovered by mathematicians Leonhard Euler and Joseph-Louis Lagrange where gravitational equilibrium between Earth, the Sun, and the Moon could be maintained. It was not the most stable of the Lagrange points, but it was a useful spot to keep a spacecraft parked temporarily and, as such, made for a good staging area for Firelight. Now suspended in a halo orbit above the lunar surface, the long-dormant platform slowly stirred back to life, releasing its tiny offspring like spores from a dying flower. They rose gently, emitting slight clouds of vapor for thrust as they made their way toward the approaching hulk of the Thresher.

"Bugs are online and looking good," Patricia said. "They should reach the asteroid in approximately two days."

Sara leaned in and watched the video feed from the bugs. There was nothing visible yet on the monitors, but she knew the asteroid was out there.

"Patricia," she said, "there's one other thing. Now, I don't want to rattle you, sweetheart, but there's a chance that the crew up there will be filling the craters with water ice when you get there."

Patricia looked over her shoulder at Sara. "What does that mean?"

"It shouldn't be a problem," Sara promised. "We've marked the craters that are already filled, and we'll hit them first. But, if we find ourselves in a position where we're aiming close to where they are, then we'll have to give them a little more time before we can fire the lasers. There's a delay for the video feed, and that means there's no guarantee that they won't get hit."

"And what happens if we have no choice?"

"Then hold your breath and pray you shoot better than you play volleyball," said Ned, referencing a former company event.

"Thank you, Ned," said Patricia, fixing her gaze on the video monitor and her attention on flying the bugs to their destination. "I feel so much better now."

◆ ◆ ◆

"Shaw!"

Caitlin's voice snapped him out of his daze, the end result of ceaseless hours of laborious work in a harsh environment. He blinked his eyes a few times and stretched his neck.

"Sorry, Boss," he said. "I'm getting a little punchy, I guess."

"It's all right," Caitlin said. "I know you're pulling a double out here, and we'll get you back in the rack soon. But for now, I need you on point. Just a little bit longer."

"You got it," he said, tossing her a small salute. Trudging his way back across the asteroid, Shaw returned to working the Noser's backhoe to break up more water ice.

"So did you like it?" Caitlin asked.

Shaw looked up at her. "What?" he replied.

"Being a teacher," she said. "Did you like it?"

"It had its upside," he said. "For every kid who wrote 'Shaw is a douche' on a desk, there'd occasionally be one who you could see was listening a little more intently. Taking notes instead of crumpling up the paper and throwing it when my back was turned. Coming up to me after class. After a while, I learned to try and speak to that one kid. The one light in the darkness."

"Caitlin, Shaw!" Vee's voice popped in their headsets.

"What is it?" answered Caitlin.

"You all better find a place to lie low," she said. "I'm getting word that they're about ready to fire down there. I'm pretty sure you'll want to be on the road before that happens."

"Probably right," said Caitlin. "We're just about finished here, then we'll stay put until the first round is done. Let's just hope that these little buggers make some kind of a difference."

"Difference or not," said Vee. "This is our last shot. If this plan doesn't work, then . . ."

"We're not there yet, Vee," Caitlin said.

"Fair enough," she said. "I'll let you know when the PDCO's ready to fire."

"Copy," Caitlin said before getting back to work. She looked up into the darkness of space and at Earth standing helplessly in their path.

We're not there yet, she thought. *But we're cutting it pretty damn close.*

Patricia Delgado's palms were sweating, and she felt as though the only sound she could hear was her own breathing. But she stayed focused and alert as she guided the lightning bugs to their destination. In Moscow, her partner, Dr. Kuznetsov, was also studying the path of the bugs intently, but he seemed much more relaxed and unconcerned. Even his delivery was laconic, making Patricia think of a recorded voice played back in slow motion.

"Dr. Delgado," he said, "I am reading the bugs in position above craters number one and two. Do you confirm?"

"Yes," she said, trying to shake the nerves from her voice. "Yes, I confirm."

"Very good, then," he said, and Patricia found herself thinking that, if she ever had trouble sleeping, this guy's voice would do the trick just fine. "When you are ready, we can begin firing the laser."

"Ready when you are, Doctor."

"On my mark," said Kuznetsov. "Three . . . two . . . one . . . fire . . ."

Patricia and Kuznetsov activated the laser weapons on their respective bugs, each one blasting the asteroid with 130 watts of intense heat. Rather than firing in a continuous stream of photons, the bugs' laser weapons were designed to pulse in sync with each other, delivering concentrated blasts.

◆ ◆ ◆

On the asteroid, as the lasers pounded the surface, the water ice inside the craters filled by Caitlin, Shaw, and Vee exploded, sending steam up into space with locomotive force. Although they were already a safe distance away, Caitlin and Shaw could see the craters' eruption and flinched. Although it made no sound in the vacuum of space, the geyser of steam funneling up from deep within the asteroid was nevertheless awe-inspiring. As it shot forth, the steam, ice, and rock particles caught the Sun's light, creating a shimmering display that reminded Caitlin of the massive fireworks her father would bring home during summers in Oregon, lighting them off and standing back as showers of white sparks burst into the hazy night sky. She wondered if, to the people of Earth, the Thresher now looked less like an asteroid and more like a comet. Caitlin looked over at Shaw and grabbed his shoulder.

"And you were just a *substitute* teacher?" she said.

"True greatness is never recognized in its time," he said.

Back on Earth, Patricia and Kuznetsov continued hammering the asteroid with the beams from the lightning bugs. Finally, after several more sustained bursts, they eased off the trigger and sat back, hoping that the bugs had done what they were supposed to do. A few tense seconds passed as Alex and Ned read the data that was coming through. Finally, Alex stood up.

"Thresher has been diverted by 1.6 centimeters per second!" he shouted triumphantly. "We moved it!"

On both sides of the screen, the two rooms erupted in cheers as hands were shaken, coworkers were hugged, and fists were pumped high into the air. Patricia sat back in her chair and breathed a huge sigh of relief. Even though this was only the beginning, the fact that it had worked once was enough for now. She looked at Kuznetsov over in Moscow, who was also sitting back in his chair. The formerly placid man looked exhausted and similarly relieved. She gave him a friendly smile.

"Was it good for you?"

CHAPTER THIRTY-ONE

For the next several days, things went smoothly, for the most part. The team on the asteroid worked around the clock, filling the craters with as much water ice as they could, while the two teams on Earth, Russian and American, continued beating the Thresher with lasers, forcing jets of steam upward and incrementally moving the asteroid. Technical glitches appeared from time to time, disruptions in communication between Russia and America, between Earth and the asteroid, even between Caitlin and her team. And the lightning bugs were stubborn and not always responsive. They were old, with a tendency to be ornery and uncooperative at times. Eventually, Patricia, Ned, Lebedev, and Kuznetsov learned to predict their movements and correct or compensate for their shortcomings. The four drone pilots began to feel as though they were strangely connected, not only with each other but with the bugs themselves. Whenever Patricia was relieved of her shift for some much-needed sleep, she found her dreams were in drone-vision, muddled and green, filled with jagged rocks and yawning craters.

Outside the world of the PDCO, the chaos had largely subsided, but there were new concerns to address. The news that the initial efforts had diverted the asteroid away from California was initially met with jubilation. However, the Thresher was still on course for Earth and likely to hit somewhere in the Pacific. Already, both Hawaii and Mexico were planning evacuation procedures as talks of tsunamis dominated the twenty-four-hour news cycle. Ecologists were also speaking up, asking the world to not just consider the human cost of an asteroid strike, but the countless plant, insect, and animal species that would become extinct if any of the islands in the Pacific were washed away. The island of Tonga, deemed by some to be far enough away from the potential impact zone to suffer the least amount of damage, briefly became a haven for residents of the South Pacific looking to escape disaster, its main port of Nuku'alofa soon bursting with ships large and small as everyone swarmed there to take refuge.

In addition to seeking safe haven on Earth, many people were trying to get off-world in search of asylum on the Moon. However, the available launch facilities were simply unable to meet the sheer volume of passengers seeking a way off the planet. Translunar docks across the world were choked with people demanding to be taken on board any ship, no matter how small. The fact that the majority of craft capable of making the trip had already left was immaterial. They believed that money would talk, even if no one was there to listen.

While some were interested in saving their own skins, there were others who were willing to volunteer their time and their crafts to travel to the asteroid and mount a rescue mission. Unfortunately, for those would-be Samaritans, the velocity at which the Thresher asteroid was traveling made such a mission a practical impossibility.

As fast as the world tried to process the potential impact, the game changed twice as fast. Every blast from the lightning bugs and every burst of steam from the asteroid's craters caused a shift in trajectory, which meant that an entirely new point of impact was created and the whole process started all over again. The erratic bursts of steam coupled with the lightning bugs' equally erratic blast patterns had now shifted the asteroid's course so that it would potentially strike somewhere near

Kiribati. But that would only be the beginning. The small island nation would be completely wiped out. However, the disaster zone would still spread far and wide, with effects being felt around the globe. In a revelation that was as surprising as it was disturbing, most of Australia would be affected by a massive electromagnetic pulse that would disrupt power in every city and village within fifteen hundred miles of the impact. Additionally, the atmospheres around all these areas would be ionized, rendering all communications, from cell phones to the Internet, completely useless. Shock waves would also be of grave concern, with ground shocks toppling bridges and buildings and tearing roadways apart and blast waves swatting airliners out of the sky and sending ships plummeting beneath the tides. Once the asteroid struck the ocean floor, it would send debris and evaporated seawater soaring up into the atmosphere. As that debris, now heated to around nine thousand degrees Fahrenheit, returned to Earth, fire would literally rain down on every area within the disaster zone. The debris that did not come back to Earth would remain in the upper atmosphere, where it would blot out the Sun in the affected areas. Over time, that debris would eventually cool, forming spherules that would pepper the surface of the planet like hailstones. Earthquakes would be felt as far away as China, and volcanoes would spontaneously erupt in Indonesia. The asteroid's impact with the seabed would also create a massive crater, which would displace millions of tons of water as it was refilled. That displacement would create tsunamis as high as 350 feet and traveling at nearly two hundred miles an hour. Coastal cities in the path of the waves would be obliterated, with the death toll potentially creeping up to the hundreds of millions. In short, while the impact of the Thresher would not be what scientists would call an "extinction-level event," there was no doubt in anyone's mind that it would mean the end of life as they knew it for generations.

◆ ◆ ◆

"All right!" Caitlin barked, startling both Shaw and Vee from sleep. "Let's get up and get moving. This is the final crater, so we're all going out there. We know what we're doing and we know how to do it. Let's make this last one count and hopefully get ourselves home."

Shaw and Vee struggled awake and began suiting up. As they did, Sara's voice popped into their ears.

"Woo-hoo!" she said, trying to bring some levity to a tense situation. "Everybody up, in there?"

"She's got a nice voice," said Shaw during the delay. "But I hope I never have to hear it again after today."

"What's up, Sara?" said Caitlin. "We're just suiting up to head out to the crater."

"Well then, I'm glad I caught you when I did," she said, "because I've got some news for you."

"Good news?" said Vee.

"When has she ever had good news?" said Shaw.

"OK, OK," said Caitlin, quieting them down with her hand. "What have you got for us?"

"Here's the thing," said Sara. "We're looking at everything we've done and everything we've got to do down here, and as you know, we've had a few hiccups along the way. Some of the bursts from the lightning bugs have been more powerful than others and some of the craters have generated more steam than others."

"Is she questioning our work ethic?" asked Shaw before being shushed by Caitlin.

"So," Sara continued, "this last shot has got to count for everything. Basically, it needs to be two times as strong on our end, and the crater has to be about two times as full on your end. Anything less and the asteroid won't miss Earth, even if they fire the nuke."

Caitlin, Shaw, and Vee looked at each other, and something passed between them. For a lot of other people, what Sara had just told them would be seen as crushing news. But not for them. They'd worked too long together and been through too much. They had all suffered losses, both here and at home. They wore the scars of hard work and hard luck, but in this moment, it came down to one simple truth: they were still a crew and there was still a job to be done. They shared a nod, and Caitlin got back on the mic.

"Sara?" she said.

"Yeah?"

"Don't worry," said Caitlin. "The crew of the *Space Invader* has got this."

Chapter Thirty-Two

They were almost done when the rover finally gave out.

"Dammit!" said Caitlin after her third attempt to get the vehicle's electric motors up and running again.

"What did you expect?" said Vee. "This thing wasn't meant to run as long or as hard as we ran it. I'm actually amazed it lasted up to this point."

Caitlin looked over at Shaw.

"What do you think?" she asked, breathing heavy from exertion. "Is it enough?"

"It's going to have to be," he said, "unless you want to start working by hand."

They looked out at the vast crater, now close to bursting with several tons of water ice. Caitlin shook her head.

"We've done everything we can do," she said. "No matter what happens, no one can say we didn't. Now let's call Sara and—"

"Guys!" Sara suddenly screamed into their headsets. "You've got to get out of there now! The lightning bugs are in place, and if we don't use them this instant, it's going to be too late."

"What's happened?" Caitlin asked.

"We're out of time," she said. "We'd hoped you'd be done and back before now. But we've got to act now or there's no way the asteroid can be diverted in time."

"Hold on, Sara," said Caitlin. "Our rover's given out. I don't know if we can make it back in time for—"

"You're out of options, Caitlin!" Sara yelled.

Realizing that Sara was serious, the three miners began to make their way back to the *Alley Oop*. Looking ahead of them at the vast landscape they had to navigate, Caitlin wondered if all their efforts had been in vain.

◆ ◆ ◆

Back on Earth, Patricia had steered the lightning bugs into orbit above the asteroid for what she hoped would be the final time. On the monitors, everyone could make out the blurry outline of Caitlin, Shaw, and Vee bouncing their way across the landscape back toward the lander.

"Holy God," said Alex. "They're still out there?"

"Lightning bugs are in position," said Patricia. "It's now or never."

"I concur," said Dr. Lebedev in Moscow. "We must act this instant if we stand any chance of diverting the asteroid."

Sara hesitated a moment, watching the three of them running for their lives.

"Sara?" said Alex. "We need—"

"Fire," she said, closing her eyes.

Patricia complied, hitting the button on the Firelight's control panel and activating the lightning bugs' onboard laser system.

On the asteroid, there was no beam of light, no sound effect that let the crew know that a massive pulse of concentrated energy was being sent down at double the force of its predecessors. The only clue they had was the monstrous funnel cloud of steam that began rocketing up from inside the crater, silently blasting its way up into space with unimaginable, nearly awe-inspiring force.

"Damn," Vee said, unable to help herself. "Now that's a lot of steam."

"Not good," yelled Shaw. "Not good at all!"

"Move! Move! Move!" Caitlin screamed. She began hop-walking back as, thanks to the incredible heat generated from the laser, a second crater of ice erupted, knocking them forward. If it wasn't for the RCS on their suits, all three miners would have been ejected off the asteroid's surface before they had a second to react.

As the shattered bits of the asteroid floated out into space, the crew noticed glints of reflective material slowly turning over and over, catching the sunlight like tiny diamonds.

"What the hell was that?" Caitlin screamed.

"Something very bad," Shaw said. "I think the bugs hit a vein of iron that must be running underneath us."

"Meaning?" Vee asked.

"Iron conducts heat," Shaw said. "This whole asteroid just became a bomb."

Back at the PDCO, the team was frantically trying to decipher what was happening. Between the video delay, the disruption from the lasers, and the steam blasting everywhere, it was next to impossible to see anything. Patricia found herself flying blind, unsure of what to do.

"Keep hitting the asteroid," said Sara. "We can't afford not to."

"But what about the crew?" she asked. "I can't see a damn thing."

"Caitlin Taggart has been in worse scrapes than this," she said.

Alex shot her a baffled look. "Really?" he asked.

"OK, you know what I mean," said Sara. "This isn't the time! Hit it again, Patricia! Now!"

◆ ◆ ◆

Battered again and again by the bugs' lasers, the Thresher's final crater continued to disgorge its contents, ejecting rock, ice, and steam off the surface and slowly forcing the asteroid off its course. Meanwhile, and unbeknownst to the people back on Earth, the heat blasting the subterranean vein of iron was causing the asteroid to buck and heave from multiple eruptions. In the distance, Caitlin could see the *Alley Oop* as they drew closer.

"Push it, everyone, push it!" she cried out. "Almost there!"

"We're going to make it!" said Shaw. "We're going to—"

Before he could finish his thought, Shaw was struck by an errant pulse from one of the bugs' lasers. He didn't have time to think or react. There was only a brief flash of heat and Shaw was cosmic dust.

"No!" Caitlin shouted.

Caitlin and Vee couldn't take more than a second to process what had happened. The Thresher was still vomiting steam and rock particles violently into space, and as the heat propagated across the surface, other craters decided to join in the cacophony, forming jets of sublimated ice that popped up as the two bounced frantically across the asteroid. As the lander was just within reach, one of the rogue jets caught Vee in its wake and pushed her up and off the rock so fiercely that it forced her left leg behind her at an impossible angle. Vee didn't even need to speak. The anguished look on Vee's face told Caitlin all she needed to know. Before Vee could meet the same fate as Diaz, Caitlin reached out and grabbed for her, yanking her back down by using the thrust from her own suit. They crashed back down to the surface.

"Oh no you don't," she said, pulling Vee close. "Not you too!"

Vee ordinarily would have had a witty comeback, but the agony from her injured leg had rendered her unable to speak. Her face was a mask of pain, and no sound came from behind her clenched teeth, even as she tried to speak. Caitlin threw her friend's arm over her shoulder and continued to hop-walk across the asteroid, plumes of steam punching up through the ground alongside every step. Another jolt and the two lost their footing. Were it not for the jets in their suits, they would have been lost to the void.

"We've got to get out of here now," Caitlin told Vee. "Or you and I are going to be permanent residents."

Her voice was weak, but Vee spoke nonetheless.

"Leave," she said, her voice ragged and breathless. "Just leave me here."

As the asteroid was coming apart around them in an explosion of heat and steam, Caitlin froze.

◆ ◆ ◆

"What is it?" Davidowitz asks.

"Roarke's been tagged," says Caitlin, frantically racing over to the fallen soldier, who's on the floor clawing at her bleeding neck.

"Must've gotten caught in the cross fire," says Davidowitz.

"Looks that way," says Caitlin as she tries to wrap the wound as best she can. "She's not going to last long. We've got to get her out of here."

"Roger that," Davidowitz says as Ben races in.

"We've got to move," he says. "Enders are locked on our position. They're headed right for us."

He looks down at Roarke, bleeding helplessly in Caitlin's arms.

"Oh shit," he says. Caitlin nods.

"Yeah," she says. "You're right. We've got to move."

With bullets shredding the air around them, Caitlin and Ben carry Roarke out into the street where a Bradley Fighting Vehicle lies discarded outside the safehouse. They climb in with Ben behind the wheel. Davidowitz mounts the M242.

"Let's go, Ben!" Caitlin shouts. "Drive it like you stole it!"

Ben forces the BFV into gear, and they career through the wreckage of the city.

"Enders coming up fast!" shouts Davidowitz, pointing to the cars streaking their way up the street, undoubtedly loaded with explosives.

"Hit 'em with the sabots!" Caitlin yells back, and Davidowitz gladly obliges. Sabot rounds, rather than exploding on contact, punch through the target using mass and velocity, more like an arrow than a bullet.

Davidowitz stops the Enders in their tracks with round after round from the M242 as the heat generated by the piercing of armor creates a pressure wave, sending fragments of metal everywhere.

Inside the BFV, Caitlin grabs a walkie to call in the air strike.

"Echo Twelve to Viper Strike actual, requesting air strike on target five hundred meters from current position! Danger close!"

"Viper Strike actual to Echo Twelve," comes the voice over the comm. "Copy that. Splash in thirty seconds."

"Let's move it, Ben," Caitlin screams. "This place is going to be a big-ass hole in about thirty seconds."

They race out of the city, pulverizing insurgent vehicles as they do. Overhead, they hear the approaching missile strike, a roar of displaced air that grows louder until it bursts as the incoming rocket pulverizes the compound. Rubble and debris scatter everywhere, and the force of the shock wave nearly rocks the Bradley off its wheels. Inside, Caitlin holds Roarke's head in her lap, trying to keep her stable. She can feel the life draining out of her.

"Hang on, Roarke," says Caitlin. "Stay with me, kid. You're going to make it, OK? Roarke? Roarke!"

Roarke tries to say something, but the sound that comes out of her damaged throat is close to inaudible. Caitlin leans in closer, cradling Roarke gently.

"What?" she asks softly. "What is it?"

"Emily," Roarke says as her voice grows faint. "My name is Emily."

Chapter Thirty-Three

In the White House Situation Room, the president and his staff continued to monitor the activity on the asteroid closely, as they had for the past six days. The tension grew with each passing hour as everyone present considered how much was at stake in the operation and what the outcome would be if it failed. As the lightning bugs went to work and the steam clouds generated by the displaced water ice began to erupt, the video transmission from the asteroid was suddenly interrupted.

"What just happened?" asked the president.

"We're not sure," said Bob Lee, the president's science advisor. "It seems we have a loss of signal. I'm reaching out to the team at the PDCO to find out why and see if I can get a situation report."

As Lee left the room to assess the situation on the asteroid, Alan Kittredge leaned in to address the president, his face serious.

"Mr. President," he said in an ominous tone, "we need to seriously consider the nuclear option."

The president hesitated, trying to take in the sheer weight of what was being asked of him. For the first time since he considered running for president, he finally felt he understood the great and terrible power of the office. It was the power to move nations, to change the course of events, and to shape history. But it was also the power to make decisions, which if wrong by even a small margin, could impact thousands if not millions of lives. It was a power he no longer wanted and perhaps was never qualified to wield in the first place. But, want it or not, for the time being, it was his to wield.

He sighed and rubbed his temples.

"Mr. President . . ."

"How long until the asteroid reaches the point of no return?"

"A couple of hours, sir," said Kittredge. "But in this instance, with everything that needs to happen, even hours aren't enough. We must act quickly, or we are facing a monumental catastrophe."

"This isn't a decision I can just make on the spot, Alan," the president said.

"With all due respect, sir," Kittredge replied, "I believe that on-the-spot decisions are what define this office."

"Do you know I'll be the first president to deploy a nuclear weapon since Truman?" he argued. "I need to have all the information before I can make that choice."

"Truman knew the consequences of his actions," said Kittredge. "And, again sir, I say this with respect, I believe he knew the consequences of inaction as well."

The president paused again, looking at the screen in front of him. He squinted at the static, as though by scrutinizing the pattern he could divine the answer to his problem. He knew already how history would judge him. The question in front of him now was could he temper that judgment even slightly by making his last act in office count for something?

"I'm giving them more time," he said at last.

"Mr. President, please . . . ," began Kittredge.

"I know what you're saying, Alan," said the president. "But I'm not prepared to launch a weapon with that kind of destructive power until we're absolutely certain that this crew has failed."

"You're taking an incredible gamble," Kittredge said. "One that may have grave consequences for the planet."

"I understand that," the president said. "And I'm willing to accept those—"

Dr. Lee burst back into the Situation Room.

"I've just gotten off the phone with the PDCO," he said. "They've lost contact with the crew on the asteroid. They're trying to track its trajectory now, but it's too soon to know if they successfully diverted it before it reached the limit."

Almost in unison, every head in the room turned to the president. At first, he felt ill, but then that sickly feeling was replaced with a kind of resolve. He took a breath and looked hard at Alan Kittredge.

"Get on the line with the United States Strategic Command," he said. "Let them know we're deploying the nuke."

Although Earth was still intact, on the Thresher it was the end of the world. The asteroid continued to be rocked by the force of the blasts from the lightning bugs and the resultant steam. *Shaw's plan worked like a dream,* Caitlin thought, *maybe even better than expected.* Caitlin looked at the chaos around her and then down at her wounded friend.

"Sorry, honey," she said. "You don't get to play the martyr today."

She pulled Vee up, draping her arm around her shoulders, and continued to hop-walk back to the lander as the asteroid shook and burst around her. Arriving at the *Alley Oop*, she forced open the hatch and hoisted Vee inside. Once she'd climbed in herself, she helped Vee into one of the seats and out of her suit. Vee screamed in pain as she did and Caitlin apologized profusely, assuring her friend that it had to be done. When Vee's EMU suit was off, Caitlin took a look at her leg.

"The good news?" she said. "It isn't broken. Your kneecap is just dislocated. The bad news? I'm going to have to try and pop it back into place. And you're not going to like me for it. Ordinarily, I'd leave this to a specialist for fear of tearing tendons and whatnot. But we've got a long way to go, and you've got to be as close to one hundred percent as I can get you, OK?"

As she talked, the asteroid was rocked by more explosions of steam.

Jesus, can they give it a rest?

"Just do what you've got to do," said Vee.

"All right," said Caitlin. "Straighten out your leg for me and sit up."

Vee did as Caitlin had asked, and trying to work fast, Caitlin grabbed the side of her friend's knee and slowly began to slide the kneecap back into place. Vee gasped sharply as Caitlin worked, squeezing her eyes shut and clenching her teeth.

"I know," Caitlin said. "Kind of redefines the word 'pain,' doesn't it?"

"Oh yeah," said Vee, her eyes still closed.

"Just don't pass out on me, OK?" Caitlin said. "I'm gonna need you to get us home."

A few more attempts at moving the kneecap, each of which obviously sent the needle on Vee's internal pain meter well into the red, and it was back in.

"There," Caitlin said, giving the injured knee a gentle pat. "You're not going to be able to put much weight on it for now, but it'll do until we get you home. Now let's try and find you some kind of brace."

Searching around the cabin of the *Alley Oop*, Caitlin sighed in relief as she found the perfect solution. No matter how advanced human society became, she thought, the need for duct tape would remain eternal. She scrambled for the med kit. Fumbling it open, she dug through the box before she came across what she was looking for, a morphine tab. Sometimes the old ways were still the best. Clambering back over to Vee, she handed the tab to her friend and began wrapping her knee with the tape.

"Here," Caitlin said, as Vee began to squirm in pain from the wrapping. "Put half under your tongue. It will help with the pain but still keep you alert enough to help me fly this thing home."

Vee nodded and grabbed half the tab and slid it into her mouth, where it dissolved instantly under her tongue. Almost immediately, her face changed as the pain drained away. Caitlin patted Vee on the shoulder.

"There we go," she said. "Now sit tight while I try and get us out of here."

"Caitlin?" Sara said suddenly on the *Tamarisk*'s comm. "Caitlin, are you there?"

"Yeah," said Caitlin. "I'm here and we're about to take off."

"Thank God!" said Sara. "We thought you were all dead."

"No," said Caitlin, thinking of Shaw. "Not all of us."

"If you're planning on getting out of there, you'd better do it now."

"I know," said Caitlin. "The asteroid is really rocking . . ."

"It's about to get a lot worse," Sara said. "The president has given the order to deploy the nuclear warhead. It's about to launch!"

Chapter Thirty-Four

After the president had officially authorized the use of the nuclear weapon, things began moving very fast. Since they were in the White House, there was no need for his military aide to produce the Football, the case that traveled with the president at all times and contained the nuclear launch codes as well as the authentication codes for the nation's entire nuclear arsenal. In addition, given that this was a special set of circumstances, the president was not required to review the attack options, which were specific orders designated for specific targets. Instead, he needed only the Gold Codes, a series of numbers that identified the president as commander in chief and allowed him to authenticate a nuclear launch. The codes changed daily, and as such the president was required to memorize his personal number. The codes were kept on a small plastic card called the Biscuit, which the president was required to keep on his or her person at all times. For all the security around the Football, precautions regarding the Biscuit were somewhat less stringent. When President Reagan was nearly assassinated by John Hinckley in 1981, his clothes and personal possessions were taken by the hospital staff before surgery. It was only hours later that his staff found the Biscuit tossed into a bag with the rest of his items. There were also rumors that Bill Clinton had misplaced the Biscuit during the last days of his presidency in 2000.

Now, with the launch of the largest nuclear weapon ever built about to take place on his watch, the president reached into his pocket and withdrew the Biscuit. He snapped the card's plastic covering in two, removing it and unveiling the list of codes. Scanning down the list, he found and identified his code to Roger Bennett, the chairman of the Joint Chiefs of Staff. Bennett nodded, acknowledging the president's authentication, then asked for confirmation of his order.

"I give the order to deploy," said the president.

"Under the two-man rule, the order to deploy must be confirmed," said Bennett.

At this point, Alan Kittredge, who as secretary of defense formed the other half of the two-man unit known as the National Command Authority, stepped forward. He confirmed his name and title and authenticated his own code on the Biscuit. Although he had been advocating for this course of action, now that it was upon him he looked green and uneasy, the pallor of someone who has helped to set in motion events whose consequences he only partially understood. Once his code was confirmed, the order to deploy was relayed to the National Military Command Center at the Pentagon and then on to the crew of the missile silo.

More than two hundred feet below the Iowa pastureland, the crew of the missile silo enacted a procedure that had gone unchanged for more than a century. The technology had become more sophisticated, but the steps needed before a nuclear missile could be launched remained the same.

Over the silo's primary alerting system, the crew received an Emergency Action Message, authorizing the use of nuclear weapons. The EAM squawked out a coded message using numbers and letters from the NATO alphabet, which two crew members were then required to take down. After receiving the message and writing it in their separate notebooks, both men immediately compared what they had written. The codes matched, which meant the message was authentic. From this point on, training kicked in and the two were focused only on the job that needed to be done.

They raced over to the safe at the far end of the silo's command center, retrieving the authenticator cards they would need to further verify the message's authenticity. Once they had that verification, the two inserted their launch keys. The keys were placed on two different control panels spaced far enough apart that it would be impossible for one person to turn them simultaneously. This had to be a two-person operation, and both had to be completely in agreement. The missile commander turned to his deputy.

"On my mark," he said, his face completely neutral. "Three . . . two . . . one . . . turn keys."

Both men turned their keys at once, and the panel lit up with the green message light: "READY TO LAUNCH."

The keys were spring-loaded and had to be held for five seconds before the launch could be completed. After five seconds, the display flared again with a second message: "LAUNCH ENABLED."

Inside the silo, sunlight filtered in as the massive overhead door was retracted. The missile slowly began to smolder as power was transferred from the silo to the missile's internal systems. The internal guidance systems were then activated, directing the weapon toward the asteroid. A few seconds later, the main engine kicked in and fire burst from the missile's massive engines, slowly pushing it upward into the morning sky.

In the White House, Kittredge received confirmation from Strategic Command.

"Launch confirmed, sir," he said.

The president took a seat and folded his hands involuntarily in prayer. "If I'm right, let me be right," he said quietly. "And if I'm wrong, let me be forgiven."

Chapter Thirty-Five

"He what?" Caitlin shouted.

"He's launching the Thunderclap!" said Sara. "It's probably on its way to you now."

"Jesus Christ," Caitlin muttered to herself. "Could just one thing go right on this mission?"

"You need to get out of there now!"

"I'm working on it, I'm working on it!" shouted Caitlin. She turned to Vee.

"You ready to get out of here?"

Vee smiled and nodded weakly.

"Then let's do it," said Caitlin. "Sara, we're preparing for launch. We will try and contact you when we're off this rock."

"Good luck," said Sara. "And God bless . . ."

Caitlin started the launch cycle, pressing screens and swiping madly as she prepped the ship for takeoff.

"How are you feeling?" Caitlin asked Vee. "Are you clearheaded enough to give me a hand?"

"I think so," Vee said. "The morphine's keeping the pain at bay for now. But what about that pyro problem? Are you sure you fixed it?"

"I think so," said Caitlin. "I'm pulling power from some other systems long enough to push a sufficient charge through the separation system to hopefully fire the blade."

"What other systems?"

"Guidance and navigation, life support . . ."

"Life support?"

"It's just until we're off the surface," Caitlin said. "Then everything should even out."

"OK," said Vee. "But will it work?"

"We'll find out when we launch."

"Wonderful," Vee said.

The two women ran through the prelaunch checklist as quickly as they could, the asteroid heaving around them.

"Valentine," Vee said suddenly, her eyes not leaving the control panel.

"What?"

"Valentine," she said again. "That's my name. Valentine."

Caitlin gave her friend a look. "That's not so bad," she said. "The way you kept it hidden, I thought it was going to be much, much worse."

"It was pretty bad to me," said Vee. "Got teased about it every day in middle school. I know you know what that's like."

"I do," said Caitlin, hearing an echo of "Moon girl" rebound in her memory.

"Anyway, figured if I'm going to die, I may as well die without any secrets."

"You're not going to die," said Caitlin, continuing to prepare the *Alley Oop*. "Ascent engine is armed. Get ready . . ."

"What about you?" said Vee. "What's your big secret?"

"Oh," Caitlin said absently, still focused on the tasks in front of her. "I was a virgin until I was twenty-five."

Vee leaned back against her headrest. "Shoot," she said, closing her eyes. "Some secret. I could have told you that."

"Nice," said Caitlin. "Hold on. In three . . . two . . . one . . . ignite!"

Caitlin hit the switch, and all the lights inside the cabin dimmed as available power was funneled into the umbilical severance system.

There was a hollow bursting sound as, in an instant, the pyros fired and the wires tethering the two stages were severed. For a moment, the *Alley Oop* sank down instead of up. Vee and Caitlin had a second to look at each other in terror before the engine ignited fully and the lander sprang upward, now fully free of its moorings. In one swift motion, like a shot put hurled from the hand of an invisible giant, the *Alley Oop* burst up and away from the surface of the Thresher for the last time.

◆ ◆ ◆

"Are they away?" asked Alex.

"Yeah," Sara said, "I think so."

"Well that's some good news. And here's some more."

He handed Sara a printout, grinning widely.

"The force from the last burst, combined with everything we've been doing over the past several days, has diverted the asteroid by a velocity of about twelve centimeters per second! We did it!"

Alex looked at Sara's stricken face and tilted his head slightly in confusion.

"Um, the way I played it out in my head, this was the part where you jumped up and down in excitement, maybe cheered a little bit," he said. "Did a dance, you know? I wouldn't even have said no to a hug . . ."

"Haven't you heard?" she asked him.

"No," he said. "I've had my head down trying to get these numbers back from the asteroid. What's going on?"

"The president," Sara said. "He's launched the Thunderclap. It's on its way to the asteroid now."

Alex's expression changed so that it matched Sara's harried face.

"We've got to call the White House," he said.

In the Situation Room, the president and his advisors were watching the Thunderclap pull up and away from the silo when Dr. Lee came bursting in, red-faced and panicked.

"The PDCO just called!" he said. "The asteroid has been diverted. It's going to skip harmlessly off the atmosphere!"

"My God," said the president. "We've got to abort the missile strike."

"We can't do that, sir," said Kittredge. "It doesn't work that way."

"What do you mean?" the president asked. "You don't have some button or an abort code? Something that stops it cold or causes it to self-destruct?"

"Maybe in movies, sir," said Kittredge. "But only an insane person would actually put something like that in a nuclear missile. What if the abort codes fell into the hands of the enemy?"

"So what are our options?"

"I'm afraid we don't have any," said Kittredge. "The missile will detonate when it reaches the designated altitude. We can only hope now that the effects will be relatively harmless. All space stations and functional orbital platforms have been alerted and have EMP countermeasures in place, and all transit from Earth has been temporarily suspended."

"What about the asteroid?" asked Lee. Everyone turned to look at him.

"Come again?" asked the president.

"The asteroid," Lee repeated. "Yes, it's been diverted for now. But if the nuke detonates on the wrong side of the asteroid, the force of the blast could shift its course again, sending it right back into our atmosphere."

"Explain it to us like we're six-year-olds, Dr. Lee," said Kittredge. "How exactly can that happen after everything we've done?"

"It's *because* of everything we've done," Lee said. "The heat from the lightning bugs and all the discharged steam from the craters has resulted in a ton of material being ablated from the asteroid's surface. It's now belching out rock, water vapor, and ice particles as it moves by us. All of those are enough to confuse the missile's radar system and cause it to detonate too early or too late. And if that happens, there is a chance it will send the Thresher back to Earth."

"Jesus Christ," said the president. "What I wouldn't give to be back in Alabama right now . . ."

"I may have a solution," Lee said. "Secretary Kittredge is right. The missile doesn't have an abort code or fail-safe button, but that doesn't mean we can't create one."

"Go on," the president said.

"Every missile is equipped with an internal clock," said Lee. "The clock specifies when each ascent engine should ignite and cut off. If we can hack into that clock, we can reset it."

"Reset it?" asked the president. "What the hell will that do?"

"We can trick it, Mr. President. The missile is set to ignite the second stage four minutes from now. If we can reset the clock and make it think that it's later, we can trick it into firing three minutes from now while the first stage is still attached."

"Destroy the missile in flight?" the president said. "Won't that set off the nuke?"

"I'm not going to lie to you, Mr. President. I'm not entirely certain," Lee said, a look of honesty on his face. "If the explosion is hot enough or powerful enough, it definitely could. But the chances are unlikely. Back in the twentieth century, a Titan missile exploded in its silo in Arkansas and nothing happened, so . . . fingers crossed, Mr. President."

"So, just so I'm clear on what's being pitched here, you're talking about a possible nuclear explosion in the upper atmosphere of the planet?" the president asked. "Won't that be just as disastrous?"

"Not necessarily," Kittredge opined. "It's been done before. During the First Cold War in the 1960s, American bombers detonated a series of nuclear bombs about two hundred and fifty miles above the planet in what they called fishbowl events. It'll play hell with the electronics on the surface, but there's nothing we can do about that I'm afraid."

"Can we warn anyone?" the president said. "Cities? Towns? First responders?"

"We're talking minutes, sir," said Lee. "Call whoever you can in that time."

The president shot Secretary of State Katz a look.

"On it," she said, and ran from the room.

"Dr. Lee," said the president. "Do whatever you have to do."

Lee nodded and turned to Kittredge.

"Mr. Secretary," he asked, "do I have your permission to hack into the missile's guidance system and reset the clock?"

Kittredge looked surprised that Lee would even bother to ask.

"Well, hell yes you do!" he sputtered. "What are you even asking me for?"

"Just trying to go by the book," said Lee, opening his holopad and starting to punch the keys. "I don't want to die in ADX Florence because I neglected to follow protocol."

His fingers moving like a virtuoso musician, Lee quickly hacked into the missile's guidance system. Kittredge watched him, a somewhat disconcerted look on his face.

"You can do this from a holopad?"

Lee gave him a sideways glance. "If more people knew what they could do from a holopad, this world would be far less safe," he said. "OK, I'm in! All right, looks like the mission clock is at four minutes . . . so let's just move things up a bit . . ."

With a few deft keystrokes, Lee reset the missile's clock, deceiving the onboard guidance systems into believing they were farther into the launch than they actually were. On the other side of the world, where it had already traveled in preparation for its rendezvous with the Thresher, the Thunderclap responded to its new instructions perfectly. The second stage began to fire while coupled to the still-burning first stage. The reaction was almost instantaneous, with heat and liquid fuel erupting out from the sides of the two attached stages. The fire raced up the side of the missile. When it could no longer withstand the sundering forces, the Thunderclap missile exploded in a spectacular fireball. Unfortunately, the warhead, heated by the extreme temperatures from the burning ascent stages, also ignited and detonated in an airburst approximately eighty miles above Papua New Guinea. Residents there, as well as throughout Indonesia and parts of Australia, were immediately plunged into blackness as the EMP generated by the explosion wreaked havoc with every electrical system, from cell phones to onboard computer systems in their cars. In exchange for the inconvenience, they were rewarded with an incredible light display as the weapon's charged particles mingled with the planet's magnetic field, creating auroras for hundreds of miles.

Back at the PDCO, Sara sat in her office with her hands folded, waiting to hear news from either Caitlin or the White House. She thought about everything that had happened since she first received that distress call from Caitlin Taggart. In some ways, she wondered if she was the same person. She had spent so much of the last decade just looking forward, not daring a glance back over her shoulder. After college, Sara had vowed that she would never let anyone come between her and her goals again. And over the years, she had held fast to that vow. It had served her well. But since the stranded crew on the asteroid had first called to her, things had changed. Suddenly she understood what Caitlin had said about how she'd felt when her daughter was born. There wasn't time to think about yourself or your own problems, because someone was depending on you to act. In some ways, Caitlin Taggart had given Sara her life back. She supposed she loved her for that, and she hoped she'd get the chance to thank her in person.

As Sara contemplated these things, Alex came into her office with a relieved expression on his face.

"What've you got?" Sara asked.

"They were able to detonate the missile in the upper atmosphere," he said. "Not an ideal solution, and the EMP screwed up a lot of lives in the southern hemisphere, but the trajectory of the Thresher wasn't affected. It's still going to miss us."

He looked at Sara's face as he relayed this news and suddenly looked annoyed.

"You know," he said, "if this is how you react to good news, I'm just going to start coming in with bad news and see how that plays out."

"The EMP," Sara said. "Anything within the blast radius not armed with countermeasures will be completely disabled, right?"

"That's how I've been led to believe they work, yes."

"Caitlin and Vee are still in the *Alley Oop*."

Chapter Thirty-Six

As the world was trying to avoid engineering its own destruction, Caitlin and Vee continued their steady course back to Earth aboard the *Alley Oop*. While the threat of being arrested for illegally entering Terran space was no longer an option, they still had no guarantee that their ship could survive reentry. So far, Shaw's grim prediction that, without the protection of the Mylar insulation, the *Tamarisk* would be seared by the Sun's light had not come to pass. However, there was still the heat shield to contend with. With that in mind and with them growing closer and closer to Earth, Caitlin was trying to hail someone from ICC to see if they could be towed in.

No response.

"This is escape lander *Alley Oop* calling ICC control, can anyone hear me?"

"It doesn't sound like anyone's listening," said Vee.

"I'm thinking everyone's hunkered down because of that big damn missile that the president launched," Caitlin said. "Or it could be something on our end. Maybe the onboard communication system has finally given out. I doubt this ship was designed to take this kind of pounding. Or last for as long as it has."

"You could be right," Vee mused. "Or it could just be that legal or illegal, no one is interested in coming out for a capsule carrying a pair of immigrants."

"Sad but true," Caitlin agreed. "Whatever the case is, it doesn't paint a very rosy picture for our return home. We're gonna have to do this the old-fashioned way. Let's start the reentry cycle and see if we can—"

Before Caitlin could finish her sentence, everything on board the *Alley Oop* blinked out at once, leaving them in darkness save for the sunlight reflected into the viewports as well as the light from Earth. Shocked and confused by what had just happened, they both made their way to the windows, Vee with considerable effort, and looked out to see if they could divine what had happened. Looking down, they could make out ribbons of green and blue unfurling in serpentine lines across the planet's atmosphere.

"What is that?" Vee wondered. "The aurora borealis?"

Caitlin shook her head. "No," she said. "We're over the South Pacific. I think we're looking at the aftereffects of the president's new toy."

"The nuke?" said Vee. "So that was an EMP that just hit us."

"Looks that way," said Caitlin. "Which means we're dead in the water and no one knows we're out here. And with all our systems dead, life support is going to give out. On top of that, thanks to the ionization in the atmosphere, all our communications are now officially dead and gone."

"That's all very bad," agreed Vee. "But here's something worse. We're coming up on the atmosphere, but we're still upside down relative to Earth, right?"

"Right," said Caitlin, slowly getting the picture.

"Without thrusters to turn us over or the guidance computer to tell the ship when to do it, we're going to enter the atmosphere on the opposite side of the ship's heat shield."

"Which means that we're going to burn up in about thirty minutes," said Caitlin.

"Uh-huh. If that."

"OK," said Caitlin, starting to assess options.

"We could always bail out," said Vee.

"Are you kidding?"

"Half kidding," Vee said. "Yuri Gagarin did it. He never actually landed the *Vostok 1* spacecraft back in 1961. He ejected from the ship at twenty-three thousand feet and parachuted to Earth."

"Well, if it's all the same to you," said Caitlin, "I'd rather explore alternatives."

Vee rubbed her temples as though trying to draw an idea to the surface. Then an idea dramatically hit Caitlin.

"You're gonna hate me for this," she told Vee, "but I'm gonna need you to get into your EMU suit and come outside with me."

"What are we going to do?" asked Vee, giving her a tentative look.

"Whatever we can."

Around the world, the mood was one of triumph and euphoria at having avoided annihilation. In nearly every city, all work had ceased and the streets were teeming with revelers celebrating the Thresher's near miss.

In the areas affected by the nuclear blast's electromagnetic pulse, relief was swift and came from a variety of sources. The president sent in everyone from the Red Cross to FEMA to the Peace Corps, and other nations joined the call as well, extending a hand in whatever way they could. There was still a lot of political maneuvering to be done, given the fact that the US president had detonated a nuclear weapon over Oceanian airspace. The circumstances surrounding the launch and the diversion of the asteroid meant that government officials weren't prepared to go to war over the incident, but they did expect the president to roll up his sleeves and clean up the mess he'd had a hand in making, something he was more than willing to do. For him, it was a matter of atonement.

The only thing left for him to do was address the nation. However, he had insisted on waiting until he knew the fates of the two women who had escaped the asteroid.

"I want to know if I need to welcome them home as heroes or honor them as martyrs," he told his staff.

Unfortunately, no answer was yet forthcoming and the news from the PDCO was grim. No one had heard from the *Alley Oop* in more than six hours.

◆ ◆ ◆

In the time it took for Vee and Caitlin to get into their EMU suits, the *Alley Oop* had come down even farther. The two women had a flicker of hope when the ship's instrumentation came back on, but those hopes were dashed when they saw that the reentry protocols had been wiped from the hard drive as a result of the EMP.

"Jesus," Vee said when she took stock of this new development. "How much did Ross spend on this bucket anyway?"

"Less than he did on his wardrobe, I can promise you that," said Caitlin.

With no reentry protocol and the guidance system also failing, they had no choice but to go with Caitlin's plan. She and Vee would have to make their way to the outside of the *Alley Oop* and tether themselves to the ship's hull. After that, Caitlin said they could attempt to use the thrusters in their suits' onboard RCS to try to generate enough force to turn the ship over. Whether the two women could do that before they entered the atmosphere or even do it at all was a legitimate concern.

With both of them ready, Caitlin depressurized the ship and opened the hatch. Moving gently so as not to jostle her knee, Vee drifted out into space and anchored herself to the ship's hull, slowly beginning to work her way back along the outside of the *Alley Oop*. Caitlin pushed her way up and out of the lander and tethered herself before taking a moment to look around her. Below, Earth spread out like an incredible, majestic tapestry. The green and brown of the continents slid into the deep blue of the oceans as white clouds floated above them. In all her time spent in space, she'd never actually taken the time to appreciate what her home world looked like from up above, so small and helpless, a glass ornament suspended above a yawning black abyss.

"Now just remember, we have to be careful out here," warned Caitlin. "Material that they blasted off from the asteroid could still be floating around. It could come up from anywhere and tag us before we know it."

"I'll be sure to duck," Vee promised.

Caitlin fired the jets on her suit gently, moving aft until she'd reached the tail end of the craft, where Vee was already waiting. Once Caitlin was there, she and Vee grabbed on and positioned themselves to ensure the best possible thrust.

"OK, girl," Vee said to Caitlin. "This is your show."

"You ready to do this?" Caitlin asked.

"Let's go," Vee said. "Starting thrusters now."

With precise, gradual movements, the two women began firing the thrusters on their suits, first to port, then starboard, then forward and aft. Whatever direction Caitlin and Vee needed the ship to move in at that moment, they were able to guide it with expertly timed jets of exhaust. Little by little, as both women worked, the *Alley Oop* began to respond. It was stubborn, for sure, but it was beginning to come around. Vee shouted triumphantly.

"Ha ha!" she exulted. "She's starting to give up the fight. I knew we'd get her to turn around! I knew we—"

Before she could finish, a small shower of micrometeorites, no doubt remnants of rock broken from the Thresher, collided with Vee, slicing through her tether and knocking her off the *Alley Oop*. The larger pieces were followed by a school of smaller rocks that peppered the hull of the ship like bullet hits, many of them punching through and damaging the craft irreparably. It was only through sheer luck that one of them hadn't torn through Caitlin herself. She pulled her way along the *Alley Oop*, using the damaged craft as a makeshift shield against the barrage of micrometeorites and scrabbled her way back inside, calling for Vee over her headset mic.

"Vee?" she asked, then asked again, this time yelling her name. *"Vee!"*

There was only static in response. Frantically, Caitlin looked out of the viewport and saw a sight that made her stomach turn. Vee turning helplessly end over end as she tumbled away from the ship and into Earth's atmosphere.

"No!" she screamed. "*No*, God, please no!"

Grief, anger, and rage swarmed up inside her like a cloud of angry hornets. She pounded the damaged instrument panel, the ceiling, the walls, anything that her fists could get to in her frenzy, screaming and cursing as she did. When the fight had left her, she floated there helpless and alone, crying for her friend and at the notion that she had now completely failed. Her crew was gone. She would never see Emily again. Never set foot on her home planet again. All her efforts, everything she had tried to do, it all had led to this, and it had all been for nothing. The unfairness of it all struck her again and again like waves, crashing over her and threatening to drag her out in their merciless undertow.

In the second before the grief consumed her, Caitlin had a flash. She thought of late nights, skinned knees, first thunderstorms, and the smell of the street after a summer rainfall. She thought of playing princess, playing doctor, playing soldier, playing at being whoever you wanted to be, even if it wasn't something real. She thought of flashlight tag in the summer, sleeping beneath too many blankets in the winter. Of wood smoke and firelight and old stories that were retold and new stories that were made up on the spot. Of favorite games and new games that made no sense but existed only because they made you laugh. She thought of learning how to ride a bike, her father holding the seat until she was ready and then letting her go, standing at the end of the street as she rode a little farther away. She thought of all these things in an instant, a lifetime of memories passing in a warm glow.

She thought of Emily. And she knew she wasn't done yet.

Just then, the ship's master alarm began to blare and the calm, impassive female voice of the main computer began speaking, repeating the same announcement over and over.

"Danger. Proximity alert. Danger. Proximity alert."

Caitlin looked out of the viewport and saw what the computer was talking about. She was getting dangerously close to Earth. She had to act before the ship entered the atmosphere. If she didn't do something, anything, she was going to be incinerated in a matter of minutes. She recalled sitting in Ross's office in what felt like another lifetime, and hearing him talk about a "zero-limit" option. It didn't make sense to her at the time, but she thought that, if anyone on Earth, the Moon, or anywhere in between was at the so-called zero limit, it had to be her.

Screw it.

Caitlin floated to the back of the ship, breathing heavily and pushing herself along the walls as the alarm blared and the computer continued its three-word intonation. Shedding her EMU suit, she quickly slid into one of the drop suits. It cinched around her body like the counterpressure outfits she'd worn on the Moon. Sleek and aerodynamic, the drop suits were designed for a last-minute bailout from a damaged spacecraft above Earth. That last part was key. Earth. The suits had only been designed to function once the wearer had entered the atmosphere, as no one had yet been able to create a suit capable of withstanding the intense heat and friction of reentry. Searching quickly through the ship's supplies, Caitlin's eyes finally landed on the object she was looking for.

"Oh, good," she said in a strangely detached voice. "They have a MOOSE."

Proposed by General Electric in the 1960s, the MOOSE (Manned Orbital Operations Safety Equipment) was basically a foam-filled bag that could act as a makeshift reentry vehicle, carrying a single astronaut to Earth in the event of a catastrophe in space. The MOOSE worked simply, with the astronaut climbing inside the bag outside of the damaged ship and filling it with foam. The craft would then use a small rocket engine to deorbit before plummeting back to Earth, with the MOOSE protecting the occupant using the foam and its small heat shield. Neither NASA nor the air force was interested in the MOOSE at the time, but as travel to and from Earth became more commonplace, the idea had been revisited at the turn of the last century and they'd been increasingly seen on in-and-outbound spaceflights.

Yanking the MOOSE, still in its suitcase, from the emergency locker, Caitlin pushed her way forward until she reached the hatch. She depressurized the cabin and stepped outside. Below her was Earth, unfurling in a riot of color. In a flash, she thought of a verse from *Alice's Adventures in Wonderland*, a book she still had every intention of reading to her daughter.

In a Wonderland they lie,
Dreaming as the days go by,
Dreaming as the summers die;
Ever drifting down the stream,
Lingering in the golden gleam,
Life, what is it but a dream?

Caitlin opened the case that contained the MOOSE and climbed into the awkward, ungainly bag. She could only imagine how ridiculous she looked. At once the foam released, encasing her like a mummy. Using her hands, she toggled the switch that activated the twin-rocket engine. It sputtered to life, forcing her up and off the *Alley Oop*, which tumbled away from her and began its fiery descent into the atmosphere.

As Caitlin punched through into the air above Earth with a sound like distant thunder, the heat shield on the MOOSE immediately went to work and began slowing her descent, forcing the heat away from her as the foam kept her encapsulated. Unfortunately, this particular MOOSE hadn't been updated or inspected since a time long before its current occupant had learned to walk. Buckling under the intense heat of reentry, the MOOSE, well past its sell-by date, began to flake away around her. Caitlin looked left and right wildly, breathing heavier and heavier as she watched her escape vehicle disintegrate. Then, in one final glorious burst, the MOOSE blew apart, leaving her completely exposed.

Shit.

Were it not for the drop suit, the cold and lack of oxygen would have killed her outright. Tumbling through the sky, Caitlin tried to keep her wits about her and hugged her knees to her chest in a classic cannonball position. At once she flipped over so that she was falling facedown instead of on her back, her arms and legs spread-eagle. Caitlin Taggart found herself in an uncontrolled free fall more than twenty miles above the surface of Earth.

Chapter Thirty-Seven

Within thirty seconds of the MOOSE tearing away from her, Caitlin found herself accelerating to almost seven hundred miles per hour, fast enough to break the sound barrier. In order not to be decimated by colliding shock waves in the air in what was called shock-shock interaction, Caitlin had to try to position herself in a head-down, arms-at-sides bullet formation, no easy task at the speed at which she was traveling. She forced her body to cooperate, but it didn't want to respond. She'd once heard a skydive from space being described as swimming without touching water; she now understood what that meant. She waved her arms and legs helplessly in the air until she was finally able to correct her angle and point herself like a missile directly at the ground.

Caitlin tried to regulate her breathing, doing whatever she could to keep the oxygen flowing through her body. Given the spontaneous nature of the jump, she obviously hadn't had any time to "prebreathe," or take in oxygen for hours before jumping, to avoid buildup of nitrogen in the bloodstream. As a result, due to the low-pressure environment of her drop suit, Caitlin was quite possibly inviting a serious case of the bends when, or if, she made it to the ground.

Looking out of her faceplate, Caitlin tried to orient herself. The horizon shook with the force of her descent, and she felt as though she could hear the wind whistling around her as she nose-dived faster and faster toward the ground. The Sun was a thumbprint on the sky. Below her, all she could see were clouds. She had no idea if she was over land or water or about to smash into the side of a mountain. She also didn't exactly know where she was over Earth in general. She thought she had spotted desert below her while climbing into the MOOSE, but the cloud cover and the suddenness of the jump didn't allow her the time to orient herself. So whether it was the Mojave, the Gobi, or the Syrian Desert, she had no idea. She could be diving into a rescue or something far, far worse.

Finally, she hit denser air that began to slow her descent to a more manageable 120 miles per hour. It was then that she hit turbulence, sending her into an uncontrolled and violent spin. Caitlin's suit alarm went off in her ears as she tried in vain to orient herself. She couldn't see the horizon, and the Sun went from thumbprint to smear in her vision, flashing in and out of her sight like a strobe light.

Fighting against g-forces as well as the urge to pass out, Caitlin reached out and activated the small emergency chute on her suit. The alarm silenced as it fired out and slowed the spin enough for her to gain her bearings. The canopy was designed only for use in extreme situations and, as such, wasn't connected to the main chute. Having served its purpose, the canopy was released from its moorings inside the suit and went whipping away.

Caitlin came down through the clouds, and she could see roads and highways carving their way through hills and valleys, and neighborhoods dotting the landscape in neat, symmetrical patterns. Off in the distance, she could just make out a thin sliver of ocean and, closer, but still far away, the dusky-orange spires of the Golden Gate Bridge rose from a bank of San Francisco fog. She hit the main parachute. It unfurled above her like a sail and slowed her down instantly. As the chute caught her, it yanked her up hard and forcefully, digging into her shoulders and underneath her arms. When it did, Caitlin screamed. Part of it was the pain, but the other part was defiance. She had made it. She wasn't going to die on the Moon, or the asteroid, or in orbit above Earth or falling to its surface. She was going to survive, and she was going to see her daughter again. Even if it meant she'd have to crawl over glass back to Washington, DC. One way or another, she would see Emily again. She screamed again, a loud, triumphant yell that she hoped let the entire world know that she was back, and back for good.

Grabbing the links on her parachute to steady herself, Caitlin allowed herself a moment to absorb the view. She smiled. This was her country. And not just her country, but her planet, her world, her home. Everything she had been through in the last year had shown her that people could no longer be separated by boundaries and borders or solely identified by race, creeds, or allegiances.

Before Caitlin could contemplate the view any longer, the ground came up to meet her. Grabbing the links and yanking them downward, Caitlin slowed her descent and made contact with the earth. Despite her attempts at a soft landing, she still came down with a forceful impact, tumbling and rolling into the dust gracelessly. She lay on her back a moment, breathless and panting as her chute slowly fluttered to the ground behind her. The Sun's rays passed through her helmet and created small rainbows in her peripheral vision. She also thought she heard birds singing somewhere in the distance, but couldn't tell for sure, partially because her helmet was dulling her hearing and she hadn't heard actual live birds in more than a year.

Sitting up with some effort, Caitlin slowly unlatched her helmet and drew it off her head, tasting the air as she did. Almost immediately, her head swam. Real air was absolutely intoxicating, filling her lungs with its sweetness and replenishing her entire body in a vigorous rush.

For a while, she just sat there in the dust, hugging herself as she laughed and cried, the sun warm on her skin and the sound of the wind and birds and trees in her ears. She struggled to her feet, her legs shaky after having been in one-sixth gravity and then the almost zero g of the asteroid. She felt like a newborn foal just learning to stand. But she didn't let it deter her. After a few tries, Caitlin eventually found the strength to walk—hobble—until she came to a small county road that was more dirt than asphalt. Unable to will her legs to carry her any farther, Caitlin tumbled into the dirt and waited until a truck came shambling along. She pushed herself to her knees and weakly stuck out her thumb. The truck slowed down, and the driver, an elderly man in a checkered shirt and CAT tractor hat, eyed the strange hitchhiker.

"You need help, miss?" he asked.

"Yes, I do," Caitlin said, still somewhat dazed and giddy. "I just came here from space."

"Yes, well, folks tend to do that these days," the old man said. "Can I give you a lift?"

"That would be great," Caitlin said. "Where am I, anyway?"

"Lone Pine, California," said the old man. "Hop in and I can take you as far as Bakersfield."

Caitlin worked her way to her feet, using the truck for purchase, and then climbed into the cab. Buck Owens was singing "I Don't Care (Just as Long as You Love Me)" on the radio. The old man studied Caitlin as she shifted awkwardly in the passenger seat, trying to get comfortable while still in her drop suit. He chuckled at the sight, shaking his head, and then put the truck in gear and steered back out onto the road.

"You know, ma'am, you're pretty damn lucky you got here when you did," he said as they got moving. "You know we almost got hit by an asteroid?"

"Yes," said Caitlin as she watched the pine trees roll past her window. "I heard something about that."

◆ ◆ ◆

"I thought you were heading out."

Sara was standing at the door of Alex's temporary office. He looked up from his holopad, then at his phone and, noting the time, quickly began gathering up his things.

"Yes, I am," he said, somewhat frantically. "I've got to be on a flight back home in the next two hours. I've got a whole life there that I don't even remember. What about you? When's the last time you saw your home? Or even the outside, for that matter?"

"I'm going to stick around a little longer," she said. "Wrap things up."

Alex walked around his desk and put his hands on her shoulders.

"You know you did everything you could for her, don't you?"

"Keep telling me that," Sara said. "Maybe one day I'll believe it."

"We pulled off something impossible here, Sara," Alex said. "But there's a difference between the impossible and the miraculous. The odds were so stacked against that crew from the beginning that I'm amazed they got as far as they did."

"I'm not," said Sara. "It's like I told Caitlin. She was a fighter."

"And I know you know all about that," Alex said.

"Damn straight," she said, and returned his smile warmly, though it didn't last.

"Do you remember what we promised each other, the last day of college in our senior year?"

"That you would never again take me to another jam band concert as long as we both lived?"

"Yes, but after that," Alex said.

"Truthfully, right now, I don't remember anything from before Caitlin decided to call this office," Sara said. "So please fill me in."

"We promised each other that we'd take on the world together," said Alex.

Sara paused a moment, catching a glimpse of her twenty-two-year-old self in her mind's eye. A reflection in a smudged mirror. She *had* made that promise, hadn't she? But a lot of promises made in the warm afternoon of youth turn smoky and disappear when twilight approaches. She gazed at Alex, wondering how the years had turned so quickly, and additionally, how the wheel had landed her in practically the same spot again, standing across from this man to whom she'd made a promise to in another lifetime.

"Yeah," she said at last, "I remember that promise."

Alex pointed to the TV screen behind her where one of the endless parades of twenty-four-hour news channels were celebrating the salvation of Earth.

"Take a look," he said. "I think we finally made good on it."

Sara looked at the screen, seeing the jubilation around the world, the people from disparate nations, religions, cultures, and orientations all standing together in streets and plazas, dancing, embracing, welcoming the second life they'd been given. It did not ease the sting of losing Caitlin, but Sara had to admit that, for the first time in a long while, she truly felt better.

"Come on," Alex said, standing up and grabbing his jacket. "Come with me to the airport, and I'll let you buy me a drink before I have to go home."

"Thanks," said Sara. "It's a tempting offer, but I'm going to hang here for a little while and make sure we've got everything buttoned down. And then I'm going to drive to Ashburn and try and figure out how to tell an eight-year-old girl what happened to her mother."

Alex looked as if he was struggling for something comforting or wise to say. But before he could speak, Ned suddenly came bursting into the room.

"Sara!" he said. "Sara! There's someone on the phone for you."

Sara's stomach tightened. "Who?" she asked.

"I don't know," Ned said. "Some old man. He says he's in a bar outside of Bakersfield, California, and that he's got someone who wants to talk to you."

A flutter passed between Alex and Sara.

"Put him through to Alex's line," said Sara, barely able to contain the excitement in her voice.

The phone beeped once, and Sara immediately put it on speaker.

"Hello?"

The voice that answered did not belong to an old man, but instead was the one voice that Sara Kent had been certain she would never hear again.

"I know Bakersfield is a long way from DC," said Caitlin Taggart, "but if you're up for a road trip, I still owe you a beer!"

Chapter Thirty-Eight

Caitlin had been back on Earth for three days and already she wanted off. She had been picked up by a fleet of black SUVs outside her motel in Bakersfield and whisked to a private airport where a Gulfstream was waiting to take her, not to DC and to Emily, but off to Dallas, where she had spent nearly forty hours straight being grilled by the lawyers for Core One Mining, which, as she had learned, was filing for Chapter 11 in the wake of this disaster. Initially, it seemed as though they were going to hold her responsible for the loss of the ship, the escape lander, and the life insurance policies on the crew members. Additionally, they were hinting that she'd be on the hook for the trillions of dollars in future earnings that were lost when the asteroid was diverted.

"What we are looking at here represents a substantial loss for the company," the Core One lawyer, who, to Caitlin, looked distressingly like Dr. Bunsen Honeydew from the old *Muppet Show*. She supposed she was tired and punchy from her ordeal on the asteroid, as there was nothing funny about her present situation. Nevertheless, looking at the round-faced, squinty-eyed man nattering away in front of her, Caitlin fought the urge to giggle.

"I understand that," said Caitlin, "but, quite frankly, that isn't my problem. We were given a dangerous assignment with faulty equipment and no time to prepare. The *Tamarisk* itself could not have been flown legally and was operating with an outdated fuel system. I'm actually shocked we didn't disintegrate in lunar orbit."

"Be that as it may," Honeydew began, "we need to find out—"

"No. I'm through answering questions," Caitlin barked. "I did the job that was asked of me, in spite of everything that was working against me and my crew . . ."

At the mention of her crew, Caitlin paused and took a second. It was still hard to think of them and how they had all perished so that she could be sitting here, breathing air that didn't come through a recycling system. And now, after everything they'd gone through and sacrificed, instead of being reunited with her daughter, Caitlin was stuck in a gray, antiseptic room in Texas arguing with this balloon-faced shyster over who was going to get stuck with the bill. She took a deep breath and went on.

"My crew and I," she continued, "we took on the job and we assumed the risks. Everything else is on you guys. If a cargo ship goes down in a storm in the Atlantic, the shipping company doesn't pin it on the crew, do they? No, they take the hit and move on."

This brought forth a sardonic chuckle from Honeydew. He shifted in his seat and began scanning through his paperwork.

"It's interesting to me how quick you are to assign blame," the lawyer said, "when we have testimony from a member of your crew that places the burden of responsibility squarely on one set of shoulders. Namely, yours."

"Wait," said Caitlin, trying to get a handle on what the lawyer had just said. "A member of my crew?"

The lawyer seemed especially pleased that he was in possession of information that Caitlin was not. His head popped up, revealing an expression of pure delight.

"Oh, you haven't heard?" he said. "Indeed a Miss . . . Beckett. Valentine Beckett."

Vee, thought Caitlin in shock, consumed by a wave of emotion. *Vee is still alive.*

"Yes," Honeydew went on, licking his thumb and turning the pages of the file. "After the accident in Earth's orbit, she drifted for fourteen hours before being picked up by a rescue tug out of the London star docks. And she's had quite a story to tell. Not only did you insist that she, along with her husband and Freddy Diaz and Ellis Shaw, accompany you on this mission, but that it was also your idea to land on the asteroid as well as deploy the solar sail, which, as we know, cost Mr. Diaz his life."

"The RCS on Diaz's suit failed!" said Caitlin. "That's what killed him. A suit that was supplied by Core One—"

"The fact remains that three people are dead, Ms. Taggart, and people are going to want answers," Honeydew said. "At the very least, they're going to want someone to be held accountable."

"So that's what this is?" Caitlin said. "You're going to throw me to the wolves to ease your own consciences?"

Honeydew stared at her evenly, the look of a hungry animal waiting for his master's command. Just then his phone rang, startling the both of them. He angrily snatched it up and put the receiver to his ear.

"Yes?" he asked in an irritated tone. As soon as the other person on the line spoke, his entire demeanor changed. Caitlin didn't recall him saying anything other than yes during the conversation, but to her it seemed as though he went through every possible tone in his delivery. From fearfulness to deference to shock to dismay and then, ultimately, acceptance. The rather one-sided conversation finished, he set his phone down.

"Thank you, Ms. Taggart. It seems as though we have everything we need."

"Care to tell me what that was all about?" Caitlin asked.

"It seems that a . . . settlement has been reached," the lawyer said, clearly dismayed at being denied the chance to carve Caitlin up. "And, as such, Mr. Ross wishes to avoid any further . . . negative publicity from this incident."

"Mr. Ross or Senator Ross?"

The lawyer pursed his lips in a failed attempt at producing a grin. "My client," he said, trying a different tactic, "would like this matter resolved quietly and quickly. With that in mind, Ms. Taggart, you are free to go."

"Thank you," Caitlin curtly said, and pushed the chair out as she stood to leave, still in quiet turmoil. When she reached the door, the lawyer called after her.

"On one condition," he said.

There were always conditions when it came to the Ross family, she thought. She turned around to face the lawyer.

"And that would be?"

"You must never, ever attempt to profit from this," said the lawyer. "No speaking engagements, no book deals, no movie rights. If you so much as tell this story in a public library, my client will have no choice but to react swiftly. And, I'm afraid, harshly."

"Is that so?" said Caitlin. "Well, please tell your client that I consider any profits that come from this incident to be little more than blood money. Ask him if he's prepared to live with *that*."

Having said what she needed to say, Caitlin turned on her heel and walked out of the room, her footfalls echoing off the concrete walls as she did.

As she walked through the lobby of Core One's headquarters, Caitlin tried to put together everything that had transpired during her debriefing. Mostly she tried to process the fact that Vee had somehow survived against all odds. Before she could even begin to consider how, she saw someone across the lobby and called out her name.

"Vee!"

Vee was busily making her way across the lobby aided by crutches and a knee brace. A pair of suit-clad lawyers walked on either side of her, one female and one male. At the sound of Caitlin's voice, all three swiveled their heads. The lawyers' faces tightened immediately, and both attempted to usher Vee out of the building even faster. Vee, however, brushed them aside and turned around, coming toward Caitlin.

Caitlin found her steps picking up as she made her way across the lobby to her miraculously resurrected friend. Caitlin was so glad that she wasn't dead that her arms were already fanning out in preparation for a hug. Vee's body language, however, was less than receptive. She remained cool and businesslike, the demeanor of one stranger greeting another. Caitlin saw this, and her pace immediately slowed, her arms returning to her sides.

"Hey," was all Vee offered.

"Hey, yourself," said Caitlin. "You're alive."

"Looks like it," said Vee. "Those EMU suits are built to last."

"For sure," said Caitlin, rather lamely. "It's good to see you. Really good. I thought you were gone."

"Yeah, you too," said Vee. "Look, I gotta . . ."

"Go, go," said Caitlin. "We'll catch up soon."

"Right," said Vee, and turned to leave.

"Why'd you do it?" Caitlin asked suddenly. "Why did you say all those things up there? Things you know aren't true."

Vee paused, keeping her back to Caitlin, then turned slowly as though on a revolving pedestal. Efficient with her crutches, she marched back toward Caitlin purposefully, her green eyes locked on her. When she had crossed the distance, she leaned in close.

"I knew the risks going in," Vee said. "We all did. But it turns out knowing the risks and living with the aftermath are two different things.

You get to walk out of here, get on a plane, and fly back home to your daughter. But me? Where do I go? Who's waiting for me? On the asteroid, we did what we had to do to survive. We worked together just like we always did. But all that's over now. And here we are, back on Earth. Everything is different. My husband was a loving man, and he's dead, Caitlin. Tony's gone. Someone has to answer for that."

"Even if it's me?"

"I think it *should* be you," said Vee. "Don't you?"

And with that, Vee turned and moved through the lobby to rejoin her legal team, exiting the building without bothering to give Caitlin a second glance.

From Dallas, Caitlin flew (this time commercial, although on the government's dime) to DC, where she was slated to meet with the PDCO for a debriefing similar to the one she had just endured at Core One. She hoped this particular meeting would be somewhat less painful, given that they knew the lengths she and her teammates had gone to, to stop the asteroid from hitting the planet. The uncomfortable meeting with Vee was beginning to recede in her memory, yet continued to sting as she thought of their time together on the Moon.

The flight was blessedly uneventful. Although the world now knew that there had been a team of miners on the Thresher and said team of miners had been instrumental in keeping it from striking the planet and that two of those miners had, against impossible odds, survived the entire ordeal and made it back to Earth, what they didn't know was what any of them looked like or who they were. That information was being kept strictly classified, and if Core One and Senator Ross had their way, it would probably remain that way for the foreseeable future. Personally, Caitlin was fine with that arrangement. Fame was not anything she had ever sought out. But it secretly pleased her to think of how Diaz would react to the idea of celebrity being snatched away immediately after it had been bestowed upon him. The tirades he would have unleashed at the Dark Side—drinking on someone else's chits, no doubt—would have been endlessly entertaining. As the plane made its bumpy descent into DC airspace, Caitlin found herself wishing that she could have had the chance to hear them one more time.

Walking through the terminal, Caitlin scanned the area, looking for the telltale driver with her name scrawled on a white piece of paper and probably spelled with a *K* and a *Y*, as was usually the case. She searched around the baggage claim area, watching other travelers being whisked away by limo drivers, cabbies, and gleeful family members, but could not find anyone who was waiting for her. Then she heard a voice from behind her. One she had gotten to know very well over the last several weeks, only this time it was clean and bright, not filtered through the chop and hiss of the *Alley Oop*'s speakers.

"Caitlin?"

She turned and saw Sara Kent waiting there for her. Instinctively, Caitlin reached out and hugged her like an old relative. Sara, although probably expecting a warm welcome, was nonetheless taken aback by the suddenness of Caitlin's embrace. Still, she affectionately returned the hug.

"Good to see you too, partner," she said.

Caitlin stepped back, already getting emotional, but held on to Sara's shoulders.

"I can't believe you're here!" she said. "I would have thought you guys would have sent a car or something."

"Well," said Sara, "they had one lined up, but I had to come see you myself. There was a time when I thought this meeting would never happen, so it only seemed right for me to be the one to bring you home. And I wanted to give you this."

Sara reached into her bag, extracted a bottle, and handed it to Caitlin, who turned it over in her hands to read the label.

"Autumn's Hunt Vineyards," she said.

"Napa Valley," said Sara. "Now that you're back, maybe you should take some time for the little things."

Caitlin slid the wine bottle into her shoulder bag.

"You got it," she said, and this time she knew that she meant it.

"Good," said Sara with a smile of her own. "But the wine wasn't the only reason I came to get you myself."

"Oh?" asked Caitlin. "You mean there's more?"

"There is," said Sara. "You see, there's someone else here I'd like you to—"

"Mom!"

Whatever pretense Caitlin had about staying calm or composed during the meeting fell away in an instant. As she saw her daughter running toward her, her face aglow and her eyes alight with happiness, Caitlin fell to her knees, now sobbing openly in complete and total joy. She felt as though a firework had been ignited inside her chest, and when Emily ran into her arms and they embraced at last, it burst in a shower of elation so strong and so powerful, Caitlin was sure her daughter could see the swirls of color.

"Hi, baby girl!" she said through her tears. "I can't believe it's really you! I thought I was never going to see you again!"

"I thought so too," said Emily, burying her face in her mom's shoulder. "I was so scared."

"So was I, honey," Caitlin said. "So was I."

Emily looked at her mother with curious, studying eyes. "Were you scared you were going to die?"

"Yes, baby, I was," Caitlin said. "But I was more scared that we'd never be together again. And that would have been so much worse."

They hugged again, even stronger this time, and Caitlin melted. All the pain, agony, and trauma she had endured since the day she left

Earth more than a year ago dissipated like breaking fog, burned away by the glow of her daughter's love. Now, at last, she could say that it was truly over.

As she hugged her mother, Emily looked up at Sara.

"I'm sorry," she said. "I hope I didn't spoil the surprise."

"Sweetheart," said Sara, wiping the tears from her own eyes, "I think you nailed it."

Chapter Thirty-Nine

The word eventually did get out. Caitlin and her crew's identities were leaked to the press and soon she found her face, as well as the faces of Vee and the friends and loved ones they had both lost, splashed across every TV, computer, smartphone, and tablet display in the country. As the only survivors of the mission, Caitlin and Vee were separately bombarded with questions daily. Vee had decided to use her public profile to raise awareness of the treatment of Moonborns and the desperation that had led *Tamarisk* crew members to undertake the asteroid mission. She started a nonprofit organization and began working with leaders on both Earth and the Moon to help improve the immigration process and create opportunities for Moonborn travelers that they might otherwise never enjoy.

Caitlin did not attempt to turn her ordeal into profit either. She was cordial and polite when asked about what happened on the Thresher, but declined every TV interview, book deal, and movie producer who came around looking to bring the story of the incident to life. She wouldn't have tried to benefit from what happened even if Core One hadn't made its threat. The idea of getting wealthy off something that had killed most of her friends, and cost her another, turned her blood cold. What she did take, however, was a job offer to become director of operations at a small, up-and-coming He-3 mining company outside

Seattle, with the proviso that lunar travel was out of the question. She and Emily had packed up everything and moved to a small house on Whidbey Island. It was old and needed some work, but Caitlin didn't mind. She had the time.

Shortly after moving in, Caitlin undertook her first home-renovation task, replacing the house's previously installed artificial intelligence system with one of her own, the one and only souvenir she had decided to electronically retrieve from her stay on the Moon. Caitlin noticed how well Ava seemed to take to her new surroundings. Her voice even seemed to have a little lift to it. Life on Earth seemed to agree with her. She supposed it agreed with them all.

Ben was happy with the new direction Caitlin's life had taken. He'd even offered to move up to Seattle to help her get settled in, an offer she'd politely passed on. After Eric, the Moon, and the asteroid, she needed to find out who she was again on her own before she could even think about starting something with anyone else. She knew the consequences of rash decisions.

Of course, as was the case with any sudden change in lifestyle or behavior, Caitlin's new direction wasn't without its share of detractors.

"Why did you take that job?" Sara had asked during one of their many weekly video chats.

"Why not?" said Caitlin. "It's a good job with good pay and better hours. And I don't come home covered with Moon dust every night. Believe me when I tell you that's a perk and a half."

"Fair enough," Sara said. "But with your new celebrity status, you could work just about anywhere and ask for anything."

"I suppose." Caitlin shrugged. She looked out her window at Emily scavenging along the beach, searching for whatever treasures the sea may have brought her that morning. "But I've got the job I want right now."

◆ ◆ ◆

When the media eventually realized they weren't going to be squeezing any blood from the rather obstinate stone that was Caitlin Taggart, they turned their collective attention to a far more interesting target—Lyman Ross and his father, the good senator from Texas. Core One Mining was dragged through the mud in both the court of public opinion and the actual courts themselves. The media had a field day with the angle of Core One using "illegal immigrants" to perform dangerous, deadly, and of course, unlawful mining procedures. A congressional panel was convened to investigate the incident thoroughly, and Caitlin and Vee were forced to testify on several occasions, recounting minute by minute the ordeal they had experienced on the asteroid. Since this was most likely the only time Earth would see the survivors of the Thresher incident give their accounts of the events that had captivated the world's attention, their entire testimony was broadcast and live streamed around the globe. Transcripts were featured in every news outlet available and shared and reshared across social media platforms from Earth to the Moon and back.

"We weren't doing it to get rich," Vee said in one of the many hearings that were broadcast on a never-ending media loop. "We weren't doing it to become famous or be pioneers in some bold new enterprise. We were doing it because we had to. Because, for some of us, it was our only shot at getting back some of the life we had lost."

Whenever their paths crossed during these hearings, Caitlin and Vee were cordial and friendly, but there was a barrier between them now, one that was insurmountable. Too much had happened, both on the asteroid and in the time since they had returned. In the loss of their friendship, the Thresher asteroid had claimed its final victim.

Core One Mining could not hold up under the pressure of the sustained media pounding, the consistent probing of Congress, and the endless public demonstrations against the company. They closed their doors quickly and quietly, with little fanfare and no public statement. Lyman Ross took a job in his father's office, a position most suspected was designed solely so that Hamer Ross could keep close tabs on his son and ensure that he didn't attempt anything that stupid ever again.

Caitlin's testimony cast a stark and unflattering light not only on the practices of Core One Mining but on the policies of the White House itself. Although the president had repealed the lunar embargo, and negotiations between Earth and its nearest neighbor had begun anew, the fact that the situation had even been allowed to become as dire as it had was of grave concern to the nation, which was also still reeling from the revelation of Ark City. Those who had opposed the president's election in the first place relished the opportunity to say "I told you so" to anyone who would listen. On the other side of the aisle, those who had endorsed him as their candidate were now wiping the egg off their faces, trying to explain how they could have supported a man whose disregard for policy and protocol nearly brought about the end of the world.

The president himself, however, was enjoying a momentary spike in approval ratings thanks to his last-minute change of heart and his efforts toward stopping the asteroid, as well as everything he'd done to help the Oceanian nations in the wake of the nuke's detonation. He was also staying true to his word and stepping down once the fervor from the asteroid crisis had subsided. However, he maintained, he would not leave before all his work was done. His last act as president was to give NASA the resources it needed to launch telescopes and probes out to the asteroid belt and beyond to scan the stars for anything that might put Earth or the Moon in danger. He also ordered that even more funding be directed to the Planetary Defense Coordination Office to combat and respond to potential threats looming out there in space. He also appointed someone to run the NEO Program in the DC office, someone who had firsthand experience dealing with these kinds of threats and had shown the wherewithal and courage to face them head-on—Alex Sutter.

On his final day in office, the president sat at the Resolute desk, composing the letter for his successor, in keeping with the tradition of the presidency. As he finished and was signing the letter, Jason Keating walked in.

"Sorry to disturb you, Mr. President," he said. "I just wanted to let you know that Marine One is waiting for you."

"Thank you, Jason," he said, standing up and walking around the desk. He shook Keating's hand and pointed to the desk.

"She's yours now," he said. "And all that comes with her."

"I think I'm ready, sir," he said.

"I have no doubt," the president said.

"What about you?" asked Keating. "What are you going to do next?"

"I don't know," said the president, answering honestly. "I've spent so much time chasing power that I don't know if I know what to do with the world, any more than it knows what to do with me. I guess for now I'll just . . . be quiet."

"Are you going to miss this office?"

The president gathered up the last few items from his desk. He picked up a picture of his wife and tucked it into his briefcase.

"Not really," he said as he walked out the door. "I don't think it suited me all that much."

On a bright morning in May, the press, public, and a host of military personnel and foreign dignitaries gathered at the unveiling of a memorial cenotaph in Arlington National Cemetery for the three miners lost on the asteroid. Everyone, both present and watching at home, listened as the country's new president, Jason Keating, spoke. These would be the first words he would ever give as the commander in chief of the United States.

"None of the three who were lost in this disaster had ever served in any military capacity," said President Keating. "But all of them gave their lives not only in the service of their country but of the entire world. There can be no greater honor, no sacrifice more worthy of praise than that. But their deaths also cast into sharp relief the dangers of limited thinking. Because of the policies and practices of this office, five people were forced into a position where they had to put their own lives in jeopardy to try and get back that which was taken from them. And, of those five brave, selfless people, only two of them came home. That notion brings shame to the office of the presidency, and having spoken at length to my predecessor, I know he will carry that shame with him all the rest of his days. He has told me as much, and he is content to live with it. However, all of that said, today isn't about me, my predecessor, or the office to which we were both appointed. And, to be fair, it isn't about these three brave souls, at least not exclusively. In actuality, this day is about all of us. It's about each one of us turning to the other and asking ourselves . . . what would we sacrifice everything for, as they did? How much do we believe in the things we hold dear, and how much are we willing to risk to preserve them? See, we've been given a second chance. We have avoided annihilation, and the world has been allowed to continue turning for a little longer. So what are we going to do with that time? Are we going to continue squabbling over trivial and meaningless disagreements? Are we going to spend our lives in the ceaseless pursuit of material things? Or are we going to turn to each other and finally come to the realization that we are all in this together? That here, in this little patch in the arms of a vast galaxy, here is where we must make our stand, and make it as one united people?"

He pointed to the cenotaph, which was bedecked with flowers and ribbons from nations around the world who had paid their respects. President Keating went on.

"These three people are asking us that question right now," he said. "And I believe we owe them an answer."

He stepped away from the podium and took a seat between the new First Lady and Vee, who looked elegant and mournful dressed all in black, her emerald eyes rimmed with tears but still stoic and watchful as she looked out over the crowd. As the president sat down, Vee gave him a courteous nod and the First Lady took his hand in hers. Overhead, four fighter jets streaked through the air. Suddenly, the second plane from the right pulled up abruptly, shooting upward into the sky as the other planes continued in the classic missing-man formation. The president and all military personnel stood and saluted as a fife and drum corps played "Amazing Grace."

In the back of the cemetery, far away from the prying eyes of the press and public, Caitlin Taggart stood and watched the jets soaring above her. She stood at attention and saluted, offering respect and a silent prayer to her fallen friends. She looked over at Vee, but, given the distance between them, couldn't be sure if her old friend saw her. Not that it would have mattered much if she had, she supposed. Caitlin liked to think that someday, when they'd both had a chance to gain some distance from all that had happened, they might find each other again. It was only a thought, a nice thought, and was enough for now.

Above the planes, Caitlin could make out a sliver of moon hanging indifferently in the midmorning sky. There was a time when she might have looked at the Moon and been plagued with dread, thinking of her yearlong internment there and the tribulation she'd endured to escape it. But now, it was just another object in the sky, worthy of a glance, a passing thought, and little else.

Turning her eyes away from the sky above her, Caitlin looked down, focusing her attention on the person at her side. She reached down and squeezed Emily's shoulder.

"Ready to get out of here?"

"Almost," Emily said. "I want to see the Last Campaign memorial."

"Oh *really*?" Caitlin asked, realizing how much she sounded like her own daughter when presented with a task she didn't want to do. "Do we have to?"

"It'll be quick," she said. "I told Kyle I'd text him a picture. He thinks it's really cool that you fought in the war."

"Who's this Kyle who thinks I'm cool?" Caitlin asked.

"Just a boy from school."

"A boy from school? And why am I just hearing about him now?"

"I don't know."

"I thought we had an agreement, young lady."

"What agreement?" asked Emily, genuinely surprised.

"No boys until you're forty," said Caitlin. "I think that's reasonable."

Emily giggled at her mother's chiding, and Caitlin squeezed her hand.

"C'mon, kiddo," she said. "Let's go get Kyle his picture."

They began to walk, and Caitlin allowed herself one last look around the cemetery. She sighed, looking around her. How weird, being in the place where so many of her friends, both past and present, were memorialized. With the Moon overhead and her daughter at her side, it was as though she was standing at the nexus point of all the events of her life.

"What are you thinking about, Mom?" asked Emily.

"What?"

"I've seen that look on your face before," Emily said. "It means you've got something serious on your mind."

"I'm just thinking about how much I love you," Caitlin said.

Emily rolled her eyes. "That's what you're always thinking about!"

Caitlin gave her daughter another hug.

"And I always will be," she said.

She took Emily's hand, and the two walked reverently into the morning sunlight. It was time to go home.

Acknowledgments

Every book is a team effort, but this one brought together an incredible group of people, each of whom helped get the project off the ground. First and foremost, I have to thank Bob Lee, who was there every step of the way to answer questions, raise ideas, and challenge me time and again about the science and its accuracy. This book wouldn't exist without you, Bob! Many thanks also to Chris Dieckman, who offered great advice at the book's outset that helped the wheels to start turning. Thanks also to Jason Kirk at 47North, who took a chance on this when it was little more than an outline, and to my agent, Jennifer Lyons, who took a chance when it was even less than that. Lots of gratitude must also go out to Chris Mari for his continued friendship and support. Many thanks and much love to my whole family, immediate and extended, who have always shown such support. And a special thanks to every family member who bought a copy of *Ocean of Storms* (or several!), came to a book signing, or took the time to promote the book on their own. I will be forever grateful. Thanks to William and James for being such good examples of what young men should be and for never objecting when Dad had to spend another night writing. And the greatest thanks of all goes to my wife, Alli, who supported this whole thing from day one, even when it seemed impossible to pull off. The only reason I believe I can accomplish great things is because I see you do it every day.

About the Author

Photo © 2016 Alli Brown

Jeremy K. Brown published his first book, *Calling Off Christmas*, in 2011. His first science-fiction novel, *Ocean of Storms*, was written with coauthor Christopher Mari and published in 2016. Jeremy has also authored several biographies for young readers, including books on Stevie Wonder and Ursula K. Le Guin. Jeremy has contributed articles to numerous magazines and newspapers, as well as special issues for *TV Guide*, *Newsweek*, and the Discovery Channel. He lives in New York with his wife and sons and is working on his next novel.